Finding Mercy

Return to Welcome, Volume 1

Bonnie Edwards

Published by Bonnie Edwards, 2023.

This is a work of fiction. Similarities to real people, places, or events are entirely coincidental.

FINDING MERCY

First edition. January 20, 2023.

ISBN: 978-0993858581

Written by Bonnie Edwards.

Table of Contents

This book is dedicated to my readers, who humble me
with their support.

Thank you, thank you, thank you for reading and sharing
your love of books.

Every story I write contains a small piece of my heart, and
every time you read my stories, I entrust that piece to you.

And for Ted, always...

What Reviewers and readers just like you are saying about
Finding Mercy...

"... I loved the whole family dynamic. I think that was the best part of this. Bonnie Edwards recreates the feel of a small town full of second chances and happy endings. **A heart-warming romance...what more could you want?"**
Highland Hussy – 5 STARS Got Fiction? (Book Reviews)

"Wow! This was more than I was expecting. Rarely is (this) level of introspection offered. This is my first book by this author, but it won't be my last."
5 STARS Badass Lioness (Book Reviewer)

"...this story has depth, emotional highs and lows, and plenty of punch in the story arc... extremely well-written and edited. **HIGHLY recommend this and her other books!** 5 Stars!" Diana Trodahl (Reader)

"Loved it!! This was a really sweet heartfelt book that you won't want to put down." 5 stars Sissy Mae Hicks (Romance Book Review)

1

BONNIE EDWARDS

"...emotions in this story are poignant and strong... the underlying love they both work so hard to ignore, will not be silenced. **I enjoyed this love story very much."**

5 stars Liza O'Connor – (author and blogger)

Chapter One

"DID YOU HEAR YOUR SISTER-in-law's back in town?"

Clay Foster's receptionist watched for his reaction from her seat across the front counter of his veterinarian clinic.

This was his dead wife's sister's first trip home in two years. "She must have blown in for a quick visit."

"Pfft, so much for making it big," Sybil commented with a glance at her computer screen.

"Out with it, Sybil. You look too delighted for this to be anything but juicy gossip." Mercy was a Hollywood success story. Everyone knew it.

Sybil crossed her arms and leaned forward. "She came home with boxes. Lots of boxes." Sybil's husband, Bud, worked at the bus depot and shared all the comings and goings of Welcome's population.

Clay leaned in to glean every nuance of meaning from Sybil's face. "Out with it," he repeated.

She licked her lips as if each morsel of gossip was filet mignon. "When Bud asked if he could call her a cab, she said no, she couldn't afford it." She hefted a disbelieving sigh and muttered, "Of all the nonsense. So"—she stretched out the word because Sybil loved telling a good story—"Bud called Nate, who showed up half an hour later. Nate didn't say a word, which, of course, is just like him, and tossed all the boxes into his pickup. Mercy didn't explain a thing, just looked miserable, Bud said."

He nodded, at a loss. It still came as a surprise that he was related, if only by marriage, to Mercy Talbot. Welcome High's golden girl: the blond, beautiful, leggy, and untouchable Mercy Talbot. The Talbot daughter who'd made a real success of her life, unlike the one who'd ruined her life by marrying him, the town hell raiser.

"That Mercy is a real glamour girl. Dilly's gonna love her. All that prettiness and sunshine wrapped up in one girl." Sybil sighed as if just knowing Mercy Talbot had somehow blessed her.

At the mention of his daughter, Dilly, Clay frowned. "Mercy won't be here long," he said. "Dilly won't get attached." Women like Mercy always had an exit strategy and somewhere more important to be.

Mercy Talbot had been as angelically perfect as his wife, Janna, had been hell-bent on personal destruction. Two sisters: impossibly different, forever at odds. He used to wonder if Janna's darkness was in counterpoint to Mercy's bright flare. But none of that mattered anymore.

It was Dilly who mattered.

"What child wouldn't get attached to a beautiful actress?"

A pulse pounded in his temple. He dreaded seeing Dilly's eyes light up when Mercy played the caring auntie. But she'd barely held Dilly as a baby. He doubted she'd show any interest now.

"I have nothing to worry about," he told Sybil.

"Still, makes you wonder why she's back in town."

He left Sybil to her musings about the reason for Mercy's return. When he stepped into exam room one, he was relieved to see nine-year-old Josh Camden holding his dog's collar. Josh's mother, Shandy, leaned against the wall, jeans tight and low slung, hips jutted. At least with Josh there, he wouldn't be alone with her.

"Good afternoon, Josh," he said. He gave Shandy a cursory glance. Her answering smile was come-hither and meant to be hot.

The dog sniffed Clay's fingers. "Set her on the table, Josh." Clay rolled her onto her back and gently checked the incision on her belly. "She's perfectly healed like I said last week." He raised an eyebrow at Shandy, who shifted her hips.

"I don't gotta lift her up on my bed anymore?" Josh asked.

"She can jump up herself." He ruffled the boy's hair.

"Thanks, Clay," Shandy said. "I wanted to be certain because you never can tell." She gave him a pout that said she wanted to be sure about his lack of response to her previous invitations. "I'd love to cook you dinner to thank you." Her eyes held expectation he refused to meet.

He shook his head. "This is Mimzi's last checkup. She's been fine for a week now."

Shandy canted one side of her lip into a defeated smile. He didn't mean to embarrass her, but she had to see he wasn't interested. Had never been interested, not when he'd taken what she'd offered all those years ago and not now. Beer and high-school hormones had gotten the best of them back then.

Clay had his regrets about his behavior that night by the lake, while her memories seemed warm and cozy. She was friendly, but she'd been friendlier since her divorce. And now that Clay had been alone for two years, she'd found numerous ways to make her approach.

He followed them out to the reception area. Shandy strode out of the clinic, head held high. Josh ran behind his mother with Mimzi's leash tight in his hand. "Thanks a bunch, Dr. Foster." He stopped at the door, turned and gave him a wave. "See ya."

"See ya, Josh."

Maybe he should have left town after Janna wrapped her car around that tree, but he'd needed to stay in Welcome for Dilly's sake. His daughter needed a woman's hand, and Janna's mother, Hope, had dedicated herself to Dilly. Janna would have laughed her ass off if she'd known that all she had to do was die for Hope to care.

Once Shandy and Josh left, he turned to the reception desk to hand off Mimzi's file. Sybil looked past him toward the clinic's entrance. A glimmer of anticipation glowed in her eyes.

He glanced over his shoulder to see what had caught her interest.

His mother-in-law, Hope Talbot, walked in leading her Yorkie. It made sense that he'd see her today, now that Bud and Sybil had told the whole town about Mercy coming home. This visit would be about damage control and putting Sybil in her place.

These two had a long history of sniping. "Hope, it's nice to see you," he said mildly. "Is there a problem with Humphrey?" The dog looked as happy as ever as he wiggled a greeting.

"He's fine." Hope sighed with dramatic effect while she pulled her credit card from her wallet. The Yorkie sat at heel. Hope liked to keep her pet, her husband, and now his daughter firmly in hand.

On a regular basis, Clay reminded himself to be grateful.

"I just recalled that I neglected to pay for Humphrey's food the other day." But her eyes shot glass shards toward his receptionist.

Sybil rolled her eyes. Great, he'd have to referee. The pulse in his temple picked up.

Last time Hope had come in, she'd been frustrated with Dilly and had taken it out in trade: one twenty-pound bag of food for having to deal with Dilly's temper for an hour. You'd think a little girl would wear herself out, but not his. No. She could wind herself up for longer and longer as if each tantrum increased her stamina.

At three and a bit, Dilly was capable of marathons.

He waved away Hope's credit card. "No need. I'm sorry I was in surgery the last time you were here." He'd been unable to step away to coax his daughter out of her temper. He was never sure who angered Hope more, Dilly or him. "There's no way I'll take payment for the dog food."

"I insist. I won't have people say I take advantage of you because we're family."

She hated admitting they were related. He was a Foster, after all. "I hear Mercy's here for a visit," he offered in an effort to soften her. Janna used to tell him Mercy was Hope's angel while painting herself as a devil child.

His mother-in-law tilted her head down as if to shush him. "She's here incognito." She slanted Sybil a glance. Sybil yanked open a drawer in her desk to pretend the conversation was none of her business. "I expect your discretion." She gave him a pointed look and with a stiff nod, included Sybil.

Sybil refilled the stapler without looking up.

Hope leaned toward him. "Mercy's waiting on a big part. This is something that will show the world just how talented she is. But it's hush-hush."

Clay nodded like he gave a shit and Sybil cleared her throat. He didn't care what Mercy was doing. She'd be gone soon, and in the meantime, he'd keep an eye on Dilly for signs of bedazzlement with her aunt.

"How long is she here for?"

"I can't say."

"Most people know how long their visit is."

Hope pursed her lips as if he'd pushed too hard. She turned to Sybil behind the counter. "Her agent's sure her big break is just around the corner," she whispered loud enough for the whole waiting room to hear. "Don't tell anyone."

"I won't breathe a word," Sybil vowed, dust dry.

"If the paparazzi find her here"—Hope went on—"we'll never get a minute's rest."

Hiding out in her hometown would do nothing for Mercy Talbot's career, Clay thought. If you wanted something, you went for it. You didn't hide and expect success to come knocking.

If Hope decided to manage Mercy's career again, he could kiss Hope's help with Dilly goodbye. Janna had often said that she and Dilly were poor substitutes for Mercy.

Janna's warning sounded in his head. *If Mercy ever comes back to Welcome for good, my mother will ditch Dilly like yesterday's news.*

Hope took care of Dilly day-to-day and saw that she went to all her classes. He was no kind of father to guide a girl through dance, singing and comportment lessons. If Dilly kept up her tantrums and crying jags, Hope might happily walk away from her daily care, especially if Mercy needed her. Dread thickened his blood. Hope sometimes created her own truth, and Mercy coming home in the dead of night on a bus was not in line with Hope's version of Mercy's life.

But it was Sybil who asked Hope for clarification. "Mercy showed up at the bus depot instead of in a limo like she usually does because she's in hiding?"

Hope clicked her tongue. "We don't want her tracked down and followed. She came in disguise. She visits as often as she can."

But could Sybil leave it at that? No. She had to poke the dragon. "Of course she visits regularly. Last time was two years ago, at the time of Janna's tragic accident." She used Hope's favorite phrase to describe Janna's drunk-driving death.

Spite burned the air and guilt squeezed his lungs.

"Sybil, you're out of line," he ground out between clenched teeth. She'd brought up how Janna died *and* the length of time between Mercy's visits.

"Take my credit card." Hope's brittle voice tore around the edges. Sybil looked guilty and contrite. She actually reached out to pat Hope's shoulder in silent apology.

Hope shook her off.

Clay took the credit card out of her hand. With a shake of his head, he dropped it into her open purse. "I'll be over to get Dilly as soon as I can. It'll be nice to catch up with Mercy," he said as kindly as he could.

Thirty minutes later, he had a free moment to head to the front desk. As soon as he walked into the momentarily empty reception area, Sybil looked up from her keyboard. "You here to tell me off?"

"You stayed on at the clinic when I took over just to torment people."

"Whom do I torment?" she demanded, although her eyes looked chastened.

"Hope Talbot for one, me for another."

"Hope and I go way back, Clay. There're years of snark between us. We wouldn't know what to do if the other wasn't around to needle," she said. "She knows I didn't mean to be hateful. That woman just gets to me with her high-and-mighty tone." Avid curiosity returned to her gaze. "I wonder why Mercy's really here?"

"And for how long?" His gut clenched. Dilly couldn't resist a beautiful, exciting actress, and if Mercy left without a backward glance, his daughter might never get over it.

He'd just gotten the pieces of his life back in order and now everything could be tossed to the wind, including his child's heart.

"And Clay, I'm awful sorry I mentioned Janna's accident. I didn't mean—"

He stalked out before she could finish. He knew exactly what she meant. Janna had run out of another argument and driven to her death in a white-hot rage.

And it was his fault.

Chapter Two

MERCY TALBOT SAT AT the sandwich bar in her parents' kitchen and flipped through the local paper. Nothing much had changed. The sports pages were full of high-school team news, a beer-league baseball team wanted a catcher and someone was complaining in the letters to the editor section about dogs barking. She sighed, happy not to be scouring *Variety Magazine* looking for hints of work.

"Hello," her dad said and hung up his jacket by the side-door entrance. From there you could go out to the backyard, where Mercy had spent most of the afternoon weeding flowerbeds. "Your mom not home yet?"

"She had errands." She flipped one more page to find the classifieds had shrunk to one-tenth their former size. They'd become irrelevant, like her. People placed ads online these days. Newspapers, like her, were yesterday's news. Even *Variety* was strictly online now.

"She kept Dilly with her?"

Mercy shrugged. "I guess." She'd avoided the child by sinking into a tubful of bubbles after weeding. She didn't need the reminder of her sister's death. Her passing hung like a pall after two years.

Nate Talbot stood in the kitchen, his large hands resting on the other edge of the counter. His nails were blunt, square, and clean.

Mercy recalled the comfort of holding her dad's hand as a child while her sister, Janna, tugged and squirmed to be released. "Thank God for your mother," he said. "I don't know who'd be taking care of Dilly if not for her."

"Most children go to daycare," she said.

11

Her dad ignored her comment and pulled a box of macaroni dinner out of a cupboard. "But this is your mom's bridge night, so. . . ." He set the box on the counter and gave her his patented I'm-a-helpless-male look.

"Fine by me. I'm not into healthy eating," she said with a smirk. Her dad was the best mac-and-cheese maker on the planet, bar none.

"Fine auntie you are, letting your niece eat this stuff," he teased, dragging out a saucepan.

"Are you kidding? I've lived on mac and cheese many times. Beans, too."

"It never got that bad, did it?" he asked over the sound of water running into the pan.

She saw no point in sharing the truth now. "Of course not, most times I ate at work. That's one of the perks of waitressing and a major reason Hollywood hopefuls wait tables. You're guaranteed one decent meal a day."

He opened the fridge and pulled out a couple of hot dogs. "And I figured all those starlets were skinny by choice."

"Most of them are." She tucked her fist under her chin and set aside the paper. "I won't miss worrying about my weight." Or the light lines that had begun at the corners of her eyes.

"You never told Mom how bad it got." His brown eyes, so different from hers, looked concerned. "You never told *me*."

"I'm a failure, not an idiot." Although sometimes she wondered if she was both.

He frowned but said nothing.

"If I'd told Mom how fast things were going downhill, she'd have been directing my life all over again. When Dilly came she was needed here. Besides, you missed Mom when she was back and forth with me."

He grunted in agreement. "Dilly changed everything. Being a grandmother meant a second chance with Janna. But when Janna died . . ." He trailed off and collected his thoughts. "I'm not sure how any of us would manage without your mother. Clay can't be mother and father and town vet all at the same time." Her dad shook his head in sympathy.

The sympathy surprised her because, during the years of her sister's marriage, contact between the families had been sparse and difficult. Hope had never approved of Clay because of his family and thought less of Janna for marrying him, which suited Janna just fine. She reveled in rebellion, in all its forms.

Dilly's birth had brought change to everyone but Janna. Hope had blossomed with pride in the baby, Nate and Clay had warmed toward each other and Mercy had taken the reins of her career.

If her indie film role in *Roger's Lie* had paid better, she wouldn't be here now. But she'd loved the pivotal role and felt proud of her work. Small comfort, but that was all she had. And maybe the new role Esme, his agent's assistant, had mentioned would pan out. Not likely, though. After all, it wasn't her agent who'd told her about it. He was too busy with actual working actors to give a damn about her hopes and dreams.

"I'm sure Clay's doing the best he can. He must appreciate the help." She needed to get off the topic of her niece and brother-in-law. Of course, he needed help raising a child. Given his background, and his parents, Hope helping out was likely keeping child services at bay. "I didn't tell you about how bad things got because you had enough to worry about."

He nodded but got busy with the classic comfort food. She warmed with nostalgia as she watched him. He was grayer, heavier in the jowls, but rock steady, as usual. "You made this meal taste special. I never did know how."

He grinned and looked years younger as he hit the broil feature on the oven. "It's all in the dogs, honey. It's all about the dogs."

She laughed. "I'll remember that." She stood and got out plates and cups. "Plastic for Dilly?" She held up the cartoon-character tumbler that she remembered. "Why did you keep this thing?"

"Your mom kept a box in the garage. Odds and ends."

"And what is with my room?" She was a cliché in this house: the adult child with a teenager's room. Trophies and tiaras from pageant triumphs lined the walls: a shrine to her early success. She'd had hope and potential. Her heart had been full of happy ambition and youthful eagerness. "Why are all my trophies still on the shelves?"

He held up his palms in a don't-blame-me gesture. "Your mom won't let them go and my garage is full of my gear."

"Sorry I had to stuff all my boxes in your garage, but it won't be crowded for long. I'll find my own place soon." Please, God, it wouldn't take long, because she couldn't afford a storage unit. She pulled her cell phone out of her pocket and set it on the counter beside the folded newspaper.

Nate glanced at it. "No calls today?" When she shook her head, he shrugged. "Their loss, honey." *Honey* meant something when Dad said it, unlike people in Hollywood who wielded the word like venom. She gave an inward shudder at the memory of her last humiliating day before she left that hellhole.

She didn't want to call her agent to see about the indie role Esme had told her about, but still, hope burned. She had to learn to extinguish that flame with a dose of reality. She would never garner the success she'd dreamt of and never be the star her mother expected her to be.

And that was Mercy Talbot's pathetic new reality. Last year, when she'd snagged her role in *Roger's Lie*, a cheaply made indie flick, she'd had reason to hope, but now her career had tumbleweeds blowing through it.

They lapsed into silence while her dad busied himself with the mac and cheese. She searched for another topic of conversation but came up empty. She'd done that a lot lately, come up empty.

"Enough about me," she said with a sigh. "How is Clay with Dilly?"

"He's good. Better than he thinks he is."

"And Mom? Is she okay with Clay?"

Nate slanted her a sidelong glance. "She steps carefully. Dilly's everything to your mother and she's keeping her concerns to herself."

For once. After seeing how Clay clutched Dilly to his chest at Janna's funeral, she had no doubt Clay was doing his best.

"Your mom takes Dilly to all the classes you took." If Nate had noticed that Mercy had avoided Dilly earlier, he hid his disappointment.

"Mom said that sometimes she gets stubborn about going." She remembered lots of children who hadn't liked dance class. They came, they tried, and they left. Their moms hadn't pushed but found something else their children enjoyed. Looking back, Mercy was glad she'd liked the discipline dance required. It had made life easier when she was a child. "Maybe Mom should lighten up on Dilly for a while."

"Might as well ask a fish not to swim."

A trickle of sympathy for Dilly made Mercy shift in her seat. "Nothing's changed then." Her mom could be a bulldog when it came to dance class. She changed topics because sympathy for Dilly wouldn't count a whit with her mom. "Not much has changed in the paper here either." She tapped the thin edition. "Even these complaints. I swear I read this letter whining about dogs barking once a week back in school."

"That must be the neighbors out by the rescue operation that Clay's involved with. There's some opposition to it."

"Clay Foster's running a rescue?" The irony made her chuckle. "Bad-ass Clay Foster is saving animals for free?" The man her sister had claimed was cold and unfeeling? A savior? She found it hard to believe. "How did this come about?"

"He got involved a couple of years ago when a dogfighting ring was busted near here."

"Poor things. But aren't dogs used like that ruined? What breed were they?"

"Mostly pit bulls. But once people heard about the place they started dropping off all kinds of dogs. Karen Bowler's overrun out there." He shook his head in sympathy. "Has been for two years."

She drew back in surprise, a visceral response to the breed. Clay had been involved since Janna's death at least. "Isn't he afraid for Dilly with those dogs?"

"He says he's not. Your mother won't allow Dilly anywhere near the kennels. We don't tell her she goes with Clay sometimes." He tapped the side of his nose in his familiar *secret-from-Mom* gesture. What Hope didn't know wouldn't hurt her.

"Two years," she muttered.

"He jumped on the idea to keep busy. As if raising Dilly and taking over a vet clinic wasn't enough to keep his mind occupied, he took on the rescue, too." Nate sighed deeply and nodded. "Clay's a good vet. Doesn't overcharge and never tries to upsell. I guess he needed more distraction from his grief. It's not good for a man with a child to raise to wallow in the past."

"He handed Dilly off to Mom."

"He didn't feel equipped to do everything on his own, and your mother, well, she needed Dilly. And Janna had dropped her off here plenty of times. Dilly was used to being here."

She nodded. Maybe Clay saw himself in the dogs: battered, bruised and unwanted. Maybe the dogs were easier to deal with than facing life without his wife. She'd bet Dilly's dance classes started after Janna died. There's no way her sister would have agreed.

"Is Clay seeing anyone?" she asked. A new wife may want some say in how a stepdaughter was raised. Hope would hate being usurped in a role she relished.

"As far as I can tell Clay keeps to himself." He reached into the fridge and pulled out a jug of iced tea and held it up in offer.

"Yes, please, I'm parched." She waited while Nate poured two glasses.

If Clay was on his own, that's how he wanted it. He'd always been attractive and had girls fluttering around him in school. But once Janna had set her sights on him, she'd made sure no other girls had had a chance.

"He and his sister, Elle, were united against the world," she commented. "She was loud and mouthy while Clay was quiet and stern, but they had each other's backs." There'd been fights and suspensions as they'd defended each other as far back as grade school. Eventually, nobody messed with the Fosters.

Nate shook his head and slid the hot dogs under the broiler. "Elle Foster left town about the time Janna and Clay got married. I'd say Clay Foster's happier with animals than he is with people."

Another cliché.

One brisk knock on the side door startled them both. "Hey there," came a low male voice as Clay stepped into the kitchen.

"You're here earlier than usual," Nate said. "I'm just getting her snack ready."

"Mac and cheese, I see."

Clay was as attractive as ever: commanding, intense, and bad-boy handsome. He was thinner than she remembered, but then she'd never studied him. *Much*. There was something dangerous and exciting about Clay Foster, and she'd preferred not to think about that. Today he wore clean pressed khakis, a vivid-red polo shirt topped by a worn leather jacket and stood with his hands on his hips, knees, and feet braced. "The Punk not here yet?"

Nate offered his hand as if it were rare to have his son-in-law in his home. Maybe Clay waited outside most of the time. "Clay," he greeted him with a nod. "Hope had an errand on the way home. They'll be here any minute."

"Nate." He shook hands with Nate and ducked his head at her, but not before an assessing glance. His intent focus was one of the few things she recalled about the teenager he'd been. That and the town's negative reaction to the Fosters. "Mercy, I heard you were back. Staying long?"

His tone was coolly objective, but his eyes said he was keenly interested in her response. Unfortunately, she didn't have an answer for him.

"You're asking the unknowable." She shrugged off the question. The question that she'd avoided all day by hiding inside her daddy's house waiting for the phone to ring. Pathetic.

He peered directly into her eyes when she hedged and suddenly she knew he wanted her gone. A spark of pique crackled and made her sit straighter. Why should he care how long she stayed?

She wasn't doing anything that might affect him. The pique burned down to curiosity just as quickly as it had sparked. She didn't much care what Clay wanted.

She glanced at her hands where they rested on top of the newspaper. "My dad makes the best mac and cheese in the world. It's his best dish, and it got me through a lot."

"Through a lot?" he echoed in a tone that dismissed the idea that she'd had her share of troubles.

She nodded. The disappointments in the pageant world could be tough on a kid. But considering *his* childhood, she decided against saying so. "Sometimes nothing's better than Dad's mac and cheese," she said vaguely, not wanting to dwell on past failures when she had a big whopper of a failure to deal with now. "Mom and Dilly should be here any minute," she repeated her dad's earlier comment and drummed her fingers on the top page of the paper.

From Clay's hesitation to take a seat and Nate's deference, these social moments must be rare, though the men should feel a bond through her niece. "Oh, I just remembered that I found something," Nate said into the silence and rushed off to a back room.

Alone with her brother-in-law for the first time ever, she was at a loss. The last time she'd seen him had been at Janna's funeral. He'd withdrawn and walked to the front of the chapel, where he'd held a sleeping Dilly in his arms as he stared down at the casket. He'd been deathly pale, unshaven, and visibly shaken.

Her mother had blamed it on a bender, but now Mercy wasn't sure. There hadn't been a hint of the wild life Clay used to live since before Dilly was born. He'd put all that behind him when fatherhood had come calling.

Janna was the one who hadn't settled into parenthood. Two years had given Mercy the distance she needed to see the truth.

"So, uh, how've you been?" She slid over to the next stool to let him see he was welcome to sit. She wasn't sure he'd take a seat otherwise.

"Busy. Took over Doc Rimmel's clinic when he retired."

"I see you keep the letters to the editor hopping mad." She tapped a chipped fingernail on the paper. She pulled her hand back. She'd noticed the chip earlier but hadn't bothered to repair the polish. "The dogs?"

"Oh, yeah." He slid onto the stool next to her but kept his back straight and his hands on his knees. "But those kennels were there for years before the new houses were built nearby. The Bowlers bred prize poodles before the rescue started up. Dogs have been there as long as I can remember."

Nate returned carrying a carved wooden chest Mercy recognized. "Janna hid that under her bed," she said when she saw it. "I hope whatever's in there isn't what I recall."

Her father shook his head. "Before she hid her pot, she kept these in here," and he opened the lid to show Clay.

"Formula One racing cars?" He lifted one out that was vintage racing green. "Retro. They look like the very early years."

"She loved them," Nate said with a voice full of nostalgia. "Ran them around the house all the time."

Clay spun the tiny wheels and pursed his lips admiringly. "Nice. They'd still take some corners."

"Dilly might like them," Nate said as he closed the lid and held the box out for Clay to take.

Clay's laugh was dry but warm. "She'll love them. Thanks, Nate." He took the box and set it on the floor. When he straightened again, he drummed his fingers on the counter.

The kitchen warmed with the scent of broiling hot dogs. Nate bent to check them in the oven. "Mom will have Dilly here any minute now," Dad said again. A lot of minutes had gone by since Clay's arrival, but who was counting?

Mercy slipped the newspaper under her arm and retreated to the living room and hoped it was far enough. She loved her mother, but this return home had made Hope prickly as hell and it just plain hurt to look at her niece. It was cowardly to avoid the child, but Mercy needed to ease into it. Her happy voice and smiles sent spears of loss through her. Dilly sounded like Janna.

But there was no escape because Clay followed her, making her feel more of a coward. What effect did his stern expression have on a young girl?

He took temporary ownership of her dad's lounger while she settled on the sofa. She picked up the remote control to aim at the TV. In that breathless moment between hitting the on button and when the picture appeared, the silence grew chill. Didn't he see she wanted to be left alone?

A game show lit the screen and the sound blared but that didn't stop Clay. No sirree. "You didn't answer my question. How long will you be here?"

She shrugged, flipped channels, and lowered the sound a few levels.

He leaned in close and slid his hand over hers to take the remote. His unguarded focus caught her and the remote slipped from her fingers into his. "I need to know because your mom's time with Dilly is good for her. With you here, Hope might—"

"What?" she cut him off, afraid of where this was going. "Ignore her motherless granddaughter?" A knot tightened in her chest. "Is that what Janna told you?" She lowered her voice but couldn't keep the ice out of it. "That our mother is capable of that?"

Clay looked over his shoulder toward the kitchen where Nate was busy stirring macaroni noodles. When he turned back to face her, his features firmed into sharp angles. "She told me about how you got all Hope's attention. She said if you ever came back, Hope would do it all over again." His hands flexed on the lounger arms. "Dilly needs her and I don't want you taking Hope's time."

"Bullshit. Janna never wanted anyone watching what she was up to. Because Janna's main concern was not getting caught." She'd never wanted their mother's attention. Janna had rebelled against whatever attention she got. Frustration rose as Mercy remembered the arguments and strife that filled their home during the worst of Janna's teen years. "Of course my sister put her own twisted spin on our home life."

"Bud down at the bus depot is married to my receptionist. You remember Bud and Sybil?"

Bud. Shit. At her nod, he went on. "Sybil tells me you arrived with all your goods in boxes. Far cry from the way you used to come to town."

"So? What of it?" She hadn't lied or put on airs. She didn't recall saying a word to good old Bud. She'd sat on the bench and waited for Nate to come get her. Oh, wait, she had to ask Bud to call him because she couldn't waste money on a cab.

"Either you haven't told your mother you're home for good, or she's under the mistaken impression that you arrived in the dead of night for a reason. She's been all over town telling people you're hiding from the paparazzi because you're waiting for some huge, career-making news."

She closed her eyes and drew in a slow breath. "Sometimes my mother's enthusiasm gets the better of her."

A noise from the kitchen ended the unsettling conversation as Dilly's wail filled the house. "You can stop your crying, Dilly, it won't make a bit of difference," Hope said above the din.

Nate's voice was next. "Hey, Dilly. Somebody's waiting for you in the TV room. You go on now and see."

They heard a *thunk* and suddenly Dilly barreled around the corner in a dead run. She stopped with a screech of surprise. "Daddy." But her eyes told Mercy how shocked she was to see him here. "You're in Grampa's chair." Clearly, this was a violation.

Clay stood and made a guilty face that brought out a giggle. She was hot, her hair sticky and her face pink. "Whoa. What have you been doing, Punk?"

Mercy watched as the miniature Janna collapsed against her father's legs and held on tight. This is why he'd braced his legs when he'd first arrived. He'd been prepared for her full-on assault.

Hope stepped out from the kitchen. "Nice of you to wait inside for a change, Clay." She looked from him to Mercy. "Go on out to the kitchen, Dilly, and get your dinner." She smiled down at her. "I have my ladies' bridge night tonight."

Clay swung Dilly into his arms. He gave Mercy a measuring glance. "No thanks, Hope. We'll get something to eat at the diner. What do you say, Punk?"

"It's a shame you won't let her have Dad's mac and cheese. It's the best," Mercy said. But she knew he'd had his fill of her and wanted to be gone. She shouldn't have been rude about Janna. The dead couldn't defend themselves.

Dilly swung her head around to look at her, her hair a soft fall of curls and waves. Sweet and so *Janna* it made her heart pinch. "Mac and cheese with hot dogs is good." But her face went dubious as she considered Mercy. Her brows knit into a frown. "Who's Dad?"

Mercy perched on the arm of the sofa and looked into Dilly's questioning face. "Your Grampa is my daddy"—she patted her chest—"and he made me mac and cheese when I was your age."

Dilly looked at her own daddy for confirmation. He nodded to assure her of the awful truth: her Grampa had had way special girls before her. Thunderclouds broke out across Dilly's face, dark enough to make Mercy laugh.

"Oh, there she is. The Janna I remember."

Dilly went stiff and tears sprang to her eyes as she opened her mouth with a dreadful screech. Hope rushed to her but Clay moved fast and sidestepped. He glared at Mercy and marched out of the room. The last she saw of Dilly was her unhappy face scrunched into creases of outrage as she bobbed up and down in his arms.

AS CLAY CARRIED DILLY through the kitchen with an apologetic glance at Nate, Dilly's pretty face puckered into a full-blown crying jag. "Take it easy, Dilly," he murmured as he hugged her stiffened body. "What's got my girl bothered?" Tears tracked down her cheeks as she heaved air for another ear-splitter.

Hope followed at his heels, filling the kitchen. He headed through to the mudroom to give Dilly more space and less Hope. But her grandmother still dogged them. "She's fussy because I attempted to comb her hair after dance lessons. You'd think I was trying to murder her. The girl needs taming, I swear." He heard the unspoken threat: if Clay didn't see to taming his daughter, Hope would.

"Hey, Dilly," Nate called to her in a singsong voice and tipped shredded cheese into the cooked noodles. When he held up a wooden spoon for her, Dilly was too angry to take it. She hurled the spoon to the floor in spite.

"That's it, we're going home," Clay said. Hope was right; he was out of his depth with Dilly. His sweet baby girl had turned into a writhing, screaming fury.

He held on to his patience just as tightly as he held his child. Her over-warm arms clung around his neck as she smeared her tears on his cheek. Heartbroken sniffles filled his ears.

Mercy stood on the far side of the sandwich bar, out of the way of the tantrum, observing. "She needs a nap before we go to the diner," he explained with a shrug. "Dance class interrupts nap time."

"Nonsense, both my children gave up their naps long before this age."

He wanted to ask for whose convenience, but he bit his tongue. He was the one left to deal with a cranky child.

Hope said, "Take her home. None of Grampa's mac and cheese for you today, young lady." He'd already said they'd go to the diner. But Hope had to make her point.

When Clay stepped out of the Talbot home, Dilly slid down to the walkway and sniffled and snuffled and wiped her runny nose with the back of her hand. "I want mac and cheese. I'm a good girl," she wailed.

But there was no going back now. "You need a nap before dinner and we'll have mac and cheese at the diner." She slipped her wet, snotty hand into his with one last big gulp of a sigh. "Does Grampa let you stir the cheese into the noodles?"

"Ya-huh. I gets to."

"Next time he hands you the spoon, you take it and help him the way he wants you to. *Without crying.*" He'd made a mistake showing up earlier than he normally did, but when the last two appointments of the day canceled, he'd wanted to get here to see what was happening with Mercy. He knew nothing more than he had before.

He held in a smile as he watched Dilly stamp her feet to show how angry she was. Mercy had been right. His Dilly was a teeny tiny Janna.

God help them all.

IN THE KITCHEN, HOPE raised her eyebrow at Nate. "Did anyone call for her today?" she asked as if Mercy wasn't right in front of them.

The question was directed at her father, but Mercy answered. "I'm not expecting calls, Mom." Not exactly true, but hoping and wishing were a far cry from expecting. Some part of her clung to the indie role that was up for grabs. The one that Esme, her agent's assistant, had mentioned in passing; washed-out hag or no. Maybe that role suited her more than ever. "You have to let it go."

Her mother bit her lip and a frown line appeared between her perfect brows. "We'll see. Your agent will come up with something, he always does. He'll find out what a loss it will be if Mercy Talbot walks away from her career."

Her mother wasn't ready to hear that it was the career that had stumbled off, leaving Mercy in the dust. The indie role Esme had mentioned was chaff in the wind. Esme had heard a glimmer of a rumor that financing had firmed and casting would soon begin. Esme was confident Mercy had a shot at being *a washed-up hag*. But that would mean spending money she didn't have on bus fare and a hotel for the audition. She couldn't face asking Hope and Nate for the money to go. Being at rock bottom meant there was no point digging herself in deeper. *Roger's Lie*, while fun and demanding hadn't done a damn thing for her career.

"Aren't you running late for your bridge game?" she asked her mother to get her off the depressing topic of Mercy's prospects. She smoothed her hands down her jeans and spied the box that Clay had left on the floor by the sandwich bar. Relieved at a viable escape, she picked up the chest and hurried out. With luck, she'd catch Clay before he left.

He was backing his SUV into the street when she waved him down. He stopped and the passenger-side window opened. "You forgot these." She held up the box. "I get the feeling you don't come over all that often, and I don't know where you live to deliver them."

"Same place the Fosters have always lived."

"In that trailer? Out in the woods?" she blurted. The questions hung in the air for a full second while his eyes narrowed. She wanted to sink into the asphalt. Heat flared in her cheeks at her gaffe.

"Something like that," he said dryly. His knuckles whitened on the steering wheel.

She searched for a way to recant the message between the words. *The Fosters are trailer trash.* But she came up with the worst possible thing.

She shrugged as if her unspoken message was nothing. As if his family was nothing. "Oh, well . . . here you go." *Lame.*

"I'm a good girl," said a sniffley voice from the back seat. Mercy peered through the dark-tinted back window to see her niece glaring back at her, cheeks wet and lips wobbly. "I a good girl," she screamed at Mercy for all she was worth.

"Of course you are," she said to the child but looked at Clay.

"She gets like this sometimes," he explained with a helpless shrug. "Anything can set her off. I've got to get her home. Thanks for the toys. She'll like them when she calms down. Tell Nate thanks again."

"Sure, maybe she'll fall asleep in the car." She'd heard somewhere that car rides could soothe a child. She stepped away from the vehicle and watched as Clay drove off, not sure what she'd just witnessed, but certain the episode had played out many times before. Dilly had been happy to see Clay, had talked to Mercy, had asked questions and then Mercy had mentioned Janna. After that, all hell had broken loose, as if comparing Dilly to her mother had enraged the child.

But how could looking like Janna send Dilly into a tantrum? Janna had been a beautiful child with soulful brown eyes.

She looked at the house where she grew up, lived in by the people who loved her most and wondered how she should deal with them now.

Hope had lied to all of Welcome about her return. Her room looked the way it had when she was fourteen. Her niece, who should be a source of joy, seemed to bring out more anger and frustration than comfort. Hope had claimed combing Dilly's hair had set her off this time, but Mercy wasn't sure that was right. Running the scene back in her mind, she doubted her mother's version.

Her childhood home looked the same, but inside was a maelstrom of grief, anger, guilt and lost dreams. She'd made everything worse by coming home. Clay assumed she'd take her mother's attention from Dilly and she couldn't blame him for thinking so. Janna had poisoned his mind and put that concern into his head—a terrible seed to plant.

Surely he saw that Hope had transferred her pageant ambitions to Dilly. Why else would her mother invest in dance and singing lessons?

Her dad, bless his heart, seemed the same. Right now, he'd be wondering what to do with his mac and cheese.

When she walked inside, Hope was pushing the noodles into the trash and then, with a theatrical gesture that painted a destructive pique, she tossed the broiled hot dogs. And let the lid of the trash can fall with a clattering slam. She brushed off her hands to let Mercy see she was pleased with the job. *Drama, thy name is Hope.*

"Your father's grilling steaks tonight." She smoothed Mercy's hair and then tucked an errant curl behind her ear. She clucked, clearly dismayed that hair had escaped her headband. "You never did use enough hairspray."

Mercy moved away and got plates and cutlery out for supper. "Dad said you have bridge tonight."

"That's after supper."

Nate took steaks outside to the grill.

"How am I supposed to find a job when you've told people I'm leaving for some big role?"

Her mother tore at the lettuce. "You don't need a job here. Your agent will call." She whacked at a juicy red radish. "You're an incredible talent and any day now you'll get your break. Isn't that what I always said?"

"That doesn't make it true." She backed away and turned to leave. "Sometimes potential doesn't pan out," she muttered as she marched down the hall that led to the bedrooms.

"What was that, honey?"

"Nothing, Mom, just a home truth I took too long to see." She stepped into her bedroom and closed the door. She leaned against it, hands still on the knob, hating that she'd practiced her oldest trick with Hope: avoidance. Walking out of the kitchen was the worst kind of cowardice.

She was beginning to see a theme in her daily decisions. She squeezed her eyes shut against the pink-and-white frill explosion that was her room. Ruffles, lace, glittery trophies and cheap tiaras the size of chef's hats filled two walls. Still more filled her closet and blanket box at the foot of the narrow canopy princess bed.

What would it take to make her mother believe their dream was dead? No answer came to her in the mausoleum her mother loved. Instead, Mercy felt the urge to escape the frills and reminders of her past successes. This *couldn't* be all there was to her.

It can't be everything. It can't.

But what if it is? What if this is all there is of Mercy Talbot? All there will ever be? She battled back fear and opened the door at her back.

In full retreat, she crossed the hall to Janna's old room and leaned on the doorframe. At seventeen, Janna had moved out in a blind fury that ended the battles between mother and daughter. Days later Hope had transformed Janna's room into a sewing room. Mercy opened the closet door and found her old costumes in cotton bags and organized racks of sequins and rickrack.

Hope had been indecently happy because with Janna gone, she'd had room for a cutting table and organized shelving. Hope had never asked Janna to come home. Nate had tried, but she'd refused.

The battles had ended, but Mercy had learned that to defy Hope was to lose her. She'd never stood up for herself when she should have. It had been easier to avoid confrontation.

Things had to change. Mercy had to change them.

Janna had been the one to take life on and live it full bore. She never compromised or fretted about what their mother would say.

After moving out and quitting school, Janna had moved in with Clay Foster and that was that. In the years that followed, Mercy got sporadic reports from her parents on how Janna and Clay were the wildest pair in town. A Vegas wedding had cemented them. Hope had sniffed that they could've had the decency to allow the family a real wedding. But she hadn't hosted a party to celebrate, either.

Hope had begrudgingly given her son-in-law credit for stepping up the way he had when Dilly was born. But that hadn't stopped her blaming him for Janna's drunk-driving accident. The funeral had been brutal, and Hope had raked Clay from head to foot over allowing his wife to leave their home that night.

Clay had stood, still as stone, and allowed Hope to rant until Nate had taken his wife by the arm and led her away. One glance at Clay's eyes had told Mercy what she needed to know.

He'd agreed with every word her distraught mother had said and it was eating him up. Clay today was a grieving husband, a busy single dad running a hectic vet clinic parenting one hell-bent-for-leather little girl.

He'd changed from teen bad boy to upstanding professional and caring father. A part of her wanted to add *sexy as hell*, but she shied away, appalled that she'd noticed.

To dispel further inappropriate thoughts of her *brother-in-law*, Mercy joined her parents and ate salad and steak and talked of nothing more important than whose daughter got married and who among the Talbots' friends got divorced or retired, or both. There appeared to be an uprising among some of the longtime wives when it came to spending day in and day out with their newly retired man underfoot.

"We don't have to worry about any of that, though, do we, Nate? Not with all I have to do with Dilly. She keeps me running, I tell you." Hope sliced into her steak. "You remember how much we bonded through all our trials and tribulations on the circuit, Mercy. That's what I want with Dilly."

"Bonding." A bite of potato caught in her throat and Mercy washed it down with a sip of water. Her mother called all those pageants, dance lessons, all that *judgment*, bonding. "Maybe Dilly is too young. Why not wait a year and see how she does then?" Too late, she remembered her father's comment about asking a fish not to swim. She caught his eye and made a face.

"Nonsense," Hope said. "You started as an infant. I'm actually behind with Dilly's training. If Janna had cared one whit, she'd have let me handle Dilly sooner, but no." She blinked and Mercy saw a suspicious sheen in her mother's eyes. Had Janna kept Dilly away from them? Her parents had never complained. Keeping Dilly from their parents wasn't something Janna would share with Mercy.

It had been two years since Janna's death—far too soon to talk about her without emotions running high. Grief rose in her throat. "Sorry, Mom. Pass the salad dressing, please."

Nate contributed to the conversation by telling Hope about the toy car collection. "Dilly will like running them around. Remember I built that track for Janna?"

"I remember." Hope reached across the table to slide her hand over her husband's. She squeezed his heavy knuckles and Mercy excused herself, too touched by her parents' pain to watch them tiptoe around it.

Back in her room, her resolve returned as she surveyed the pile of boxes that had traveled with her on the bus. Her whole life right here. Everything she'd worked for. She slid out the box-cutter blade and set to work slitting the tape that held each box closed.

She turned on the clock radio to hide the sound of her unpacking. When she had a handful of books to display, she crowded the trophies on one end of a shelf. They were clean. She took a better look around. Nothing in the room needed dusting.

Hope cleaned in here on a regular basis. This room was a shrine, while Janna's had been reassigned.

Surely her parents could use her old bedroom in some other way: a den, or workout room or a more adult guestroom. But Hope's treadmill and weights stood in the back sun porch, gathering dust while Hope came in here and cleaned the detritus of Mercy's young life. Absurd.

When she looked up from her unpacking, night had stolen the day and her room reflected who she'd become: a failed actress. She took the empty boxes to the garage and then flattened them for recycling.

She was here to stay until she got a job that paid the rent. She blew out a big fat breath in one go and accepted the truth. She had to find a job: one that paid decent money, not tips. Counting her severe lack of skills blackened her mind, so she quit. Hopelessness could end her job search before it began.

She glared at the perfectly clean shelves. After she moved out Hope could dust the trophies until her dying day, for all Mercy cared.

According to Clay, Bud and Sybil had informed the whole town of her failure. Failure was why she'd shown up in the dead of night at the bus depot with all her worldly goods in neat, square boxes. She stacked the last flattened box on top of the others against the garage wall. Her dad deserved his space.

She leaned into a back stretch with a sigh and heard her mother in the sound. *Oh, shit.* She looked like Hope and now she sounded like her, too.

But Hope clung to a glory that didn't exist, while Mercy accepted the end of her career. The way to get Hope to see the truth was for Mercy to build a new life.

For the first time in this long, long day, she felt more like herself. Tomorrow she'd wander through town and say hello to anyone who wanted to chat. She'd be honest about her reasons for returning and blunt about her prospects.

By the end of the day, she'd have sniffed out a job, figured out what to do next, and squelched the rumors her mother had started about why she'd returned.

Tomorrow would be a brand-new day with a brand-new Mercy.

Chapter Three

MERCY HAD BEEN ALL over town, checking out every lead she had for a job. Nothing.

People she knew, people she'd hoped wished her well, refused to consider her. She'd asked at the beauty salon, but Betty-Jean had laughed and pretended she'd hired a high schooler when the sign looking for daytime help was still in the window. Betty-Jean had made a point of grabbing the broom and sweeping Mercy out the door.

Other shops had been less humiliating, but she was still jobless.

Which brought her to Day's Hot Grill. The diner on the edge of town was famous for its mile-high meringue. No more than a logging camp cook trailer when it started over seventy years ago, Day's Hot Grill was now a local landmark for visitors, locals and people passing through. Various additions and upgrades had added tables and an outdoor patio, but the original trailer still stood and the counter stools were full.

Day's was a greasy spoon, no more, no less. And now, with luck, Mercy would wait tables there. She had experience. Much higher end, of course, but she was a quick study and would pick it up on her first shift.

She climbed out of her dad's pickup and flung her faux designer bag over her shoulder. Maybe she should toss her sunglasses back in the truck and tie her hair back off her face. She didn't want to look too Hollywood.

Jeeze. She was fretting about applying for a waitressing job in a greasy spoon. She'd never felt this pitiful in her life. If yesterday was a long, long day then she needed to rethink her definition of long.

She squared her shoulders, fluffed her hair, slipped on her sunglasses and slicked on some lip-gloss in the truck's rearview mirror. Her makeup was still dewy fresh and with the glasses on, she gave off a successful aura. She pinched her cheeks, although it was unnecessary. Throwing a net over the butterflies in her stomach, she climbed out of the truck for one more try at a job.

Before she got to the door, she could smell the fryers, a hint of burnt coffee and bacon. The sign said breakfast was served all day. No kidding. She would go home at night smelling of fried food and be happy about it.

She pulled out her best smile as she stepped inside. No one turned to look at her. People were used to the busyness of Day's doorway.

The lone waitress motioned her to the counter and she walked up to the counter and slipped onto a stool.

Belinda, the waitress and the granddaughter of the original camp cook, eyed her. "You're Nate Talbot's girl," she said. "What can I get you?"

"Pie?" she requested as a heavy mug was set at her place. Belinda sloshed coffee expertly into the china with a highhanded flourish. "And coffee," Mercy said, as the coffee settled.

"Apple, lemon meringue, bumbleberry?"

"Lemon, thanks, I don't want to miss out on your meringue," she said with her warmest smile. It worked because Belinda's eyes warmed right back at her. Mercy reached out to touch one finger to the back of Belinda's hand.

"What else can I do for you?" Belinda queried.

"Call me Mercy." She looked around and leaned in. She should've yanked her hair back to the nape of her neck, done without the glasses and removed all trace of her dewy-fresh makeup. She was overdressed and overdone to work in here. Her butterflies escaped the net and beat against her stomach lining in a bid for freedom. "I, ah, I'm wondering if you need another server?"

"What? You mean *you*?" Belinda's eyes went from warm to mirthful in a blink.

"I have experience," she said, too anxiously, too earnestly. She'd revealed more than she should. Right there, in Belinda's eyes, she saw refusal before she could breathe again. Just as quickly, she rattled off the names of the places she'd worked in Hollywood. Not one of them qualified as a greasy spoon.

"But Nate and Hope were in here yesterday, telling me how you're waiting until you're called for your next part. Some big movie, right?" She laughed and smiled as understanding dawned in her gaze.

Before Mercy could correct Hope's misinformation—again—Belinda nodded. "Oh, I get it! Do you want to research your role? Pretending to be a truck-stop waitress or somethin'?"

"No, not at all." This had gone sideways faster than most of her conversations today. Before she could gather her wits, Belinda patted her cold hand where it lay lifeless on the counter, a victim of shock.

"I'll be right back with that pie." Then Belinda drifted down the counter, sloshing coffee refills into china mugs as she went.

Mercy dug into her pocket for change. Not enough. The pie and coffee would come to more than she had. She waved at Belinda. "I'll pass on the pie. I need to keep my weight down." It was all she could say. Pride wouldn't let her announce to a diner full of customers that her mother had lied and that Mercy Talbot was out of options.

"You actresses are as bad as those skinny-mini models," Belinda chided and clicked her tongue. The counter patrons all laughed.

What passed for coffee was bitter. Or maybe it was just Mercy's frame of mind.

MERCY'S RETURN STILL worried Clay three days after he'd gone to the Talbots' place. Apparently, she'd been looking for work and come up empty. Somehow, Sybil had gleaned the details of each failure, including a humiliating rejection at the recycling depot. It appeared that Mercy wasn't qualified to sort paper from plastic. What he didn't need to see was the glee in Sybil's gaze when she reported the fiasco. He finished writing his notes in the file on the litter of Siamese kittens.

The next time Sybil shared one of her rumors, he'd point out that it wasn't Mercy who was bragging about her big break: it was Hope. Mercy had never been one to brag about herself. Lots of people talked about Mercy, but she rarely did.

He'd pointed that out to Janna once. Big mistake. His comment had enraged her.

Sybil buzzed through to him with one terse comment. "Your sister-in-law's here." By the time he got out front, Sybil was smiling widely and pouring Mercy a coffee from the office pot. Sybil never shared that coffee unless she wanted something. In this case, it was Hollywood rumors. Her avid interest gave her away. Sybil was an indiscriminate gossip, everyone and anyone was fodder.

"Tell me. When you met Sly Stallone . . . is he as buff as he looks in his Rambo movies?" Sybil's voice went breathy.

Breathy on a woman her age was too— he controlled a shudder that his receptionist wouldn't appreciate, and stepped into the office.

Mercy flashed him a grateful glance, but replied to Sybil, "Yes, he's a fit and interesting man. I admire the way he got *Rocky* off the ground back in the day."

That last part sounded genuine. "Mercy, it's nice of you to stop by."

She stuck out her hand as if to shake his, but he clutched the file he held. When she blinked in surprise, he relented and took her hand in a light clasp.

Warm, firm fingers and a smile that reached her eyes gave him a start. He released her hand. "Sybil's sharing her coffee? This is a surprise. She shares it when she wants something." He leveled a look at his receptionist. "Like useless gossip, or a day off, or a favor."

Mercy bit her lip then took a sip of coffee. "Mm, I can see why you keep this wonderful brew to yourself." Another wide smile warmed her eyes. "And please call me Mercy."

Clay took a longer look at his unexpected visitor. Rounded shoulders, downcast eyes, flushed neck. Mercy needed to talk, not chat with Sybil. He motioned her to his office in the back. There were no chairs for visitors. He moved files around on his desk until he had room to perch. He slid his chair across the floor toward her. She took the seat and slumped as if Atlas had transferred the world to her shoulders. "What's up?" he asked.

She pinched the bridge of her perfect nose and sighed. "Damn, I hate sighing. It sounds martyr-like. And too much like my mother." She glanced up at him with a self-deprecating air. "I hope you're okay with me dropping in here. I'm sorry for taking time out of your schedule."

"But, you're here. What's up?" He glanced at the clock. "I've got a few minutes."

"I couldn't face going home." Her lips tightened for a microsecond. "There, I said it. I'm having a hard time with moving back into my folks' house." She raised her hands, fingers poker straight. "I never imagined having to do that. And here I am, living in my old room that's decorated exactly *like my old room*." She shook her head. "It's all still there. Trophies, ribbons, tiaras. The room's more crowded because I've moved in, but it's all still there." Her eyes widened as if she couldn't believe it herself.

"A shrine?" He'd never seen more than the kitchen and living room in the Talbot house.

"What does it say about my parents that within days of Janna moving out, my mother turned her bedroom into a sewing room so she could make my costumes?"

He blew out a breath. "I don't know. I have no idea what it means." But he did. It meant Janna had been right. Hope had loved Mercy, her perfect daughter, more.

At least *his* parents had been evenhanded in their neglect of him and his sister. Equal opportunity neglect meant it wasn't personal, just life in the Foster household. He shut out the memory. "Maybe it means your mom needed the space?"

"That simple, huh?"

"No. Families never are," he said. He and his sister had been close once, united against their parents, but he rarely heard from Elle now. "Don't look to me for answers on family. My own was a mess."

She nodded as if she understood.

The nod angered him. No one understood but Elle. And now, after all this time, even that was questionable. He moved to stand because the buzz of anger made him antsy. He didn't discuss family. Ever.

"I'm, um, looking for a job," she said. "You don't have one hanging around empty, do you? Because I'd love to fill it."

Shock that she'd ask him, of all people, made him sit back down on the desk. He rubbed his chin. "No, I don't. All full up." The idea of any of the Talbots coming to him for help seemed ludicrous.

"Oh. I'm not qualified anyway. But if you ever need a great smiler, I'm your girl." She tossed another of her eye-warming smiles at him to prove her point.

The room and all that was in it stilled: his breath, her smile, her eyes and then, his heart. Jesus, she was beautiful.

She blinked and the world was in motion again, a reminder that this woman was trained to make people believe anything she wanted them to.

"If I ever do a TV spot for the clinic, I'll have my people call your people," he quipped and tossed her a smile of his own.

She blinked again and stood quickly. "Funny," she said in a dry tone. "Then you'll be calling my mom. I'm not sure my agent's aware I still exist." She backed away and turned to open the door. With one hand on the knob, she looked back at him. "You have a beautiful daughter, Clay."

"Thanks, she's more beautiful when she's not bawling. I'm not sure what her problem is lately. She used to be much easier to deal with."

"Infants have simple physical needs. Dilly's not that baby anymore. She's old enough to think for herself." She shook her head. "Not that I know anything about children, of course." She turned the doorknob to open it. "I'm sure I'll see her at her best sometime soon."

"I don't know anything about children, either. But if you go to one of her pageants with Hope, you'll see her win."

A grimace crossed her face faster than a blink. But that couldn't be right. "Maybe I'll do that," she said softly without a smile. "Well, I'll go, but if you hear of a job, please let me know."

"About that," he said, holding up a hand to stop her exit. "Maybe people are reacting more to Hope's daughter asking for work than Nate's kid asking."

"You mean this is about my mother?"

He rubbed his chin in consideration. "If Nate Talbot's kid needed a job, people would bend over backward to help her out. Not so for Hope's famous daughter."

"This isn't just her lying about me and my non-existent career? It's about her lording it over people for years?" She put her forehead to the door. "I don't have a prayer."

"I'll keep my ear to the ground. If I hear of anything, I'll put in a good word for you." It was the least he could do. And his offer had nothing to do with her smile or her incredibly blue eyes. Which at the moment looked moist and over-the-top grateful.

"Thanks." She turned to leave and then stopped. "I didn't mean to upset Dilly the other day by mentioning how much she looks like Janna. It's been bothering me that I upset her."

"Don't blame yourself for a moody toddler. She was tired. She misses her nap when she goes to dance class."

"If you say so." She looked doubtful.

"Parenting books say some kids her age still need to sleep mid-afternoon. Dilly's one of them. I wish your mom would reschedule her dance classes, but she knows best." The proof stood in front of him. "After all, it worked for you."

She looked steadily at him while she processed that. "You do understand that my mom can get too focused. When she gets like that, she closes her mind. It's true that she taught me that focus can help you achieve your goals, but sometimes it pays to be flexible." Her eyes never wavered from his and he had the uncomfortable feeling there was more here than met the eye.

"Sure," he said because he couldn't probe for what she didn't say. They were virtual strangers, linked by the memory of a woman two years gone. He scrubbed a hand down his face. "There are days I'd love to grab forty winks. Maybe that's where Dilly gets it."

OUTSIDE THE CLINIC, Clay's comment rang in Mercy's mind. He believed Hope had Dilly's best interest at heart and that all the work she demanded would pay off for Dilly. He also clearly expected that Mercy would return to her career because all her training under Hope's tutelage had prepared her for success. She rolled her eyes at that.

The irony made her cringe inside. Hadn't Mercy begged him for work? Hadn't she made it plain she was a colossal failure? None of her years of work had paid off. He shouldn't look to Mercy as an example. Not when she'd been this close to signing that contract—she shut off the thought as too humiliating.

Mercy smacked her palms against her dad's steering wheel. He'd need the truck back soon and she'd have to go home to Hope and her smug assumptions that Mercy's agent would call and put her career on track again.

Home to Nate and his quiet concern that made him look at her as if he wanted to fix things if only he knew what was wrong.

Home to her bedroom, still full of trophies and little-girl lies. She started the truck. Main Street was the same as she recalled it. People still parked in front of stores and ran in for a quick purchase. She drove past the bakery and noticed that the upstairs office space now contained a real estate office. The sign read "Hughes Realty."

Parking spots were hard to come by, proof of how busy the shops were. Someone here must need a pair of willing hands, but Hope had convinced the whole town Mercy was headed back to Hollywood.

She pulled into a side street and called Esme, as if to prove there was nothing left for her in L.A. Calling was better than doing nothing, better than sitting here in a stew of regret and way better than humiliating herself looking for work no one in this town would give her. When Esme answered in her clipped tone, Mercy hesitated.

"Speak in three seconds or this line goes dead." Clearly, Esme was used to clients with second thoughts about calling.

"It's Mercy Talbot, Esme." She drew in a calming breath. "The last time we spoke you mentioned a role in an indie production. The mother who'd lived hard?" *AKA washed-up hag.*

"Oh, right. Sorry, honey, the investor pulled the plug. Financial difficulties." She clicked her tongue. "But don't give up, there's still hope for another investor."

"Sure. Thanks, Esme. Call me if anything happens."

"Of course I will, honey."

There was that word again. *Honey*. It meant something when her dad used it.

After the call she never should have made, she drove past the pet supply store. Pets. Her mind kicked straight back to Clay. She hadn't expected him to hire her. Not really. She'd just needed to vent.

Clay's comment about being Hope's daughter niggled at her. If he was correct about people holding grudges against Hope and taking them out on Mercy, then she was in a worse position in Welcome than in L.A. At least in L.A. she had the right kind of experience in the right places. She should never have come home.

Now she didn't have the bus fare or rent money to move back.

She passed through several neighborhoods she remembered and breezed by the high school without a second look.

Her return had shown her that there was more to Clay's marriage to Janna than a good girl gone bad. She had to wonder which of them had been the bad influence. If Mercy hadn't returned to Welcome she might still view her sister's husband through Hope's jaundiced eye.

She hadn't forgotten the time Janna and Elle Foster had been arrested for brawling in a bar on the outskirts of town. Apparently, Clay's sister hadn't cared much for Janna's influence on her younger brother. Hope had been too appalled to mention the episode, but Nate had been devastated and called Mercy. *Brawling, of all things. God, Janna, what were you thinking?*

When Mercy had asked that question, Janna had blown her off for a month. Things between them became more strained as Mercy accepted their distance and put extra energy into her career. It had been far too easy to move away from Janna.

Real conversation with her sister didn't resume until after Dilly was born, and by then Janna wanted out of her marriage. She'd claimed the marriage had gone from wild fun to terrible. Janna's partying had left ill-prepared Clay to take care of Dilly while trying to get through veterinary college.

In a deeply troubling way, Janna had been jealous of Clay's dedication to school, and worse, resentful of the way he bonded and cared for their baby. Mercy recalled one phone call where Janna had been furious that Doc Rimmel had taken an interest in Clay. The old vet helped him in every conceivable way. But that was just the start of her complaints that time. Janna had gone on to whine bitterly that Dilly reached for Clay first.

Guilt washed over her for not seeing the truth at the time. Janna was disappointed in motherhood and wanted out.

If Janna were here today, she'd see Clay as a wonderful father, a capable and admired veterinarian. Mercy liked him and surely her sister would, too. If their marriage had ultimately failed, Janna would admit that Clay was a good man.

She returned to the idea that she liked him as a brother-in-law with a kind face. He was someone to vent to in a town full of petty vengeances and old hurts. That was all she felt for Clay.

The slow-moving warmth that had crept along her skin when they'd shared that look meant nothing more than like. It was good to like the father of your niece. Liking Clay brought the family closer and made their relationships stronger.

For Dilly's sake, she hoped they could all be friends.

CLAY PULLED INTO THE driveway at his in-laws' house and turned off the ignition. He waited a few seconds, considering whether or not he wanted to go inside again. He hadn't bothered for the last few days because Dilly had been outside with Mercy when he'd arrived. But today was wet and overcast and Hope said Dilly might catch a cold, and runny noses didn't win pageants.

Mercy's visit had surprised him this afternoon, in ways he didn't want to contemplate. Still, he smiled at the idea of a shrine in her bedroom. Somewhere Janna was kicking up her heels and saying, "See? Told you." He shouldn't be fascinated with whatever was going on in Mercy's bedroom, but he was. If Dilly had seen the trophies, surely she'd have mentioned them.

He climbed out of his SUV and walked to the side door. He gave the door one hard rap and then stepped inside. Dilly's sweater hung on her toddler-height hook and her shoes had been kicked off in a tumble.

When she walked the soles of her sneakers lit up like a pimped-out low-rider, but she loved them. "Is the Punk in here?" he called.

"Daddy!" she squealed and raced toward him. He scooped her up and let her hold both sides of his face. She loved to squish his lips into a pucker before giving him a wet smacker. Sometimes she held him there while she blew raspberries against his mouth.

God, he loved having a girl. Her firm, strong body, her girly giggles and complete trust allowed shivers of love to fill him. He lived for these moments: when her face was so close to his he could count her overlong eyelashes, taste her breath (sweet from apples today), and smell her sweaty, overworked body. With eel-like maneuvering, she loosed herself from his hold and slid to the floor. Tugging his hand, she pulled him through the kitchen to the living room.

"Hi, Clay," Mercy said from where she sat cross-legged on the floor in front of the coffee table. Pieces of a child's puzzle were laid out on the tabletop, waiting for Dilly's hand.

"We're not done here. There's a duck that's missing his nose."

"Ducks gots beaks," Dilly explained with a hearty sigh as she knelt beside her aunt and reached for the last piece. She patted it into place and turned to look up at Clay with triumph in her eyes. "See, Daddy? A beak." She tapped the duck with one finger and looked as prim and pleased as a teacher.

"Duck beaks are called bills, honey. They're wide at the end, and they use them to find food in the water. Beaks are sharp and are used by birds that don't swim like ducks." He'd show her the difference when they got home. "We'll look at them later."

But Mercy beat him to it. "Like the robin picture, Dilly. Remember? A robin has a pointy beak." She dug through the other puzzle pieces in the box and held up a robin's beak.

"What's a eagle gots, then?" She looked from Mercy to Clay.

"A great big beak," they responded at the same time. Then Clay added, with his hands up like claws, "And talons for grabbing."

Dilly squealed and launched herself under the table so Clay couldn't swoop in and snatch her up. Mercy's eyes lit with laughter as she joined in with a serious case of grown-up giggles that set Dilly off even more.

Clay got down on the floor, reached in and tickled his daughter into fits and dragged her out into his arms. When he stood, she tried the face squeeze thing again, but he dodged her hands, which made her laugh harder.

"Hey, how about we see Aunt Mercy's room where she keeps all her prettiest things?"

"Yay." Dilly's screech deafened him, while Mercy tilted her head and considered his request.

"Sure," Mercy said to the invitation to her room. "I'm surprised Grammy hasn't given them all to you, Dilly," she said with a sly look.

He looked toward the ceiling in defeat. She had him. Now he'd have to find room for all Mercy's trophies. And Janna? Was hissing at him and throwing darts at the back of his head. He should have thought twice before speaking. Still, this was a chance to see Mercy's private domain and show Dilly how much fun she could have at dance class. If she saw the results of Mercy's hard work and effort . . . but maybe at three and a bit, he was expecting too much.

There was one way to find out.

He turned and headed down the hall toward the bedrooms, immediately lost as to which door was hers. "To the right," Mercy said from behind him. "The sewing room's on the left."

"Janna climbed out that bedroom window to sneak out with me," he said for Mercy's ears. He shut the memories down. Today was about Dilly.

Mercy mouthed, *I know*, and leaned around him to open the closed door. He caught her scent, something light and pretty that smelled expensive. He buried his nose in Dilly's neck and blew a raspberry there. She shrieked and jumped down, running full-tilt into the room. One leap, a bent knee and there she was, atop Mercy's bed. She laughed and bounced, trying to catch the ruffles that hung from the canopy.

"Oh sh—" he bit off the expletive and gawked. Meanwhile, his less-than-impressed daughter did her best to jump high enough to yank down the whole canopy. Her chubby arms stretched but she was a good foot short. "You're too close to the edge, Dilly. What have I told you about using furniture as a trampoline?" He stepped into the center of the room and turned to survey the blinding glut of sparkly crap. "Holy shit," he muttered low enough to hide from Dilly.

"What'd I tell you? It's scary in here," Mercy gave him a low-voiced rejoinder. "Dilly, honey, get down and let me show you all my trophies. I took dance lessons at the same studio where you go." She walked to the shelf where she'd crowded the trophies to fill one end.

He noted that Nate had installed track lighting to illuminate the trophies in the best light. He flicked the switch and the sparkle was near dazzling, but he felt no burning ambition to see the same thing in Dilly's room. He just wanted her happy.

His daughter slid off the bed, pressed her back against the side and went suddenly, eerily still as she stared up at her aunt. "No," she answered Mercy's question about the dance studio and then popped her thumb into her mouth, a comfort she used on rare occasions. It was mostly a sleeping habit, and during the day she forgot about it. She wrapped her finger to cover her nose and settled against the bed. She stacked one foot on the other and waited.

"Here are my trophies and tiaras," Mercy said with a flourish to draw Dilly's gaze. She walked over to lift one three-foot-high monstrosity off the shelf.

Dilly looked but didn't move. Her mouth moved harder on her thumb. She flashed a look at Clay and he conceded. "You don't want to see them?"

Her fine, barely-there brows knit into a crinkle. "No," she whined around her thumb.

"Okay, maybe some other time." If she'd ever seen them before, he now understood why she hadn't mentioned them; she wasn't impressed, and from her rising mutinous expression, would never be impressed. He looked at Mercy, who'd wisely halted halfway across the room. "Some of those things are as tall as she is."

Mercy tilted it out away from her to get a better look. "You're right. I'll put it back right now. How's that, Dilly?" she asked after she'd returned the piece to its crowded place on the shelf.

Dilly shrugged and leaned harder into the side of the bed. With a yelp, she dashed into Clay's legs and hung on to his knees as if Mercy had turned into an ogre. She wedged her face into his kneecaps and rubbed her wet mouth and nose against his khakis.

"Time for home, Punk," he said with a breezy ruffle of her hair. His next words were for Mercy. "I change clothes at work. I can't have her sticking her face in dog slobber."

"That's considerate," she said. "And healthy."

He swung the Punk up into his arms and headed out into the hall with a parting shot. "We'll take a rain check on taking the trophies off your hands then."

"Oh, gee, thanks," Mercy responded in a droll tone.

THESE TROPHIES HAD to go. Dusted or not, cherished by Hope or not. They were holding Mercy back, freezing her into a place and time that would never come again. It was unhealthy to keep them.

As if they mattered.

As if they mattered more than Janna. And there was the crux of it. Janna was gone and all that was left of her was Dilly: a living, breathing trophy for the one success of her sister's life. A stab of grief made her slide to the floor, where she buried her face in her palms and breathed in deep, fighting the tears that burned.

Janna.

She remembered, then. Bath time shared with her big sister. Janna, holding her down for tickles, sharing her secret stash of candy hearts at Valentine's Day. Janna, giving her the pink one that said: "I love you." Janna with her pretty brown hair curled and dusted with sparkles that she hated, but Mercy loved.

Janna's lower lip thrust out in mutiny as she smashed one of her first trophies into jagged pieces. She'd cut her hand. Daddy, rushing in to help stop the bleeding before Mommy saw it on the pretty, white carpet in Janna's room. Mercy swept her hand into the fibers of that carpet, remembering how everything had been moved from Janna's room into hers.

Even this carpet.

Mercy lay on the floor and stared up at the ceiling. She covered her eyes with her palms and pressed back the tears. "Oh, to hell with it," she muttered and let them flow. They welled and slid down into her ears and then farther down through her hair. She imagined a sea of tears washing away Janna's blood from her cut hand, the salty wash a cleanser for all the harm done to her sister.

Her crime? Being herself. She'd been strong. Determined. Mercy had wanted to be like her, until the drugs and the boys and the drawn-out battles with their mom.

Nate had been a silent witness to the upheaval. He should have spoken up more, said something, found a way to diffuse the anger.

Maybe he'd tried, but Mercy saw no evidence of it. And she couldn't ask. No matter how she phrased it, she'd come off sounding accusatory.

Unless Clay had some insight. Surely he and Janna talked about their childhoods.

But why bring all that up now? What was done was done. No amount of questioning would change things.

Nothing anyone said could bring her sister back to her. Not the sister Mercy preferred to remember. Not the young girl Janna had been.

She doubted anyone would want the crazy-wild woman back if her behavior was the same. Life with Janna had become an angry swirl of promises and lies and disappointment. She'd suffered all those things and could imagine what Clay had borne.

Oh, how her parents had wanted Janna's baby to sort her out. Mercy had had some hope of that happening as well, in spite of the teary, boozy late-night phone calls from Janna after Dilly was born.

Mercy could hardly recall those conversations. They were convoluted rants that circled ugly, stupid demands. She couldn't count the times Janna had said Mercy had ruined her life.

Her tears dried tight on her skin, her heart awash in pain.

There'd been no fixing Janna, no fixing anything.

She rose on her elbows and glared at the trophies. Then she remembered the boxes. Her parents' voices grew closer as they said goodbye to Dilly. She heard the gate to the garden close and latch behind Clay and her niece.

Clay. What should she do about her growing appreciation of the man? Just seeing him with Dilly warmed her. He was gentle and sweet but struggled with self-doubt. She could see why he leaned on her mom for help. Dilly missed her mother and Hope was willing and able to take on daily care.

Still, something wasn't right about this arrangement. It wasn't lack of love or commitment. Dilly was loved deeply from all sides. She considered the lackluster response to the trophies and tiaras. Clearly, Dilly had seen them before and wanted no part of them. *Like Janna.*

Before her parents could come inside, Mercy raced to the garage and grabbed the stack of broken-down boxes she'd set aside for recycling. She found a roll of packing tape stuck on a nail over Nate's tool bench and took the items to hide under her bed for later. She straightened the bed skirt. She'd have to wait for a time when Hope was out of the house before she moved the gaudy pieces out of her room.

THE NEXT AFTERNOON Mercy was still carrying boxes out to the driveway when Hope slammed the minivan to a halt and jumped out at the end of the driveway, leaving her car door gaping and the engine running.

"Mercy. What's all this?" She walked the line of boxes, counting. "All of them? I can't believe what I see." She kept her tone low, a hint to not let the neighbors hear an argument.

"It's clear enough. I want these out of my room."

"Pick them up right now. I will not have the neighbors gawking." Her mom smoothed her jeans and her hair and spun to see who was looking out their front windows, watching. "Look, there's Jenny Swanson standing in her living-room window holding her afternoon glass of wine." And then more to herself than Mercy, she muttered, "Who's she kidding, that woman needs a tumbler." She narrowed her eyes. "It's no wonder her husband fools around," she added.

"Too late to hide this from the neighbors, Mom. Carrie Ann from up the block walked by with her mother and they helped me line them up. Her mother's got that motorhome that's in Carrie Ann's driveway. You and dad should take a tour of the thing. It's incredible."

"You're trying to get a rise out of me with that ingenuous expression."

"Sorry, but you taught it to me." Mercy tilted her head and widened her eyes. Hope's anger shimmered like moonbeams on waves and Mercy softened. "I can't take everything inside. The shelves are down by now."

"What are you planning to do with them?"

"I'll take them to the dump first thing in the morning," she promised with a light kick to one of the boxes.

"That's your Ultra Supreme Empress from Texas. Remember the work that went into getting it, not to mention the time and money." Her face stricken, she leaned against the hood of the van. "How could you?" she whispered. "Everything we worked for is here."

"Years ago," Mercy said exasperatedly. "Everything we worked for *years* ago is here."

"Grammy. *OUT*," Dilly screamed from inside the still-idling van.

Mercy rushed by Hope and slid open Dilly's door. "Okay, Punk, let's go see Grampa."

"Don't call her Punk. I prefer you use the long form. My granddaughter's name is Adele."

Mercy allowed the child to run up the driveway to the backyard gate, her shoes flashing neon-blue lights. She barreled past the boxes without sparing the shiny trophies a glance.

Mercy then climbed into the minivan and waited while Hope gathered her composure and stepped aside. Head high, Hope guided her into place while Mercy crept up to park.

"I'll just come out here after dark and take them all back inside," Hope vowed as Mercy tossed her the keys and sailed past.

Her mom taught her *that*, too: a strategy that had gotten under the skin of her competition, especially as the girls had grown older. There was nothing like confidence to strike fear into the heart of the other contestants. They'd all hated Mercy. They'd never imagined a girl from Washington State swooping in and taking it all away.

"How could you do this?" Hope whispered.

"Easy." Mercy turned back, took a step toward her and Hope straightened. "I have to move on with my life. And you should too."

"You had talent, beauty, poise. And now you come back here begging for jobs all over town. It's a slap in the face," she said as Mercy listened with her shoulders back and chin up. "A slap in the face," she repeated with heartbreak in her voice. "I've done all I can to minimize the damage from this ridiculous job hunt. Mercy Talbot working in a diner? Over my dead body," she announced. "I'm taking you to Dr. Withers to find out what's going through your head."

"I'd like to see you try." Mercy crossed her arms and leaned in filled with determination. "For the first time in my life, I'm thinking for myself. I *see* what I am, Mom. I am aware of what I've become: a failure at everything we aimed for. I need to rebuild from the ground up. You can help me or not. But I *will* do it."

Hope reached out, but Mercy stepped back and then stalked away. It appeared it no longer mattered what the neighbors heard because Hope raised her voice. "Honey, you need help. Maybe anti-depressants or anti-anxiety meds. *Something.*"

Chapter Four

AFTER THE SCENE IN the driveway with Hope, Mercy followed Dilly into the backyard. Her niece headed for a pile of freshly turned garden soil. She squatted, her bottom an inch off the ground. As Mercy drew nearer she heard Dilly talking softly. "Oh, poor worm, are you looking for your mommy? Do you want to go home?"

Mercy watched as Dilly poked a hole in the soil and then picked up the worm to place it in the hole. Carefully and with gentle pats of her chubby fingers, Dilly buried the worm, helping it, she supposed, to find its way home.

If someone offered me that kind of help and direction, I could find my way.

When Dilly saw Mercy's shadow fall across the pile of pungent soil, she started and turned her face up with a fearful expression. "I a good girl," she exclaimed in a voice Mercy recognized as step one on Dilly's personal path to defiance.

Or maybe it was her path to freedom.

Maybe Dilly was telling them more than they were hearing. "Of course you're a good girl. You're a very good girl." Mercy squatted beside her and felt the stretch in her thighs. "Auntie Mercy needs to do more squats, but for now I'll sit like this." She settled on the ground and crossed her legs.

Dilly's eyes went wide. "You get dirty on your bum," she chastised, using her grandmother's scolding tone.

Mercy laughed and pulled Dilly into her lap for a cuddle. "I don't care," she said as if getting dirty was as natural as rain. "I can get clean again."

Dilly considered the comment with all the focus she could muster. Then the sun broke out on her face, lighting up Mercy's heart in the process. Then with exquisite precision, her niece brought her fingers, dirt and all, to each side of Mercy's face.

Her cheeks flattened between Dilly's hands and Mercy did what she'd seen Clay do. She gave Dilly an exaggerated pucker, which was soundly and lovingly kissed with a juicy, wet mouth that tasted of sweet, red licorice.

"I see Grandma still uses licorice as a bribe."

Dilly smoothed her thumbs across Mercy's eyelashes and gave her face a close inspection as if she wanted to memorize every line and pore. Her sweet breath seeped out between their faces and Mercy drew it in.

Oh, Janna, you will miss so much.

Dilly patted her cheeks gently and whispered. "I make you clean." With sweeping motions, Dilly cleared Mercy's cheeks of bits of soil.

"Thank you, sweetie."

"You welcome," she said seriously.

"Now, let's go see what Grampa has for you."

"Pizza."

"No matter what it is, we need to wash up first," Mercy said as she stood. Dilly giggled and swiped her hands across Mercy's bottom, which, according to Dilly, was too dirty. The bum swiping soon turned into a race for the door. Mercy ran in circles around her niece and Dilly won with a happy screech.

Her dad had expanded his culinary skills to include pizzas made with English muffins that were perfectly proportioned for a child. Dilly insisted that Mercy take a bite of hers first. "Mm-mm, good."

While she watched Dilly chatter happily with Nate, Mercy marveled at her niece's sweet nature. "Dilly helped a worm find its way home in the garden soil," she told her father. And then she'd kissed her until-now-absentee auntie. Kissed Mercy with the sweetness the very young possessed. She blinked at sudden moisture in her eyes as her chest warmed.

And just like that, she fell: into love, into family ties, and into a commitment to see this girl child grow and become the woman she deserved to be.

Hope strode into the kitchen through the mudroom, fury stiffening each muscle, her face red and blotchy.

"Hi, Mom, you're just in time for pizza."

Hope took in the happy scene and froze in the middle of the kitchen. She glared at Nate, splintering the conversation with her starched expression. "You will put the shelves from Mercy's room up in the garage. Our trophies will go there."

Nate slid his hands to the top of the sandwich bar and spread his fingers wide. He turned his face down to stare at the floor for a long moment as the clock ticked several times in the silence. Amazingly, Dilly held her chatter as her grandfather considered his wife's demand. "No can do, Hope. We agreed that the garage was my space and I don't have room for those dust collectors. But I'll take the shelves. I need more storage in there anyway."

Mercy didn't want her father taking the flak for her, but before she could speak the kitchen wall phone rang. Since she was closest, she picked up, hoping, in the most cowardly way, that the call was for Hope.

It was Clay. "I've got an emergency at the rescue kennels and I have to go right now. Can you keep Dilly for a while longer?"

"I'll bring her to you. Will that work?"

"Sure. I'll meet you there." She hung up. "I'll need the keys to the van to take Dilly to Clay. I need directions to the rescue kennel."

"I do not allow her to go there. They have pit bulls in those cages." Hope's mouth turned down further.

Mercy raised her eyebrows. "If Clay said to meet him there, I'm sure it's safe enough." Still, she wondered how safe it could be. If one of those dogs got out, she shuddered at what could happen.

Nate spoke up. "She's been there before, Hope. Lots of times." The blotches on her mother's face went redder at the news.

"I don't believe you," she said under her breath. "She'd never keep a secret from me."

"Beau," Dilly chimed in and climbed off her stool. She raced past her grandparents with her hands held high in excitement. Then she waited by the door, wise enough not to run outside without an adult.

Hope dampened a paper towel and wiped pizza sauce from Dilly's mouth while Mercy grabbed her purse and ran a comb quickly through her hair. Her mother noticed and sighed. "No lipstick and grubby jeans. I taught you better than that."

Never go anywhere without looking your best.

With a frown at her mother, Mercy slicked on a colored lip-gloss. "Happy now?" she asked.

Some secret feminine part of her cheered that she'd taken a moment to fix her hair and lips. Not for Clay, of course, but for herself. *Tell yourself another lie.*

She opened the screen door to usher Dilly outside. "Do you like the dogs, Dilly? Are they all nice?"

"Yes, yes, oh yes."

"Who is Beau?"

But Dilly looked back at her grandparents and said nothing, a familiar stubborn set to her chin.

Mercy had to trust Clay enough to give the rescue kennel a chance. Still, she'd be extra careful until Dilly was with her father.

Once in the car, Dilly relaxed and chatted happily.

"Do you like your dancing teacher? Is she nice?"

"Ya-huh."

"Do you have fun dancing?"

Silence.

"It's not fun?"

Silence. Maybe Dilly didn't have the words to explain mixed emotions. Mercy was certain the dance teacher made it as fun as she could for children Dilly's age. But what if Hope put undue pressure on the child? Flashes of the epic arguments her mom had had with Janna made Mercy grip the steering wheel hard. She pried her fingers loose and forced her muscles to relax.

"Let's sing a song," she suggested and Dilly happily obliged with the theme song to her favorite television show.

The complaints about barking dogs that had been in the paper came to mind as Dilly entertained herself. Mercy recalled that the rescue was run by a former poodle breeder's daughter who'd inherited the kennels. The breeding kennels had been the Fosters' closest neighbor. Clay and Doc Rimmel became acquainted through the breeder, which explained how Clay had gone from bad boy to veterinarian student. Three miles out of town, they were minutes from the trailer where the Fosters lived. Clay and Dilly stilled lived on the Foster property.

Mercy's memory filled with a dark tangle of overgrown brambleberry canes and tall cedars and pines that made a forbidding shield from curious eyes. Any time she'd been out that way when she was a teen, she'd hated the look of the property. Dreary shadows and dark windows had given her shivers imagining what happened behind the screen of thorns.

She'd hated the idea of Janna living out there. Clay had been as forbidding and dark as the place where he'd lived, and Mercy had never looked at him without wondering what went on behind his inscrutable expression. That is, until her sister's funeral, when he'd shown his loss and confusion. Guilt had been etched into his face.

The Clay of today was different, though. Seeing him with Dilly had made her wonder if loving Janna had brought about the change or if it was having Dilly.

Not a question to ask a busy widowed father. How did you come by this happier countenance? Love for your dead wife? Or by having your wonderful child?

She turned into the driveway with the unassuming sign that read "Bowler's Rescue" and pulled up in front of a modest bungalow. She parked beside Clay's SUV. Dogs barked from behind the house. "Dilly, stay put and don't scream to get out."

Then she walked around back to check things out. If the dogs were out of their kennels and exercising, she didn't want Dilly running ahead into a pack of strange dogs. Maybe the kennel area was fenced and gated. When she walked past the bungalow she was surprised to see the layout of the kennels.

A long cinder block building with about fifteen chain link kennels protruding ran across the back of the house. Each kennel had a doggie door that gave the dog access to an interior kennel as well. She assumed the exercise yard was on the other side of the building.

Clay was kneeling inside a kennel with the gate open, running his hands down the legs of a heavy-chested white dog with a black saddle and a huge black patch that covered the left ear and eye.

"He must be the reason my mom's concerned about Dilly being here," she said as Clay noticed her approach. She kept still in case the dog took a dislike to her.

"Beau here is a lover, not a fighter," he said as the pit bull raised his head and gave the side of Clay's face a long, wet swipe. The dog's wide mouth curved upward into what Mercy could only call a smile. He groaned as if the luxury of being petted was a rare and precious thing. Clay rose to face her and if she wasn't mistaken his gaze slid from her feet to her head in a glance so quick she might have missed it if she hadn't been looking.

"Cute," she said, none too sure her description was apt. She stayed clear of the open door. The dog in the next kennel was a jet-black standard poodle while the one on the other side was a terrier cross who looked the worse for wear. She trembled in the corner, giving Clay and Mercy the cold shoulder by staring fixedly at the ground. "That one looks terrified." But something about the dog pulled at her and she walked toward the kennel door.

"She's had a rough time," Clay explained. "We'll let her get used to the routine here before we approach her. She needs to understand she'll be fed on schedule every day. No exceptions."

"I'm glad she's here." Black with gray tips on her scruffy fur, the dog looked as if regular meals had never come her way. Mercy squatted for a better look, but Clay's pit bull barreled into her and slobbered all over her face, knocking Mercy out of her squat and flat on her back. More wet kisses followed while she scrambled out of the dog's reach, trying hard not to squeal and show fear.

"You're fine," Clay said around a chuckle. He offered her a hand up. "Beau's more likely to drown you with slobber than bite." She accepted his help to her feet. As he pulled her up, Beau shouldered past her legs and knocked her closer to Clay. Her chest bumped his and she had to do a two-step shuffle to stay upright. He steadied her with a hand on each arm. She smiled her thanks and stepped away but Clay held tight.

"Nice save, Foster," she said smartly. His shoulders were wider than she'd thought. "That dog's a tank."

His eyes flashed with something unreadable and he dropped his hands.

"Beau." A childish squeal broke the moment and Mercy's brain froze in terror.

She spun out of Clay's shadow and ran back the way she'd come, the way the dog was headed. "Dilly! Dilly's out of the car." She made it to the corner of the bungalow, eyes stinging, heart pounding with fear of what she'd see—

Beau, haunches flat to the ground, front legs extended, mouth grinning again as Dilly hugged his neck and kissed the side of his broad head. The dog kept still as he could, but his muscles quivered in doggy excitement.

Mercy's knees shook at the relief. Clay slammed up against her back. "What the—?"

He wrapped his arm around her chest to hold her upright and spoke into her ear, "You scared the hell out of me, Mercy. Beau loves Dilly and, as you can see, Dilly loves him back."

The proof came when her niece straddled the dog's thick shoulders and grabbed his ears like reins. She screeched in delight while Beau grinned like a maniac.

"But he's dangerous and unpredictable, and strong." It was then, in the space of those few words, that she understood that the same could be said for Clay Foster.

Janna. She'd needed the danger, the strength, and the essence of what made Clay who he was. He'd been the dark, troubled bad boy, quiet in school. Didn't cause trouble, but looked like a barrelful of dynamite just waiting for a lit match. Waiting for a girl like Janna.

Clay's arm tightened across her midsection for a fraction and for a smaller fraction she wanted to slide her hand over his to hold him there. Instead, she stepped toward Dilly and squatted in front of the dog. "Don't pull his ears too hard, Dilly. You could hurt him." And he'd swing that broad, powerful head and knock the child right off her perch.

Beau rolled his soft brown eyes at her as if to explain Dilly could never hurt him and he would never knock Dilly over. She smoothed her knuckles tentatively along the underside of his jaw, where his skin was soft. When he grinned wider, she opened her fingers and stroked him there, no longer nervous of his wide, cavernous mouth.

Then he yawned and she got a close-up look at the power in his cheeks. "His mouth is full of cheek muscles," she said as she slid in surprise to her rump. "My Go—goodness."

"Lots of power in those jaws. Beau's my Judas." Clay crouched beside her and scrubbed the top of Beau's head. "He calms the newcomers, and if they've never been socialized with other dogs, he's the one to introduce them to society."

"You're that certain he won't hurt them?"

He gave her a steady look that somehow connected her stomach to her toes, which curled tight. "We've had him since he was a pup."

"Daddy says Beau likes it here 'cause he gots a job and dogs like to be useful." She stretched the word as if testing the context.

"That's right, Punk. People need to be useful when they grow up. Useful and productive."

But Dilly had moved on to hooking her fingers into Beau's smile and trying to tickle his teeth.

Again, Mercy's heart stopped, but when Beau just shook his head, slowly and gently, to dislodge Dilly's digits, the beat started again.

"He's smart and understands she's a child." She couldn't keep the awe from her tone. Her stuttering heart warmed.

Clay nodded, but his eyes locked on hers. "But don't trust any of the other dogs with Dilly. Some of them are new, some have issues with children. The kennels have gates at each end; one outside and another inside." He gestured back toward the kennels. "The exercise yard is on the other side of the kennels. Only Beau is allowed free run on this side."

"I understand. If I see any other dog out here, I grab Dilly up and wait for help. If it's safe enough, I'll take her to the car."

"Exactly."

"But how did she get out of the car? Didn't you buckle her in?" He frowned and she read accusation in his gaze.

Stricken, Mercy visualized the complicated clasps of the child seat. "I heard everything click that's supposed to click." But she must have missed a step. "Even if I messed up the buckles and straps, surely the child-proof locks are functional." She shook her head. "I thought she was buckled in. I'm sorry." What if something had happened? A fender-bender or worse? Her heart squeezed with fear.

"It was me," a woman's voice called from behind the van. "I thought Hope was here."

Mercy looked at Clay. "This was a prank on my mother?"

He shrugged. "Karen, Mercy is Dilly's aunt and she brought Dilly out here for me."

The woman shuffled around the van and came into view, wincing with each step. "Knees worse today?" Clay asked.

She waved her hand in dismissal. "Never better," she muttered. "This is Hope Talbot's girl? The other one?"

"I'm Mercy Talbot," she responded. "Mrs. Bowler?" An easy guess. This was Bowler's Rescue after all.

The older woman leaned on the van with an expression that said she hated to show the weakness. "The pups came on their own after all. I should've waited, I s'pose, but with a first time and her being so small, I fretted."

"I'd rather get a false alarm and have things go okay than the other way around. I've already checked on her," Clay said. "She and her pups are fine."

Karen squinted and glared at Mercy. "You're the one who went to school with my Brianna."

Mercy frowned. "Brianna? Her name doesn't ring a bell."

"It wouldn't. She wasn't the kind of girl you'd notice." The sneer on Karen's face took her aback.

"I'm sorry I don't recall her. I focused on other things back then. High school is pretty much a blur."

Karen's *harrumph* spoke volumes. "You here to pick out a pocket dog the celebrities cart around like jewelry? Because I have no patience for that. Our dogs get good homes." Crossing her arms, Karen put paid to the notion of Mercy taking on a pet.

"Karen," Clay cut in. "Mercy stopped out here to deliver Dilly, that's all." His tone censured the older woman who seemed disinclined to care.

"And I came out here to get my mail," she groused and turned to shuffle up the driveway to her mailbox.

Mercy glanced at Clay who shrugged. "Pain changes people," he said.

CLAY WATCHED AS MERCY approached the kennel that contained the terrier cross. Her hair caught the afternoon sun, a million shades of light glistening in the strands. She squatted again like she had earlier. The position emphasized the flare of her hips and made her jeans dip south, exposing the dimples on her low back. He looked at his boots before he learned whether she was a thong girl or a panty girl.

Wanting to know that personal detail about his sister-in-law was wrong. Too personal, too intimate.

Too much.

She clucked and cooed, but the new arrival refused to look her way. Instead, she gave Mercy more shoulder and stared glumly at the ground. Mercy turned her head to face him. From this angle, he recognized the often-missed family resemblance between his wife and her sister. Bone structure. The sisters had the same cheek and jawline and the same wide, clear forehead. Startled, he shifted a step back.

"It looks like I'm getting the cold shoulder." Mercy's voice sounded warmly amused, and not at all like Janna's. Although Janna would've denied it, she'd most often sounded like Hope.

He tore his gaze from hers and focused on the dog and shrugged at the pose she presented. "If I can't see you, you can't see me. Dilly used to do that."

"She did? I don't know much about babies."

"Join the club. Having Dilly has been an experience." It was safe to talk about the only link they shared. Until she smiled right at him and then ruffled his girl's hair in easy affection. He clenched his hands to keep from reaching out. He wasn't jealous of her developing feelings for Dilly. What bit him in the ass was that he wanted that same easy affection. *Whoa.* He'd been way too long without a woman.

Mercy Talbot's return to Welcome had officially become a problem.

"Did you . . ." She blinked and trailed off. "Were you as hands-on when she was born as you are now?"

He nodded, refusing to say more about that time in their lives. The more energetic and demanding Dilly had become, the wilder Janna became. A downward spiral he hadn't stopped.

Hell, he'd hardly noticed how bad it was. He leaned down and scratched Beau's ears as the lie was exposed. He'd known, but he'd ignored it and hoped that Janna would step up to be the mother Dilly needed.

But he hadn't taken Beau home as a pup because of the fighting and the tension. He'd refused to take a dog into that swirling anger, but he'd left Dilly there, day after day, while he'd done nothing to correct the situation. Beau nudged his hand until he looked down into his soulful eyes.

"Good dog." Sensitive to mood, Beau was free with his affection. As he considered his own lack of affection, Shandy Camden's face swam into his mind and, just as fast, swam out again. That was not a road he wanted to travel. "Are you going back to Hollywood anytime soon?"

"Doubtful. I don't see any reason to. Not to mention I can't afford the bus fare."

"You keep saying stuff like that; I'm likely to believe it."

She gave up on the terrier and rose to her feet. "Believe it." A cloud crossed her gaze. "I'm not the talent my mother thinks I am. I don't have a career to go back to." The weariness in her eyes and voice lent the sound of truth.

If he'd been younger, less worn around the heart and looking for an easy lay, he'd tell her she was still the beauty she'd always been. But he couldn't go there, not with Janna's sister, not when he was still trying to do right by Dilly. Not that he knew what right was. "We both need to move forward."

She nodded. "Take our lessons and use them?" Her shoulders slumped.

"Something like that."

"I'd move on if I knew where to go. Right now, all I want is a job so I can move out of my parents' house." She put the ball of her thumb near her hairline and pressed. "I cannot believe I'm in this position."

The back screen door of the house screeched open and slammed shut. Karen stepped down stiffly from the bungalow's back stoop. She lumbered closer, wincing with each step. She held her face tight, but the pain must be bad today.

"She won't get knee replacements because the animals come first," he explained in a low voice. Mercy shifted as if to bolt. He touched her elbow in support. "She's fine and she loves seeing Dilly run around."

Dilly ran to hug Karen around the legs while Beau waited patiently for his pat on the head. Dilly didn't expect to be picked up. Karen's knees didn't allow for a lot of bending.

Karen was generally a cheerful soul, and he'd never seen her respond to a stranger the way she had to Mercy. Many times he'd come to her as a friend and neighbor when things had gone sour at home. Karen had offered cookies, milk and time to catch his breath. "Karen's been good to me over the years."

Mercy nodded, believing him. "I should move along," she said softly.

"She'll come around. Her knees are giving her hell today."

Karen awkwardly leaned over to pet Dilly's head while Beau nuzzled Karen's hand in greeting. His friend narrowed her eyes at Mercy. "Are you filling Dilly's head with that beauty-pageant nonsense too?"

This was a bone of contention with Karen: her constant jabs about Hope giving Dilly all the things that Mercy had enjoyed.

Mercy's eyes widened, but she said nothing. What could she say? Everyone hoped Dilly would take after Mercy and focus her energies into something positive. Everyone but Karen, who hated the idea of all the girly-girl stuff. He suspected there was another grudge against Hope in there somewhere.

"I've asked you before to leave this be," he said to Karen. He scooped Dilly into his arms and let her pucker his lips. "Okay, Punk, I'm done here for now. Let's go home." She kissed him and squirmed to get down for an equally full-on kiss for Beau.

"I remember Brianna now," Mercy said in a sudden rush. "She sat beside me in English. She was quiet, but an excellent student. I recall a wonderful short story she wrote. She had a hard time reading it aloud, though, because she was shy."

Karen blinked and gave Mercy something that might pass for a smile. "That'd be her."

"I'd like to volunteer here, if I may," Mercy added. "I have a lot of spare time these days. Do you need another pair of hands?"

Karen's face went blank with shock. Then she chuckled. "Go on home, girl. You'll break a nail in thirty seconds and run off to the nail salon."

Mercy held out her hands. Chipped, broken nails looked out of place on her, but there they were. "I'll be here between three and six." She glanced at Clay. "That way, I can bring Dilly here for you and get out of the house."

"Hope getting to you?" Karen interjected. "Because that woman gets my goat."

"Karen," he warned and lowered his voice. "You're talking about Dilly's Grammy."

She gave him a sour look. "I've got dogs to feed. Come along or not," she tossed over her shoulder at Mercy and stalked off.

He looked at Mercy, wondering what in hell she thought. "You're sure you want this?"

"I'll keep looking for work, but I need to feel useful. At least as useful and productive as Beau here." Her grin was more natural and packed more punch than her usual warm smile. Heat rose in his gut as he reacted. "You've given him a purpose, why not me?" she said. "And I have a feeling these dogs may need a kind voice." The unpracticed lightness around her lips, the sudden flash of a dimple he'd never noticed before, the self-deprecating glint in her eye made him want to reach out.

He stepped back.

"Up to you," he said with a shrug and took Dilly's grubby hand. "You were digging in the dirt again, Punk."

Beau sat at Mercy's feet, tongue lolling, lips pulled back into his happy dog face. As usual, the dog looked up at him, waiting for instructions. "Take Beau with you, he keeps the new dogs calm."

She turned to follow Karen. He stopped her with a hand on her elbow, noting again how soft her skin was. "Make sure you follow Karen's instructions closely."

"I will. I'm not like my sister. I'm much more agreeable." Her brows dropped into a slight frown. "Maybe that was my problem. I did as I was told." The unspoken *Janna never did* hung in the air.

Dilly spoke up. "You were a good girl, like me."

"Maybe I was too good, Dilly. Maybe I should have said no sometimes like you do."

Dilly's wide-eyed expression made both adults burst into laughter.

The two-minute drive to his place was filled with Dilly's chatter and kept his mind off Mercy. But not for long. By the time they'd eaten and he'd given Dilly her bath, he was consumed by thoughts of his sister-in-law.

He remembered watching the sisters arguing in front of the school; one darkly furious and the other pleading. Mercy, asking Janna to walk away from him, begging her sister to move home. Janna had done everything but spit in Mercy's eye. He'd had some arguments with his own sister, but nothing like what he saw that day. Janna had been scathingly vicious while Mercy looked battered and alone.

At the time, all he'd wanted was Janna, and he had her. He'd sauntered up to Janna and slung his arm over her shoulders and turned her toward his car. Mercy had had tears in her eyes as she'd reached out one long-fingered hand to Janna.

But he hadn't given a shit about the effect Janna's leaving home had on her family. He'd been a kid, with needs of his own and Janna had filled them.

Sorry excuse for his behavior.

While he toweled Dilly off, he considered making a call to Shandy Camden again. If he kept things cool and strictly fun, maybe they could have something.

But the idea turned his stomach into an acid factory. Shandy wasn't after fun; she wanted a daddy for her son. He couldn't blame her. Decent singles were hard to come by in Welcome. She was one of the good ones and deserved more than what he was prepared to give. Substituting Shandy for Mercy felt despicable.

He'd done enough damage to women in his life, including Shandy. He'd hurt her feelings back in high school by taking what she'd offered and never looking back when it was clear she wanted him for more than a good time by the lake. Shandy didn't deserve to be in the middle of the mess he was living and neither did her boy, Josh.

Uncaring self-gratification didn't have the same allure it once did.

Decided, then. No Shandy and definitely no Mercy.

THREE HOURS LATER MERCY had shoveled enough dog shit to last a lifetime. Her hands were sore and scraped. She held them out. Long, thin welts from doggy teeth streaked across the back of both hands and her palms had blisters. Most of the dogs had been grateful for any scrap of attention. Some had dragged joyful teeth across her skin. One had mouthed her wrist. Her chipped and broken nails would never be the same.

A sniff of her T-shirt told her she smelled, too: of dog, of cleanser, of *eww* . . . perspiration. Hers, she hoped, because she didn't want to smell of dog sweat. Really didn't.

Karen had eased up on her, but there were hard feelings there. For the life of her, Mercy couldn't recall what she'd done to deserve the rescue operator's enmity. She barely remembered Brianna, and since Karen said they hadn't run in the same circles, Karen shouldn't blame her for anything that had happened to her daughter in high school.

Not that Mercy had asked. No point opening up an ancient can of worms.

She dug in her pocket for the key fob as she walked around the house to the front where she'd parked. Her back ached and her thighs were twitchy from all the squatting, bending and shoveling. Karen had kept a smug smile on her face whenever they were near each other, but she was as busy with food, water, and doling out affection as Mercy had been.

And Karen did this twice a day. With aching knees.

Working with the dogs had served to keep her mind from wandering to Clay and her reaction to him when she'd caught him staring at her. Now *that* was a can of worms.

The way he'd focused on her mouth when they'd been talking. The feel of his full length behind her when she'd run toward Dilly and Beau. He'd slammed into her hard enough to knock her for a step, but his arm had been a steel band around her midsection when she might have fallen. She'd wanted *very much* to enfold his arm and keep him there, plastered against her back.

Warming up to Clay was fifty million kinds of wrong and she should feel sick about it. He was her sister's husband. She didn't need the reminder because she saw Janna in all of Dilly's mannerisms, not just in her appearance.

Having warm feelings for Clay Foster was plain sick.

Warped, that's what she was.

Convinced she was an attention whore Mercy fell into the driver's seat of her mom's minivan and rested her skull on the headrest. The thick scent of dog rose from her clothes and skin, their sad eyes floated in her mind's eye. They were lonely, had nowhere to go, no one to turn to. They'd been turned away, disowned, abandoned or left for dead. How bad was it that she could relate to rescued dogs?

At least they'd been rescued. She, on the other hand, was still out there, wandering. Wondering what would happen, how her life would go.

She shouldn't have come back to Welcome. There were too many people like Karen who remembered her as the girl with the world on a string.

Mercy closed her eyes and counted off ten seconds of breathing. If she hadn't come back, she wouldn't know Dilly. Already, she couldn't see life without her niece. How could a crying, uncooperative child steal her heart this fast? By squishing her cheeks for kisses, and loving her dog and being smart enough to hide that fact from her disapproving grandmother. By being Dilly.

She had to stay in Dilly's life, which meant staying in Clay's life, too. She counted ten more breaths, but still, it wasn't enough to get the feel of Clay off of her skin. Running her hands up her arms, she recreated his warmth when he'd held her.

She shook her head to clear it. Enough, she slipped the key into the ignition and turned it just as Karen lumbered by on her way to her truck. They needed dog food, so Mercy could shovel more shit tomorrow.

Karen stopped beside her open window and gave her a long, considering look. "See you tomorrow?"

Mercy nodded and wondered what it cost Karen to give her that smidgen of acceptance. But she didn't miss that it was a question. Karen still doubted Mercy would show up.

Did no one in this town believe a word she said? Hope's exaggerations were being laid at Mercy's door. The best way to show people that Mercy was not like Hope was to prove it one day at a time, shoveling dog shit.

That Clay might also notice her dedication and honesty didn't enter into her decision in the least.

Dedication to a purpose had been ingrained in Mercy by a lifetime of training and prodding. She sat at the exit from the driveway envisioning the years of lessons Dilly had ahead of her. Years of tears and frustration, of arguments with Hope as Dilly grew more resistant, the way Janna had. Mercy had told Dilly that maybe she'd been too good, too easygoing. Maybe she had. Maybe she should have taken a leaf from her sister's book and said no more often.

Karen's car pulled up behind her, ready to turn toward town to pick up her supplies while Mercy dithered. She should go home and get cleaned up, check for messages, maybe walk Humphrey to avoid her mother.

She put on her left turn signal and headed for Clay's place while Karen turned right toward town.

She and Clay needed to talk about Dilly. He needed to consider letting her take a break from the dance classes.

Butterflies took flight at what she was about to do, but turning back was not an option. On a precipice and ready to leap, Mercy drove the short distance to where the Foster property started. Nothing looked the same and she nearly missed the entrance.

All the trees and brambles were gone. No shield from prying eyes remained. Clay had turned his parents' dismal, dark acreage into a meadow of sunshine and light, inviting and friendly.

For Dilly.

Mercy sat in the minivan, pondering the changes. Again, had this change been for Janna? Or because of Dilly's birth? She'd like to believe Janna had moved out here and taken the dreary acreage in hand. But that wasn't her sister's thing.

This was Clay's doing. More warmth flowed up from her belly to her heart. He'd done this for his child. He'd done this so Dilly's home was bright, not shadowed. He'd taken the darkness away for her.

She couldn't go in there. She was too overwhelmed with all she saw. The trailer she'd glimpsed in the past was gone; in its place stood a solid-looking contemporary home that appeared to flow from a single story in front up to a full second story in the back. From the looks of it, there was likely a loft and high ceilings. A river-rock fireplace hugged the exterior wall and made her imagine Dilly, cozy and warm in front of it on the living-room floor.

Maybe she played with those racecars Nate had handed down from Janna.

Mercy liked the idea.

She sat for at least five minutes, taking in the view, wondering about their lives inside the house. Wishing again that Janna were here to live with them in this sunshine and light. Wishing that she'd appreciated Clay and Dilly, that she'd loved them, just a bit.

Janna had been preparing to leave Clay and her child. She'd been fed up with her domestic prison, as she'd called it. She'd wanted adventure, hard men, and freedom.

Confused and scared, not knowing what to do except hope for the best, Mercy had kept quiet about the drunken calls. She'd told herself Janna's unhappiness was Clay's fault. Janna said he was unresponsive and she was lonely and in a funk. Babies could do that, Mercy had told herself. Babies could make a woman blue, exhausted, and overwhelmed. Add a cold, distant husband and it was no wonder Janna found comfort in a bottle.

But Mercy had been wrong. God help her, she'd blamed a husband who doted on his baby, and that baby for her sister's failure to love them as they deserved to be loved.

Acceptance came with a tidal wave of guilt. Subduing a cry, she got her grief, shame, and anger under control. There was no going up to the house now. She was afraid of what she might say; more afraid that she'd fall into Clay's arms whether he wanted her there or not.

Her newly-discovered feelings for Clay Foster had no place in her heart, or in her niece's life. The revelation and acceptance of Janna's lack of feeling and her own failures had clouded Mercy's mind where Clay was concerned. These feelings would fade and be replaced with the normal respect and admiration he deserved from a sister-in-law.

Any person, male or female, who stepped into the full parenting role as father and mother deserved to be admired and also deserved the support they needed from family.

It's a crush, nothing more. You've had them before, you'll have them again.

Get over it.

While she was getting over it she had a battle ahead of her. Hope Talbot had taught Mercy everything she knew about relentlessly pursuing her goals. Now the fight for Dilly's future depended on Mercy. She slipped the minivan into gear, determined to make Hope see that Dilly deserved to be the girl she wanted to be and not another version of Mercy.

Dilly was Janna's daughter and no matter how Janna's life had turned out Mercy was certain her sister would want Dilly to be her own person.

That's what Mercy owed Janna, and more, owed Dilly.

Mercy was under no illusions. Not anymore. As a child, she'd gone along with her mother's plans because she'd enjoyed the attention, the glitter, the winning. She'd been a girly girl down to her sparkly pink toenail polish. As much as she'd been that girl, Janna had not.

Janna had paid a high price for her defiance. Hope had transferred her interest to Mercy, unwittingly creating sibling rivalry that had spanned the sisters' lives. Hope hadn't meant for things to turn out the way they had, but she'd been blinded by her ambitions for Mercy.

Janna hadn't planned on being a rebel. All she'd wanted was to be herself, not a picture-perfect girl child. Losing her mother's interest had turned Janna against her family and made her determined to be as difficult as Mercy was agreeable.

Nate had wanted to be a good supportive husband and a caring father. His quiet strength had seen all the female Talbots through rocky times. But his unerring support of Hope had created its own problems.

Mercy couldn't be sure that her father would speak up for her. If he did speak up and it created a rift in her parents' marriage, Mercy preferred he say nothing.

Dad had stuck to his guns about the trophies being stored in his garage, but that didn't mean he could face down his wife on a matter as big as taking Dilly off the circuit.

As for Clay, an innocent bystander in the ongoing Talbot saga: he was happy to go along with whatever Hope decided was best. He'd handed Dilly over to Hope two years ago and that arrangement worked. She understood his reluctance to upset the balance of Dilly's life.

None of them saw what Mercy saw. None of them had lived what Mercy had lived. The pageants had been tough on her. But she'd enjoyed the challenges and had grown stronger as she'd moved up through the age groups.

But Dilly was another Janna waiting to happen. Mercy was dead certain the pageants were wrong for her niece.

It was up to her to make all the adults see what she saw in Janna's daughter: a sweet girl, before she'd turned into the hellion they all remembered.

Life in Welcome was about to get interesting. How Hope would come to terms with Mercy's plan to get her niece off the circuit was anyone's guess, but whatever happened Hope would get the surprise of her life when she butted heads with Mercy. She had no idea how single-minded Mercy could be.

She'd learned persistence from Hope, and now Hope's greatest creation was about to turn on her. *Bring it on.*

Chapter Five

HER FATHER WAS WEEDING the vegetable patch when Mercy found him. Beside Nate, Humphrey lay flat on the ground until she approached. The Yorkie wagged his tail desultorily but raised his head to watch her.

"Hi, Dad. Where's Mom?" She bent to Humphrey to let him sniff her fingers. He loved the smells she brought home from the kennels.

"Your mother's making dinner. Smells like lasagna, but I didn't ask," her father said as he stood and wiped his hands of soil. "How'd you do out at the rescue?" He eyed her. "You look as if Karen put you to work."

She shrugged. "Karen doesn't like me much. Is there something there I should know?"

"Karen and your mother were in school together. Something about a boy they both liked. You went to school with her girl."

"Brianna. She was quiet but smart." She wished she'd remembered her right away. That may have helped with Karen, but she'd worry about her tomorrow when she went back. "I shoveled a lot of shit today."

"Mercy, you picked up some bad language out in Hollywood."

She snorted. "You're right because I never heard the word here in Welcome." She smoothed her hair, aware of the musky aromas she carried on her skin and clothes. "I volunteered to help at the kennels until I get work. Hard not to offer when Karen Bowler's carrying most of the load."

"And Dilly saw Beau?"

She nodded. "You've met him?"

81

"When your mother came home ranting about him, I wandered out there to see for myself. He's a handsome dog and Clay raised him. I trust him when he says Dilly will be okay." Not exactly a ringing endorsement for Clay or Beau, but it was better than anything she'd hear from her mother.

"Beau adores her. She climbed on his shoulders today and squeezed his ears like she was holding reins," she said. "He did nothing but smile."

Nate snorted. "I've read up on the breed. They're stoic and dependable if they're raised right." There were depths to her father she'd never plumbed.

"You checked up on me and Janna the same way you checked on the dogs. You knew what boys we liked, how we did in class, which of our friends were in trouble." Her dad had just been there, strong and quiet, keeping an eye on his girls. "How did you feel about Clay back then?"

"His parents weren't there for their kids. Clay and his sister ran pretty wild. Given Janna's determination, I talked to Doc Rimmel and Karen Bowler about him. They knew him better than anyone. I gave him the benefit of the doubt based on their feelings." He straightened and looked her in the eye. "If I'd seen one bruise on Janna, I'd have taken him down, but turns out his friends were right. Clay's nothing like his father."

She drew in a slow breath in surprise.

"What's on your mind?" he asked. "It isn't the dog, and I think you've come to your own conclusions about Clay."

"It's Dilly. Mom needs to back off on the dance classes, the pageants, all of it. And I'm telling her so."

His eyebrows rose. "We had this conversation earlier. There's no way your mother will give up those pageants."

"I have my reasons for asking." Which she may not have to share just yet. She'd keep Janna out of this until she needed the big guns. It wasn't smart to hit Hope with all of Mercy's conclusions at once.

"Good luck, honey. I'll stay out here awhile."

She patted his shoulder as she started for the house. "That's a good idea. I'll tell you when it's safe to come in."

He chuckled and bent to his weeding again.

She found her mother in the sewing room leaning over her cutting table, armed with her sewing shears. Maybe not the best time to rip Hope's dreams to shreds, but then, there might never be a better time.

"Hi, hard at it I see."

Her mother waved her hand over a piece of cherry red satin. "This is the best color for her eyes."

"It's lovely." Mercy looked at the pattern pieces. "A micro-mini? A tube top? Mom, what's this for?"

"New Mexico next month. It's adorable and the summer weather will be too hot for anything more."

Mercy fingered the satin. Smooth and cool to the touch, it would have a luxurious sheen under the lights. But it was too skimpy. "She's just a little girl."

"This is her cowgirl costume. She'll have to stand out. I've ordered her red boots and a matching hat. Maybe I should switch that to a sombrero," she muttered. "It is New Mexico, after all."

Mercy reached to stay her mother's hand and slipped the scissors out of her loose grasp.

"What are you doing? I need to cut this." Hope looked up at her then. "What's happened? Why do you look like that?" Her eyes, as blue as her own, went wide. "Did that dog do something to Dilly?" Her hand went to her chest as fright-filled Hope's gaze.

"No, no, nothing like that. Sorry to scare you. I just don't want you armed with shears when I say what I need to say." She gathered her nerve and set the shears on the table. "You need to give Dilly some time off."

Hope's chin firmed. "Ridiculous, we're building momentum that'll carry us right through the season. By this time next year, she'll be a star."

We'll make you a star. Her mother didn't realize it, but her words echoed those she'd heard on her last, desperate attempt at finding work in Hollywood. She shivered and looked down at the skimpy costume again.

"This is different from what you sewed for me. More extreme." Mercy wore dresses that rivaled ball gowns, and when she lost her front teeth, she adjusted her smile until her permanent teeth appeared. Today, the children weren't allowed a gap-toothed smile. They used flippers, tiny false teeth that slid into place to mask the gap.

Her mother raised her palm in a gesture that asked for the shears. "Don't be silly. Now, go take a shower." She made a face. "Decent young women would head straight into the bath."

Not to be sidetracked, Mercy pressed on. "Dilly hates everything to do with the pageants: the practice, the lessons, and the clothes. You've seen how she cries."

"Temper, nothing more." With a quick move, Hope snatched the shears and set them down on her side of the table. She arched a brow and waited, gaze dismissive.

Mercy shook her head. No one could push her out of here, least of all a crazed stage-grammy. She crossed her arms. "I took her into my room and she refused to go near the trophies. Didn't care to look at them. She doesn't want this." She waved her hand over the red satin. A sexy mini, of all things.

"Are you telling me that you didn't want it?" Hope crossed her arms and glared. Her chin jutted in anger and Mercy stepped back. It wasn't easy to go up against her mother. Hope still had the look that had kept her in line as a child.

"I wanted it." Her life had gone all kinds of wrong and she wasn't sure how. But she couldn't lay her failure at her mom's feet. "I enjoyed the pageants." She patted her chest. "If I hadn't loved it all I would've fought tooth and nail to end it. You got lucky with me, Mom. That's all. But you're ignoring Dilly's unhappiness."

Hope snapped her head back as if she'd been struck. Reality check.

When Dilly had sucked her thumb and leaned hard against her bed, Mercy had felt her obstinate nature. The whole thing had smacked of Janna and more than anything, Mercy wanted Dilly to be Dilly: not another Janna and not another Mercy, if that's not what she wanted. "Dilly wants to poke around in the garden soil, she wants to kiss her dog and race her toy cars. She wants to be Dilly and we should let her try that out for a while."

Hope threw her hands in the air and brushed past her. "I don't want to hear this nonsense. I *won't*." She left the room.

"Mom." But her mother rushed down the hall into her room and closed the door, refusing to respond when Mercy tapped lightly.

Mercy slid her forehead to the door and held back a sigh. "It's not the end of the world, Mom. I just want to see how Dilly behaves when you don't make her go to dance and singing classes. That's all." A small step, for sure, but what harm could it do?

"I've told you I won't hear of Dilly quitting. Besides, Clay's given me free rein with her. You have no idea what's it's been like these last two years."

"No, I don't." Her mom was correct. Mercy had avoided coming home. The grief had been raw and savage and she'd needed to believe things at home were okay.

"I will not give up on Dilly, Mercy, no matter what you say or how many times you say it. There. Now let that be the end of it."

But Mercy couldn't let it go. "Janna would hate that Dilly's involved in the pageants."

There was a long silence and Mercy wondered if she'd gone too far. A sob sounded through the door.

"If I hadn't given up on Janna when I did all those years ago, she'd be alive today."

The door suddenly opened and Hope's pain and despair ravaged the air between them. "I'm to blame for the choices Janna made." Hope slammed her palm to her chest. "I'll be damned if I make the same mistake with Dilly. I will not give up on my granddaughter and lose her, too."

THREE DAYS AFTER MERCY brought Dilly to the kennels, Clay pulled in to park at the rescue. He had no reason to be there other than to have this conversation, but Hope had made it plain what she wanted. Apparently, Mercy had tried to get Nate's backing on her campaign to stop the dance classes. Hope was at the end of her patience.

He should have known the peace wouldn't last.

He'd done a fair job of avoiding Mercy lately, but that had been a mistake. He should have kept a closer eye on her and done a better job of controlling his attraction.

He had to make it clear that he approved of Dilly's classes. He jumped out of his vehicle and followed the sound of Mercy's seductively low tone. As he walked he ignored the slam to his gut that her singsong voice brought on. Yes, he had to inure himself to her appeal, and familiarity would help. The more he saw of her, the less mysterious she would become.

The less mystery, the less curiosity. Less . . . less . . . less . . .

"Your mother called," he said as he approached the enclosure that housed the fearful terrier cross. Mercy was busy coaxing the dog and ignored him, but her shoulders stiffened.

Being a go-between didn't sit well. Peacemaking in his family was a lost cause. There'd never been peace and he wasn't sure how to broker one. "You need to back off on the dance classes. Dilly will come around."

Mercy squatted in front of the terrier to offer a piece of kibble. He focused on her hand rather than her backside and the way her hips rounded from her taut waist. She was in denim shorts today. He stared at the ground instead of at her long, shapely legs.

The terrier retreated to the wall at her back. "Don't push her," he advised. "Let her come to you."

Good advice for dogs and women. He'd done the chasing with Janna. He was through with that. Next time a woman caught his interest, he'd take it slow and see if his interest was returned. Not that watching Mercy had turned his mind to chasing women. Not at all.

"I'm not pushing," she said softly. "I'm coaxing. Karen says I should get my scent on her food by handling it."

"That means to use your hand when you're dishing up." He made a scooping motion, but she was too focused on the dog to see it.

The dog lifted her lips in a warning. Mercy heeded it and set the piece of kibble on the ground. Inch by slow inch, she retreated and allowed the dog room to snatch the morsel.

Her retreat shattered his best intentions to avoid ogling her. How was he supposed to *not watch* a pert, curvy bottom inch closer? He was a man, not a saint.

"Look, she's watching for more. I guess the cold shoulder's over." She dug into the dish by her foot and held out another bit, completely unaware of the effect she was having on him. He opened the gate for her to back out.

"For now, it's over. She could regress for any reason."

"She likes me."

He snorted. "She likes to eat. You just happen to be the one holding the food. If you're done tempting her and making her wait, swirl your hand through what's left in the bowl. She'll know you're the one who fed her."

She rose to her full height, flashed him a grateful smile while she brushed her palms against her thighs. "Thanks."

He was right; her legs were impossibly long and beautifully shaped, like Janna's.

Mercy bent at the waist to reach the food dish and, before he could look away, gave him a clear view of her cleavage. He stepped aside so she could exit the kennel and leave the dog to eat in peace.

Because his dog usually greeted him and he needed to fill the silence, he asked where Beau was.

"Helping Karen with a new arrival, but it's not a big deal. The owners brought the dog in. They were heartbroken, but they both lost their jobs. The dog's happy and healthy." She put her hands on her hips. "It was tough to watch, though." Her eyes went wet and she ducked her head.

"It happens. Times are tough. But a dog with no health or social issues will be easier to place in a home."

She nodded, still looking at the ground. "That's what Karen said." He suspected the dog's plight affected her more than she wanted him to see.

"You two getting along?" He shouldn't ask, shouldn't care, but Karen had been uncharacteristically taciturn with Mercy.

"Yes, things are better now that I've been here a few times." She dabbed the back of her hand to her cheek to catch an errant tear and grinned that heart-stopper of hers. Easy, loose and way too honest. "I still don't have a job, but at least I feel useful."

"I came to talk about Dilly," he blurted.

Mercy grimaced.

"You're disappointed that I trust your mother," he said with a shrug. "I'm nobody's idea of a good father." He put his hands up in surrender. "And I don't have a clue about raising a girl." Especially a feisty one like Dilly.

"But—"

He didn't want to argue, just state his case. "Your mother stepped in when I needed her most. She's stuck with Dilly and me for two long years while I got my life on track. Why would I doubt her?"

Her chin rose and for a flash, he saw Janna and Dilly in the pose. These Talbot women could spin him like a top. *Let that be another warning.*

"If you'd had a son you'd hand him off to my dad?"

"Probably not, although there aren't many men I like as much as your father. He's a good guy." He rubbed his chin as he considered. "I might be better off to say yes, I'd hand off a son to Nate."

At her surprised expression, he explained, "As much as I doubt my chances of raising Dilly well, butting heads with a son like me would do me in." They'd end up whaling on each other by the time the kid was sixteen.

What he didn't say was that having a daughter like Janna would kill him. He swallowed a knot of fear. Thank God he had Hope and Nate to lean on. If anyone could steer Dilly clear of being like her mama, it was Hope Talbot.

Hope could mold Dilly into another Mercy and he'd sleep at night.

That's what he wanted: a daughter like Mercy.

The realization took him aback as the real thing stared him in the eye. "Look, I don't want Dilly rebelling in her teens. If we can avoid that by steering her right at this point, then I'm all for these pageants. She'll be more like you than Janna, won't she?"

Mercy crossed her arms over her chest. "You think my mother can turn Dilly into another me?" She rolled her eyes. "That's the last thing Janna would want."

She'd hit a button he didn't know he had. Anger rose along with heat to his face. "Janna's not here now, is she? And if she was, she wouldn't give a rat's ass about how we're raising Dilly."

Mercy's eyes went wide and her arms fell to her sides as she processed. "You can't mean that." Her voice went hollow, but he'd started it now and he needed her to understand. "I'm aware Janna was unhappy," she said, "but she'd care very much about Dilly."

"Think about it," he snapped at her. "She was leaving me that night. Leaving us," he corrected. He turned to head for the parking lot, too sick of it all to continue the argument, but she grabbed his arm and stopped him. The place where she touched him sizzled in the afternoon heat. He shook her off as she stepped in front of him and glared into his face.

"Janna would care, Clay." She poked his chest, once. Hard. "She'd care and she'd want Dilly to be herself, not another me. Not another *anyone*, just herself." She poked him again and he noticed she still hadn't fixed her nail polish.

Each fingernail had a ring of black from her labor here. Scratches and healing welts marred the skin of her hand. She'd thrown her heart and body into the work without a care for her appearance. Karen should have offered her gloves.

"Why are you on this, Mercy? Dilly's fine and she'll get over this temper and we'll all be better for it. Please just leave it alone." How had his father-in-law managed all these women for all these years? *By keeping his mouth shut.*

"I asked my mother to back off for a few months, not forever." She set her hands on his arms to hold him still. His skin burst into flame where she touched, but—God help him—he couldn't move away. The earnestness in her voice and eyes froze him in place. "Dilly's still young, but she's unhappy when she comes home from class."

That made him settle on his heels. He frowned. "You believe it's the classes that make her cry? I thought she was moody." *Shit.* What had he missed? Hope said the crying jags were moods like her mother's and that Dilly would grow out of them.

"It's not just the classes. It's *all* the girly stuff. She doesn't like her hair being done, doesn't want the glitter on her skin. You saw her in my bedroom. She didn't respond to the trophies or the tiaras. None of it interests her." She stepped in close and beneath the hard work scent of her skin, he smelled her shampoo. Flowery and light. God help him, what a time to notice this. "And if you believe that was the first time she's seen the trophies think again."

"Dilly never mentioned them."

Mercy closed her eyes, took a big dramatic breath and said, "Because she's never liked them. She made that clear." Her eyes popped open, blue as a summer sky, filled with hope that he'd see her point.

He did. Hope definitely would have shown Dilly the trophies. Maybe more than once. "But how can you be sure Dilly won't *like* all the girly stuff a week from now?" Whenever he figured out her newest phase of development, Dilly moved on to the next.

"If she does, she'll let us know." She blinked and released his arms as if she just realized she was holding them. The fire on his skin still burned. "When I was her age, and younger, I danced and twirled in the living room. I loved the idea of being onstage and having people clap for me. I loved the music, the singing lessons, loved the shiny rhinestones. It was me, it was who I was."

"But it wasn't Janna? And it's not Dilly?"

She chuckled. "Never, not for a day." She touched him on the arm again and her palm scorched. Her eyes widened as if she felt the burn, too. He shifted out from under her hand. "Please consider giving Dilly some time off," she said.

"Okay." It was all he could give her. "I'll think about it, but telling your mother to back off sets my teeth on edge." No, Foster men were not designed for peacekeeping. He retreated to the tried and true. "Until you got here everything was fine."

"No, it wasn't fine and it hasn't been for as long as I can remember." She heaved in a breath that drew his eye to her chest, but he forced his gaze to her shoes instead.

"You've stepped in it," he said, loosening the coiled tension.

She gave an unladylike snort, which made him smile. "Yes, I have stepped in it. My mother calling you for back-up is proof."

"That's not the 'it' I meant."

She looked down. "Oh, I've given up trying to avoid it. Impossible in this place."

"I hear you." He headed for his truck before he did something stupid like try to kiss her. His *sister-in-law*.

"Just talk to my mother again. See if you can't make her see reason." And he heard a trace of Hope in her order. "She believes allowing Dilly time off is giving up on her."

He gave her a brief wave and refused to check her out in the rearview as he drove down the driveway. *Progress.* This battle of wills between Hope, Dilly, and Mercy had to come to an end. It couldn't be good for Dilly. Clay had been raised in a battleground and knew the damage it caused. He was reminded daily.

The Talbots had been frustrated raising Janna, and he understood their frustration. He'd married her and got how exasperating life with Janna could be. Stubborn and willful to the point of endangering herself, Janna had been a terror.

But Mercy? Janna had complained she was perfect. *Perfectly perfect*, and from what Clay recalled, his wife had been right. In high school, Mercy Talbot had been untouchable, ethereal in some respects. None of the guys in school had had the balls to ask her out.

Most of the time, her name was spoken in hushed tones. "Have Mercy," was muttered like a mantra as she'd walked past in the hall, her golden-blond hair flowing down her back, her hips tantalizing in a smooth sway.

But he'd set his sights on Janna: the original poster girl for Goth. As light as Mercy had been, her older sister was dark. Dyed-black hair, heavy eyeliner, and shitkickers outlined with studs made Janna look as if she was up for anything. He'd liked her edgy confidence and her brashness. At the time, he hadn't seen anything more and nothing beneath.

After they'd gone out a few times, he'd asked her to ease up on the black and she'd slowly revealed softer brown hair and gentle brown eyes he'd fallen into. He'd been convinced that was the real Janna, the soft and gentle girl she could turn into.

Still, she had claws. Her hard edges made him want to show her how wild he could get. So he had. Janna Talbot was the last woman he'd ever chased. The last woman he ever would.

And once they got married, he never saw that softer side again.

He gunned the truck toward town. He was late getting Dilly, and Hope would be anxious to hear what he'd had to say to Mercy. An anxious Hope and an upset Dilly made him wonder why the hell he was heading toward town when all his instincts told him to run like hell in the other direction.

On days like this, being a father had its downfalls.

But mostly, being Dilly's daddy was damn good.

It was her grandmother that could shake him.

Her aunt created all kinds of vibrations, some good, some bad, some as big as earthquakes. All he had to do was steer clear of Mercy Talbot until she left. After that, life would return to normal.

Dilly would grow into these classes Mercy was upset about and Hope would steer his daughter into being a fine young woman.

He ignored the thought that there was nothing in this equation for him.

HALF AN HOUR LATER, Clay found that Nate had no insight into the Mercy/Dilly/Hope triangle and advised him to stay out of it. Clay grabbed a stool and sat at the counter sipping the beer Nate had given him. "You know Mercy better than I do. Will she give up soon?"

His father-in-law joined him at the sandwich bar and took a stool. "No, she won't. Hope and Janna were peas in a pod, but Mercy's stronger than either of them."

"Forgive me, Nate, but I doubt that."

Nate groaned into his seat, his back sagging as he propped his elbows on the counter. The slanted glance Nate gave him spoke volumes.

"Let me tell you how I see it. Janna was a lot like her mother. Stubborn, willful, much easier to go along with than fight with. Neither of them saw the other that way, though. My wife never saw herself in Janna, but I did."

"And Mercy? Where did she fit?"

"On the surface, she liked the same things as Hope. The pretty dresses, the dancing, the applause. But those pageants brought out a backbone of steel that her sister never had. Janna didn't have the strength to take the rejection and the occasional losses, that's why she pushed to get off the circuit. Every chance she could, she rebelled."

"Hope couldn't take the rebellion?"

"Exactly. Same response, different stimulus."

"Rejection and loss made Mercy stronger?"

Nate nodded. "In ways her mother never saw."

"Neither did Janna. She assumed Hope washed her hands of her and loved Mercy more."

Nate rumbled in his throat as he digested the information. "Mercy was an easy child. Janna never was." He took a sip of beer. "We loved them both the way anyone loves their kids. But they were different and that meant their needs were, too. We failed to give Janna what she needed. Her mother and I see that now."

Treating the girls the same had backfired. "You think Mercy's right about giving Dilly a break?"

"Right or wrong, Mercy won't quit. That's what I think."

He ruminated while they sipped beer for a few minutes. Mercy claimed to have no career left in Hollywood, but from what Hope had said all over town, she'd fly back there on golden wings if a call came. "What about Hollywood? She gave that up."

"Has she?" Nate's lip lifted as he took the last sip of his beer. The side door opened. "Sounds like the princess has arrived."

Clay wasn't sure to whom he referred. "Princess could be any one of your women, including Dilly."

Nate chuckled. "You're right."

Dilly barreled into the kitchen, and it didn't take a Rhodes Scholar to see she was upset again. Her face was red and her hair stuck to her forehead. Fury turned her eyes to hard knots and Clay's stomach sank.

Hope followed Dilly into the kitchen. "Adele Elizabeth Foster," she declared, using her full name for emphasis, "you are *just* like your mother."

When Hope saw the men at the sandwich bar she slammed to a halt. Dilly bolted for Clay, who scooped her up in a fierce hug. Her hot face pressed against his neck and her deep sobs broke his heart.

"She's been horrible all day long, stubborn and willful and defiant," Hope explained.

Mercy stormed in behind her. "There's nothing bad about being like Janna," Mercy said in a soft, but threatening, tone. "Take it back."

Another ear-splitting wail from Dilly threatened his eardrum as Mercy crowded close to her mother, insistent that Hope bow to her pressure. "I will not take it back," Hope said. "And I will *never* give up on my granddaughter."

Clay had had enough. He stood with Dilly in his arms and faced down the battling women. "You will not argue in front of my daughter again." His voice was ice.

Hope reached out with a tentative hand, but Clay stepped out of reach, his stomach in knots, his blood boiling.

"You won't take her away from us. Please, Clay? I couldn't bear to lose Dilly, too." Her eyes were already wet with tears and fear.

"The arguments and the screaming have to stop," he said as he glared at first one and then the other of the Talbot women. He held Dilly close as he left the house.

Chapter Six

CHASTENED AND ASHAMED of their outbursts in front of Dilly, Mercy saw Hope firm her lips to prevent a burst of tears. "Mom, he wouldn't keep Dilly away from you. He knows how much you love her. How much we all love her."

"But he could." She patted her lower lashes to control the dampness that had gathered there. "I've been on eggshells around Clay for two years. He has the real power when it comes to our girl."

Nate nodded, visibly shaken by the episode. "Clay's a good man, Hope. He wants what's best for her, that's all. And you need to reconsider how hard you push the child."

Hope swung on Mercy. "This is your fault. Everything was fine until you came home and sided with Dilly."

The echo of her conversation with Clay resounded in her head. He had said the same thing. "I'm sorry I came home." If she'd had any other choice, she wouldn't be here.

"Why can't you see what I'm trying to do?" Hope asked. "I want her happy the way you were."

But she's not me. "Dilly wants to be her own person," Mercy said gently.

"Nate, you don't believe he'd take her away from us, do you? I have more work to do with her. I can't lose Dilly, Nate." Her voice broke. "I can't and I won't. Not the way I lost Janna." She sobbed and buried her face in her hands.

Nate got off the stool and walked around the island. He pulled her mother into his arms.

Mercy stepped back, leaned against the wall and closed her eyes against their pain. Hope sniffed, struggling not to break down. "Dilly needs to see how much fun she can have. The way Mercy did."

"Clay has a point," Mercy said. "Imagine how our arguments look to a three-year-old."

"I suppose." Hope shrugged out of the embrace, more in control. "I can't imagine what Clay saw growing up out there in that trailer. He and his sister."

Mercy recalled the rumors of violent drunken rages between the parents. *Those Fosters* was the term people used to describe them. At first, Janna had taken up with Clay to spite their mom. Then she married him. That was around the time of Janna's arrest for a drunken brawl with Clay's sister.

"I'll give Clay a call after you've all calmed down," Nate said.

"No, I'll go see him in the morning myself," Hope said. "What I need to say is best said to his face. And alone."

CLAY TOOK HIS COFFEE out to the back deck and leaned over the railing. The sunrise greeted him through the trees, pink fingers of light beckoning the new day. He'd been woken by a call from Hope and from the side of the house, he heard the crunch of gravel as his mother-in-law parked the minivan. The sound of her footsteps on the wooden steps up to the deck told him she'd remembered to meet him outside, away from Dilly's curious ears.

After the disagreements yesterday afternoon, he'd been shocked by Hope's call, but he was open to hearing what she had to say. Somehow they all had to come together for Dilly's sake.

Hope stepped around the corner of the house and looked around. "This is lovely, Clay," she said, sounding surprised.

"Thanks."

"It's different from what I expected."

"You expected what? That we'd still be in the trailer?"

She pursed her lips in response and then blew out a breath. "No, of course, we knew about your building out here. But I didn't realize how much land there was."

"Ten acres. The old man wanted his privacy." Digby Foster never wanted anyone to come around or know what the hell was going on out here.

Things were different now. Clay was in charge.

"Is she awake yet?" Hope asked.

"Not for another half an hour, give or take. Coffee?"

"Please, I need it. I didn't sleep a wink last night. Not after Mercy's disruption."

He nodded. "Rough night then."

She arched that haughty brow of hers and grimaced. "For the first time in decades, I left my house without my makeup on."

"Black coffee coming right up." He supposed he should have told her she looked fine, but Hope wouldn't hear him anyway.

After he brought her a mug of coffee he waved her into a seat. "No, thanks, I'll stand." She bit her lip and looked out over the lawn to the ring of trees that separated the front five acres from the back five. The old family home sat just past the trees. "I want to apologize for arguing in front of Dilly. It was wrong and childish and I'm sorry."

As apologies went this one was one of the best he'd heard. Maybe she meant it. "Childish and scary for her. I should know; I remember lots of fighting growing up."

She swung her gaze to his. "I imagine you do. I'm sorry for that. Home should be a safe haven. Heaven knows the world can be ugly and all children need a respite."

"And?"

"I'll do my best not to rise to Mercy's provocation," she promised.

"I'm wondering if Mercy has a point about the classes. Maybe it's too much pressure."

"All I want is for Dilly to be happy and fulfilled the way Mercy was. She'll catch on soon, you'll see."

He nodded but didn't speak, which brought a pleading look to her eyes.

"Please don't keep Dilly away from us, Clay. She's everything to me and Nate."

"You mean well, but sometimes you make Dilly feel like she's bad. That has to change." He'd never take Dilly away from her grandparents. She'd had enough loss and she loved them both in spite of the crying jags about the classes.

"I tell her when she's good, too. You catch me at my worst all the time." She frowned and went red in the face as she became agitated. "It's Mercy who argues. She keeps pressing me to give up on Dilly." She reached out and took a handful of Clay's sleeve. Her eyes filled.

"I tell her when she's good. Dilly's a sweet girl just as often as she's not. Janna could be sweet, too. My baby girl could be sweet as pie when things went her way." Hope blinked back tears and then dashed her fingers across her cheeks. They came away wet. "I can't lose Dilly, Clay." Her voice broke. "I can't and I won't. Not the way I lost Janna." She shook her head, sobbed and buried her face in her hands.

Hope Talbot fell apart right in front of him. Her sobs broke his heart and her anguish felt like an assault on his senses. If he lost Dilly, he couldn't bear to live, and yet Hope and Nate had stepped in to give him time to breathe and work and get through his days when they'd lost Janna.

He patted Hope's shoulder. She trembled. "We lost our girl," she said in a hollowed-out sob. "We can't lose her child, too."

"You won't lose Dilly. Not ever." He gave her an awkward hug and she accepted it and sniffled against his shoulder. He patted her shoulder some more and waited for her to catch her breath.

Hope stepped back and sniffed. "She just has to win a crown or two. Then she'll see what all the classes are for. I'm not taking her for selfish reasons." More tears spilled as she stared up at him. "This is not for me, I swear. Dilly needs to see how much fun she can have. The way Mercy did."

"I'm sure you're right." And he was. Mercy had been busy and committed all through school while he and Janna had just hung out. It wasn't until Doc Rimmel had given him the opportunity to go to vet school that Clay had shown any ambition. The morning after Janna's accident, Hope had come out to the trailer asking to help and Clay had allowed her to take over Dilly's care. "When I needed you, you were there. You've always been there for Dilly."

Clay drained his coffee and checked his watch. "Dilly will be up any minute. But I'm warning you, Hope, I don't want you and Mercy in screaming matches around her."

"We won't argue anymore." She nodded and turned to leave. Just as she reached the steps to go down to the side of the house, she looked over her shoulder at him. Her eyes narrowed. "And Clay," she said, "don't look at Mercy the way men look at women." With that warning hanging in the air, sharp and hard, she left.

Too bad Clay wasn't the kind to heed warnings. Never had been.

Still, it pissed him off that Hope noticed his undefined interest in his dead wife's sister. He'd told himself he wanted to figure out Mercy's true agenda for coming home and when she'd be leaving. That had lasted for a week. Next, he'd admitted that she had more grit than he'd given her credit for.

He scrubbed his palm down his face.

Now, *shit!* He had to admit that back in school, Mercy Talbot had fascinated him. She shone like a bright light against Janna's dark appeal. If he were brutally honest he'd admit that there'd been that one time when he'd come upon the sisters arguing . . . he'd been hit fiercely with whatever the fuck it was that teenage boys felt for beautiful girls and he'd flung his arm across Janna's shoulders and taken her to his car, and straight into the back seat.

He hung his head. He'd loved Janna as much as he could, as much as he was capable of loving back then. But that one time, it had been Mercy he'd wanted.

A WEEK AFTER THE SCENE in the kitchen with her mother and still aggravatingly jobless, Mercy stood inside the terrier's kennel with her back to the chain-link gate. She hadn't had any luck getting through to her mother about the pageants, but she'd be damned if she continued to let one pint-sized dog get the better of her. Time stopped as she slid down the links, each one making a ripple in the flesh of her back. As she settled on her haunches, Mercy rested her forearms on her knees. The combined scent of corn, processed lamb and everything else that went into kibble rose from her hands.

The terrier cross sat at the far end of the kennel beside the food dish waiting for the ritual to begin. Her fur stood up on end, the tufted points making her look like an eccentric with too much hair product. But the total package was too cute to ignore.

Until now she'd taken Clay's advice and used her hands to scoop food into the dog's bowl.

No more.

She'd get through to this dog if it took all night.

She opened one palm. Alert to the change in routine, the dog whined. With an expectant wiggle, the dog whined again and then settled to see what would happen next.

Mercy closed her fist to cover the kibble but didn't put it in the food dish.

The terrier tracked the movement of Mercy's fingers with alert eyes. She whined more insistently.

Mercy opened her fingers to offer the kibble but made no other move.

The dog settled on her belly, front paws stretched toward Mercy. A moment later, she moved her back end in an undeniable effort to inch closer. Mercy smiled and crooned encouragement as she allowed one bit of kibble to fall to the ground between two fingers.

"I'll call you Ethel," she said, "whether you like it or not." She wasn't sure why she chose the name except it was as quirky as the dog. "You have no idea what the last few days have been like."

No one in town would hire her, but everyone wished her well on her big break. "Some of them sounded like they cared." *Huh!* "Come on, girl, I need this to work. Please." Something in her life had to go right, even if it was just feeding a dog.

Ethel cocked her head as if she listened. But her eyes were on the bit of kibble resting beside Mercy's foot on the concrete floor. Another inch forward.

"You enjoy my voice? Okay, how about I tell you how bad things have been at home. My mother's not talking to me, and I haven't had a private moment with Clay in days. Just as soon as I see him alone I'll apologize for arguing in front of Dilly. My mom's furious that I stood up to her in front of Clay. She blames me for Clay getting riled."

Ethel cocked her head to the other side.

"You know Clay, right? He's the guy that's checked you over. Good looking? Nice hands? Great butt?"

Another whine.

"I see you've noticed." She widened her fingers to allow one more bit of kibble to fall. "I've caught myself glancing at his butt, too. And his kind eyes and his great body. I'm being patient with myself about that, by the way. Like with you, time is on my side. I'll wear you down eventually and I figure time will wear my attraction to Clay down to a nub." But none of this was easy. Instead of winding down, her attraction deepened whenever she saw the man.

He wasn't *trying* to catch her interest. Clay was cool, polite, and kept his eyes averted from hers. He was definitely not sending out *I'm available* vibes, at least not in her direction. Maybe he was available to other women. Maybe he was seeing someone.

Which was good.

But occasionally she caught a flash of interest in his gaze or a smile threatened to lift his lips. Those times were rare. He must blame her for the arguments with Hope. And he'd be right.

Hadn't Clay and Hope said the same thing? That everything was fine until she got involved. But she couldn't leave Dilly without support. The girl hated her classes and hated being compared to Janna.

"What would Janna think?"

The dog's ears perked up at the sound of her voice. She closed two more inches of space between them. "Back to my mother. I shouldn't say things have been that awful. I mean, it *is* more peaceful without her asking about my agent, who still hasn't called, by the way." She sighed. "In case you were wondering."

Ethel licked her chops and moved closer. "At least I'm not having any more issues with Karen." Ethel was within grabbing range now, but Mercy knew better than to reach toward her. Working well with Karen was something, at least. Ethel was next.

And Hope? Hope could wait another day. At least she'd stopped comparing Dilly in a negative way to Janna. Hearing that tone in Hope's voice had brought on hives and Mercy had had enough.

One more piece of kibble landed by her foot. Ethel was close enough to stick out her tongue to lick the morsel. When she got the kibble between her lips, she rose to her haunches and sniffed at Mercy's hand.

She tilted her palm enough that Ethel could pretend she'd won. Several pieces of kibble fell to the ground. One bounced on Mercy's shoe and Ethel got brave enough to snatch that up.

"Dilly's still fighting like a demon. She's determined to have her own way and my mother's walking around with stones for eyeballs. There is not one iota of softness in her gaze. I've never seen her like this, not even when Janna was at her most defiant."

Ethel licked Mercy's hand in a blatant bid for more kibble. Mercy lowered her hand to let Ethel eat from her palm. "There you go, girl." The soft touch of lips and tongue made Mercy smile. "Sweetling girl," she crooned several times.

When the kibble ran out and Ethel snuffled between her fingers to get the crumbs, Mercy delicately wiggled her fingers under the dog's chin. Ethel froze but closed her eyes as if enjoying the gentle touch. "Good girl, thanks for listening. You didn't offer any suggestions, but it was good to vent."

With that, Ethel sat on her haunches and allowed Mercy to rub her ears with both hands. "On my first day of job hunting, I noticed Hughes Realty in town. If it's the same Logan Hughes I remember from school, then it might be worth a try to talk to him about a job. He was nice to me when others weren't." She'd heard Logan had left for work in Tacoma or Seattle. Maybe he'd come back to town, too. "Although I'd bet he's a success. He was smart in school." She didn't know a thing about real estate, but it was worth checking out.

The sound of a vehicle arriving made Ethel back up to the far end of the kennel and Mercy rose and turned to see Clay park beside her dad's truck.

She tossed one more whispered comment Ethel's way. "Don't ask about *him*." She'd get over this stupid crush if it killed her.

He climbed out of his SUV looking determined and focused and tempting as the apple itself. And man, did she want a bite.

"Did I see you petting her?" He nodded toward the dog. No greeting, no smile, just a make-it-about-the-dog question.

"Ethel, her name's Ethel," she replied. "And yes, I'm making some headway." Finally, a success. She smiled and enjoyed a drift of satisfaction.

Clay lifted the latch on the kennel gate. She slipped out through the narrow opening. Close like this, he smelled fresh as if he'd just showered. He must've gone home before stopping by. "Why Ethel?" he asked.

He watched the dog rather than look at Mercy, but he didn't step back. She drank in his scent and felt his body heat. If she leaned against him he'd be taut across the chest, and muscular.

She tamped back her excitement at spending a few minutes alone with him and focused on his question. "I named her for the actress Ethel Barrymore."

"Never heard of her."

"She had a long career and died in the 50s. But you're not here about Ethel."

Beau careened around the corner, excited to see Clay. The soft moment between her and Clay exploded into mutual joyous greetings with the dog. Finally, Beau sat at heel and smiled up at them, tongue lolling.

At last, Clay looked directly at her, sending her stomach to her toes. "I'm here to talk about Dilly," he said.

She put up her hands in surrender or in a plea, she couldn't tell which. "We haven't been arguing around her. I promise." Her mom would never forgive her if Clay took Dilly out of her care. Fear rose as she saw doubt creep across his face. She couldn't lose daily contact with her niece. "Mostly because my mom is barely speaking to me and I wouldn't do anything to upset Dilly. She's special and sweet . . ." And Mercy loved her.

His face clouded with concern and though his eyes were turned in her direction, his gaze was inward. "But you and Hope are still at loggerheads?"

"I've decided to let it go for a while, and since she's not talking to me, letting it go has been easier."

CLAY HAD STEERED CLEAR of Mercy for a week, but he needed to get to the bottom of why she was against Dilly taking classes. This was about more than Dilly's dislike of dance. "I can understand how an active kid wouldn't want to practice dance steps. How she might not want to pay attention or focus, but she's . . . ." He let the words slip away.

She stepped toward the car. "I'm glad you're here and willing to hear me out. You are, aren't you? Willing to listen? To all of it?"

He nodded. "We'll sit in my car." As soon as he opened the passenger door for her, he knew this was a mistake. She was flushed and pretty and happy with her success with Ethel, maybe a bit excited to express her views about Dilly.

It aggravated him that he'd notice her pretty pink flush. He put his aggravation in his voice. "Dilly hasn't mentioned any more arguments in front of her, and I've asked regularly."

She settled into the seat and her face froze into a guarded look. "Of course you have."

He kept one hand on the car door and the other on the roof. The posture framed her in the car, made her look up at him and brought her eyes and face into sharp focus. Beautiful.

She was damn beautiful. And smart. And right then he understood her own sister had never known anything about her. Everything he'd believed about Mercy was wrong.

He drank in the picture of her waiting for him to speak. She looked interested, earnest in her desire to clear the air.

"I'm not used to talking about how I raise Dilly." He had no one to compare notes with about raising a child. There were times he was adrift, unsure of the best way to handle her. And Dilly was still a kid! Heaven help him when female hormones got hold of her. He was already out of his depth. She'd kill him by the time she hit fifteen.

"Clay? Where'd you go?" Mercy raised her perfect brows in question. He blinked.

"Sometimes you make me think of Janna," he said.

Her eyes shone with moisture. "I'm sure I do. Do we look alike? Sometimes as people age the resemblance becomes stronger."

"You're nothing like Janna. Nothing at all like her." He stepped back, took his hand from the roof to deny the intimacy of the moment. "The pageants worked out great for you. You learned all the things that Hope wants Dilly to know: poise, posture, confidence, how to take rejection." He stood by the door like some awkward teenager, not convinced he should join her in the car; half afraid of what he might do in the enclosed space.

Mercy snorted. "Hah! How's a snort for poise? Here's a secret, Clay." Her blue eyes held his in a serious light. "No one takes rejection well. Everybody hates it. Everybody wants to blame someone else. It's how people react to rejection that matters."

She turned to face straight ahead as if looking at him made her feel bad. Her voice changed, softened as if memories had taken hold. "I learned to keep battering at the door. That was the biggest difference between Janna and me. I got angry but never defeated."

Angry would not describe the Mercy he remembered from high school. Janna had certainly never mentioned Mercy being toughened by the pageants.

"My anger taught me how to fight for what I want. Janna gave up." She frowned as she stared off into the middle distance. "That's the biggest difference between us."

"I thought Janna was the tough one. The unbreakable one." He'd misjudged everything about his wife. He reeled at the fresh knowledge. He blew out a long breath as he sorted out all he'd learned.

Mercy was the fighter.

Janna, the quitter.

And he'd been a means to an end. Dilly, too. That end being hurting Hope and Nate.

But he couldn't explain his dark conclusion, not to Janna's grieving sister. Mercy had no idea about the misery that had infused his marriage after Dilly came. It would hurt her to hear about it now.

Mercy had fought for a career in Hollywood while Janna had fought for *him*. At least he'd *thought* Janna wanted him as much as Mercy wanted her career. But he was a tool to use against Hope. Now he understood what had driven Janna into his arms.

"You Talbot women are enough to make a man crazy."

"You're the sanest person I've met in a long time in spite of us Talbot women, as you put it. Hollywood's full of crazy. I know sane when I see it."

He had nothing to say in reply so he closed the car door. As he walked around the front of the SUV, he accepted what he'd been grappling with. Being with Clay had been Janna's reaction to her mother's rejection. Instead of trying to please Hope, Janna had rebelled and pretended that Clay was what she wanted.

She'd fooled them all. He slowed and faltered as the full impact hit him.

His entire relationship with his wife had been about retaliation. He'd believed everything Janna had said about her mother and Mercy and how Janna had been cut out of their family life. She'd wanted to hurt her mother for that perceived abandonment. And she hated Mercy. And she'd used Clay to hurt them all.

He wondered why Janna had wanted a child in the first place. When he got to the driver's door, he paused with his hand on the door handle to take another moment to come to grips with the whole sorry mess. Had she wanted Dilly to use as emotional blackmail? He remembered a comment she'd made on the day Dilly was born. *"Now Hope will have to be nice to me if she wants to see this kid."*

Christ. What a mess. He closed his eyes against the truth.

A whole lot of questions had just got answers. Two years of guilt washed away.

He opened his door and slid into place behind the wheel. He felt like a new man and wondered if it showed. He sure as hell wouldn't spill his guts about his newest realization about his wife. Not now. Probably never. He owed Janna that much and he'd never want Dilly to know. He shrugged and loosened his shoulders, feeling the lightness of a burden lifted.

Feeling free of Janna smoothed him out as if a rusted hinge had been oiled. From the time he'd closed Mercy's door to climbing in beside her, he'd become a new man. "Dilly likes you," he said to Mercy, watching her blue eyes go wide.

"I like her." Pink blossomed across her cheeks. She palmed them. "Oh, I feel warm and gooey inside."

"She makes me feel like that, too. She's so perfect, so sweet." He grinned. "Most of the time," he hedged. His child filled him up, swept him along heart-first, wherever she wanted him to go. "When things go her way." He grinned at the truth. "She's got me wrapped around her finger and some days I'm flummoxed when she shows her temper." Times like this he'd love to have a woman to talk to about parenting. Someone to bounce ideas off of.

If he wanted more from Mercy, he'd have to ask her straight out. "Your mother says Dilly needs to develop discipline. She says that dance will do that for her."

"Self-discipline comes from wanting to achieve something. Really wanting it. Dilly will never develop discipline for an activity she despises. I don't believe people are built that way. We pursue what we love with more gusto than anything we feel forced to do."

He pondered that. "Like forcing a gifted musician to go into auto mechanics?" His old man had insisted Clay was no good for anything. But once Doc Rimmel had taken an interest in him, Clay had torn into his studies like a ravening wolf because he'd loved the science and the animals. The discipline had come naturally.

"Yes." Her smile could put the Las Vegas strip to shame. "Yes, a musically gifted child should be encouraged in that area, not forced into something completely different."

He nodded, considering. "Thanks for the insight." He slipped his hands to the wheel so he wouldn't be tempted to touch her. His mind raced with a blend of Janna and Mercy, but mostly Dilly. "I'm not sure what I'll decide, but I'll consider everything."

"And you'll pay attention to when and why she gets angry? And her body language and her frustration? And you'll notice the things that she loves best to do?"

"Like?"

"Playing. Dilly has a great imagination and a deep appreciation for animals and the natural world, including worms."

He laughed. "You're right. She loves mud."

"And that's not like me at all," she said. "I was more concerned with being a good girl than getting dirty."

"And Janna?"

"Janna was a whirlwind, getting into everything she could. She wanted to learn about cars and engines and carpentry with Dad. She loved hanging out with him in the garage." Her eyes misted. "She was daddy's girl."

"Before or after—never mind; forget I said that."

She glanced his way, misty eyes and all. "I know what you mean. It's all right. Janna followed Dad around before and after Mom started taking me to pageants." She smiled kind of low and sad. "So see? Dilly's like Janna in that, too. Dilly's mad for you, Clay. You're her everything."

The burden of it nearly blinded him. The love, the overwhelming joy of having Dilly, of being responsible for his child's life—"I'm not sure I'm worthy," he said around a diamond-hard shard in his throat.

She reached to touch his arm but let her hand fall to her thigh instead. "You're worthy. I can't think of a better man for Janna to leave her child with than you."

He squeezed the steering wheel to keep from reaching for her. His wife's sister, damn it. He noticed the terrier she'd been coaxing sat by her kennel gate, watching them. He cleared his throat, more than ready to put this conversation behind them before he did something spontaneous and inappropriate. "You made progress with whats-her-name." He nodded toward the kennel. "Ethel?"

She talked freely for a couple of minutes about the dog, her face animated and flush with success. "And she let me scratch under her chin."

"And Karen?" He had to keep things impersonal. Being in the enclosed space had given him a false sense of intimacy and he needed to dispel it.

"She's come around. We're bumping along without too much snarkiness."

He glanced at her hands and resisted the temptation to bring one to his lips. "Ask her for a pair of gloves."

She put her hands up to inspect them. "I should have worn gloves, but my hands and nails are the least of my concerns these days. My mother is appalled at my condition. 'This is not how I trained you,' and 'Comb your hair and put on lipstick'—she goes on and on like I'm twelve."

Another piece of Talbot femaleness. He rarely brushed Dilly's hair more than once a day. "But Hope's not talking to you right now."

She chuckled. "True. At least she's not harping about my agent calling."

"And her not harping is a relief. But not hearing from your agent must be hard."

"I don't expect to hear from my agent, but Mom's blind where my career's concerned. She refuses to admit I'm all washed up." She gave him a self-deprecating smile. "The more I say it out loud, the more I'm convinced it's true. That part of my life is over."

Clay doubted that Mercy had given up on acting. If she were offered a role, she'd be out of here in a Hollywood second. But he wasn't here to argue with her about her acting career. He wanted to change the subject to make her stay and chat. They'd been distant since last week and this ease between them felt good. "Anything to report on the job search?"

"Maybe. Does Logan Hughes own Hughes Realty?"

"Yes. That's him. The office is over the bakery. Hasn't been open long."

She blew out a breath of relief. "Then I'll pop in and see Logan. He was nice to me." Her eyes shone as hope filled them. "Maybe he needs help in the office or something."

If she walked into Hughes's office looking hopeful and inviting, Hughes would send his own mother to the devil to have Mercy in there day after day.

His jaw went tight. "I remember Logan. Nice guy."

She stuck her hands out in front of her, fingers straight as rulers. "I'll give myself a manicure before I go. I want to make a good impression."

"I'm sure he'll be pleased to see you." His gut twisted. He just bet Logan Hughes had been nice to her. And would be again.

Shit.

Chapter Seven

THE NEXT MORNING MERCY parked in front of the bakery below Logan Hughes's office. She wasn't sure how to approach Logan. Instead of climbing out of the car to face him, she stalled by dreaming about how Clay made her want him. He'd come out to talk with her at the kennels yesterday afternoon and they'd returned to their previous friendly level of communication. It meant a lot to her that they maintain it.

She'd hoped her warmer feelings for him would have cooled by now, but his kind concern had stoked the flame. A couple of times inside his SUV the pull between them had been powerful. She'd gone still for fear she'd act out her fantasies and kiss him.

Fantasy, that's what this was. A silly hallucination she indulged in when she was alone. She drove and thought of Clay. She yanked weeds and thought of Clay. She played tag with Dilly and thought of Clay. She'd hardly slept for thinking of him and the way he'd looked at her.

Sitting in her dad's truck in full view of passersby brooding about Clay Foster would not get her a job with Logan Hughes. She didn't want to make the same mistake she'd made at Day's Hot Grill. Wrong clothes make the wrong impression, Hope claimed, so today Mercy wore a skirt, blouse, and sturdy black pumps to look more like an office worker.

Clay's veterinary clinic was across the street at the other end of the block. Not near enough to be a bother, but if things went well, she might pop in and share her news. She calmed her rising excitement and reminded herself that if the office looked fully staffed, she would act as if she'd come to catch up with an old friend.

She took one more look in the rearview mirror. There was nothing more she could do about how she looked. She tilted her head at a perky angle and cleared her throat to try out a friendly receptionist's tone of voice for phone calls. "Good afternoon, Hughes Realty. How may I help you?" She recalled Esme's dry tone and use of *honey* and grimaced. "If I start calling clients honey, I'll ask to be fired."

Maybe she needed something in between a teen's singsong and Esme's brusqueness. Something more Mercy. She tried for less perky more business. "Good afternoon, Hughes Realty. Mercy Talbot speaking. How may I direct your call?" Better.

It was early to practice her voice, but if she didn't feel the part, then it might not happen. Actor's superstition, of course, but there it was. Feel it, be it and if all else fails, fake it.

She climbed out of her dad's truck. She'd found fifty dollars tucked in the side pocket of her purse this morning. The cash hadn't been there yesterday. Her dad had noticed her trying to use sticky old nail polish last night. He must have guessed she was too broke to replace it. That was her dad, watching and caring.

In the end, she'd removed the sticky mess. Her unvarnished nails were neatly trimmed and clean and looked nothing at all like they used to in L.A. It had been months since she could afford a manicure.

Dismissing the memory of what her life had once been, she drew in a breath, ran over her telephone script one more time, and looked up at the window over the bakery. "Hughes Realty" in gold script arched across each of two glass panes. It must smell great up there with the bakery directly beneath.

In the office window, she saw Logan Hughes sitting at a desk, his hair catching the afternoon sun. Reddish blond and handsome, Logan had always been friendly. He'd never treated her the way some of the girls had in school. He'd never been standoffish the way most of the boys had been.

Logan Hughes was *nice.* A nice guy. That's what Clay had said. She hoped Logan remembered her and that Hope hadn't ruined Mercy's chances for a job with him or been difficult with Logan's mother or burned bridges with his father or aunt or anyone else he knew.

All she wanted was a chance to be Mercy Talbot, employee.

Smoothing her skirt one last time, she put on her sunglasses to hide the desperation she felt and entered the darkened coolness of the stairwell that led to the upper floor. At the top, she found two different office doors. One had the name "Women's Services" stenciled on the door. The other door near the front of the building belonged to Logan's office.

She opened the office door, stepped inside and then closed the door carefully behind her. Silent, the office was not what she expected. Logan sat at the only desk. Bathed in sunlight from the window, he glanced up as she entered.

No sign of recognition crossed his face. "Can I help you? The women's services office is at the top of the stairs."

"Logan, it's me, Mercy Talbot." She removed her sunglasses and smiled. She held onto the doorknob at her back, waiting to see the dismissive look that had become familiar in Welcome.

"Of course you are!" His eyes lit with happy recognition. "What a great surprise." He stood immediately, his face splitting into a welcoming grin. "I heard you were home, but I thought you'd be back on set somewhere exotic by now." He came toward her with his hand outstretched. "How've you been? You're beautiful as ever."

She closed her eyes for a fraction, drinking in the simplicity of seeing a kind face. Everyone else in Welcome seemed to have something against her or her mom and they had let her know it. "Logan, it's good to see you."

He clasped her hand, tugged her close and leaned in to kiss her cheek. She kissed him back. "What can I do for you?" he asked. "Looking for a property?"

She shook her head. "I'm afraid my mother has exaggerated my success, Logan. I'm not going back to L.A." The closer she got to asking for a job, the more she dreaded it.

"I always believed you'd make it big, Mercy. You're talented. I couldn't take my eyes off you when you took the stage at school. You owned it." He held her hand, took the other and squeezed them both lightly, his face alight with fond remembrance. "It's great to see you."

"That's kind of you to say." A nice guy said nice things. She felt pathetically grateful and brave enough to ask. "But I'm looking for a job and having some difficulty getting through to people that I'm here to stay."

He tilted his head, perplexed. "You're asking me if I need someone?"

Not only was he the only person in the office, he didn't have a reception desk or counter or anywhere for another employee to work. Still, she refused to give up just on appearances.

"Do you need help?" she pressed and then relented as he continued to hesitate. Maybe his new business wasn't taking off. She'd hate it if that were true. Logan deserved success. "It's okay if you don't."

"To be honest, Mercy . . ." he trailed off and then brightened. "Let's get a coffee and cinnamon bun downstairs. I missed lunch and we can catch up." He spun and reached for his phone, slipped it into his shirt pocket and held open the door for her. He left his jacket hanging on the back of his chair. His shirt was white and crisp and fit to perfection, his hair was short, freshly trimmed and he smelled of high-end aftershave. Light and appealing. Logan Hughes was the whole package: smart, successful and handsome.

Even if his new business was slow right now, she had faith he could build something great. She let go the idea of a job with him and decided to enjoy his company while they caught up on the years since high school.

Chatting on the way downstairs, Mercy felt completely at ease. For the first time since coming home, she was having an uncomplicated conversation. No background drama peppered the air, no sly comments about Hope came between them, and there was no doubting what she said.

Logan Hughes was exactly as she remembered him: comfortable, kind, and easy to talk to.

The scents of coffee and baked goods woke her appetite for the first time in days as she took a seat at the counter-height bar at the front of the bakery. Outside, the townspeople came and went from various shops, intent on their errands. She loved people-watching.

She settled on the stool while Logan put in their order at the bakery counter. She smiled as he took the stool next to hers. "Thanks, Logan. I appreciate a friendly face."

"People still treating you poorly after all these years and all your success?" He shook his head, proving how sensitive he'd been to her situation in high school.

"I was never anyone's favorite in this town." School was a blur because she wanted it to be, but the truth was she hadn't been popular. She'd been too different.

Too pretty, too busy, too polished.

Her mother had seen to all that and no one had bothered to look beyond the surface to the girl beneath. Janna had helped foster the idea that Mercy was stuck up. "But tell me about you, Logan. I want to hear it all," she said.

Half an hour later, she had his story. Successful in the Tacoma real estate market, Logan had returned to Welcome last year to be closer to his family. "My brother's got some issues and I need to be here."

This was the short version and there was a lot unsaid, but Mercy had her own disappointments. "Stuff happens," she said with a nod of understanding. "And siblings can be a challenge."

"Some more than others," he said with a wry grin. "Speaking of siblings, I was sorry to hear about Janna," he said. "I was in Tacoma when it happened. It must have been a horrible shock. I hear she left a baby girl."

"Dilly, the light of our lives. She's a sweet child but she has her moments."

He nodded and grinned. "I remember some of those same moments between you and Janna. You two were the most different sisters anyone could imagine." He said it kindly and because he'd known them both for most of their lives, his warmth took the sting out of the comparison between Dilly and Janna. Old friends were often given a pass for honest remembrances.

"Janna and I were not as different as you think." Especially given her rising feelings for one former bad boy. She and Janna had that much in common.

Logan finished his coffee and went for a refill, giving her time to relive those moments in the car with Clay yesterday. The truths they'd shared had marked a change in their communication. Once Clay had taken his place behind the wheel, their conversation had turned warm and *interesting*. She still wasn't sure what to make of it and she dared not ask Clay.

The way he'd looked at her had given her goosebumps. It was as if a mask had fallen off his face and for the first time, she'd seen the real man beneath the briskly efficient vet and busy single father. There was a man under all his responsibilities and he let her see that man.

She'd been charmed.

Logan returned with his refill, took his seat, and leaned in for privacy. "I'm not able to offer you a lot of money, but there's potential to build a good business in Welcome. If you manned the office when I can't be there, it would be a great help. I've been called away a lot lately and it would ease my mind if I had back-up."

She couldn't believe what she'd heard. "You have a job for me?" She, too, leaned closer, catching the scent of his aftershave again, feeling the warmth of his skin, seeing the interested light in his eyes.

"You wouldn't have to come in every day." He glanced around to be sure no one was eavesdropping. "And like I said, I can't pay much yet. But I would need you to answer calls for me when I forward them. No matter where you are or what you're doing. This business is twenty-four-seven and there are times I'm called away. If I can count on you to fill in, I could pay you on a scale. The more back-up I need, the more hours you get."

She closed her eyes and held onto the happy for an extra moment. "You'll give me a chance?"

"But I need you to be flexible, Mercy."

She nodded. "I get it." She touched his sleeve and grinned. "Believe me, all I do regularly is shovel poop out at the dog rescue with Karen Bowler."

He laughed and settled back on his stool. "So when can you start?"

"Now." She indicated her clothing. "I'm dressed for the part." She had old jeans and a T-shirt in the truck to wear at the kennels. She could keep office clothes with her at all times if he was suddenly called away. Like wardrobe, she could dress the part no matter where she was.

"Great, we can get you set up with a phone right away. If you have time, I'll familiarize you with enough of the business that you can take messages for now. By next month, you'll have more of a handle on things."

He was giving her a chance! "Thanks, Logan. You have no idea what this means to me."

"Right back at you, Mercy." His eyes lightened, relieved. She wasn't the only one who'd returned to Welcome with baggage. Logan Hughes needed a lifeline and, somehow, she'd just thrown him one.

CLAY CAUGHT SIGHT OF Mercy and Logan Hughes in the bakery window as he walked from his clinic to the post office. They had their heads together and faces turned toward each other. She smiled into the guy's eyes and the *nice guy* let his gaze linger on her features.

Linger.

He could walk on by; give them a nod, and move on to the post office. That would be the best course of action.

They were probably thick in the middle of a slew of happy memories. They could be trading gossip, reminiscing about stolen kisses or more under the bleachers. Maybe they were remembering how the other tasted, how their bodies had fit perfectly on the dance floor in the gym. Maybe Logan had driven her home and got to run his hands all over her and her hair had fallen to her shoulder when he'd loosened the pins that held it up.

Yes, the best thing to do would be to nod a greeting and keep walking. The worst thing to do would be to open that damn door and walk in.

He reached for the door and opened it. He nodded to acknowledge their startled glances. "Mercy." He gave Logan a steady gaze. "Logan."

"Clay." Logan stood and held out his hand. "Haven't seen you in a while. How's it going?" They shook hands. "Any thoughts on subdividing the acreage as I suggested?"

"No."

Logan settled back down to park his butt beside Mercy all afternoon, like he belonged there, letting his knee brush hers.

Mercy looked flushed and pretty, much the way she had yesterday when he'd seen her success with Ethel.

"You look happy," Clay said in what he considered an admirably controlled tone.

"I am." She lowered her voice. "Logan just offered me a job. Part-time for now." She swung her face to Logan's with a smile as wide as the Columbia River.

"With possibilities for *more* later," Logan added, drinking in her happiness. Clay's gut twisted at the display. *Fuck.*

Clay narrowed his eyes and wondered what the *more* would be. Nah, he didn't have to wonder; the interest in her and the challenge to him were clear in the set of the nice guy's shoulders and focused gaze.

"I'm having a coffee and bagel," Clay said. "Care to stick around?" He addressed Mercy.

"Oh, I would, but we're off to get me a phone and then go over my responsibilities."

Logan stood and clasped her elbow. "Yes, she needs to know the ins and outs of the business."

"I'll see you tonight then when I pick up Dilly." He wanted to snarl but maintained his cool. "Join us at the park later. She likes the slide."

She brightened at the suggestion and *bingo,* he had her. "I'd love that. She's been telling me about the swings and slides and how she's such a big girl to go down all by herself." Her smile lit the entire bakery and Logan's lips thinned.

Clay held the door for them, making certain to brush the top of Mercy's shoulder as she walked past. "See you later," he said into her ear.

Satisfied with the flush that rose to her neck at the intimacy of his whisper, he smiled and stood at the display counter and pointed at the biggest cheese-and-bacon bagel in the case. "That one," he said.

In his universe, nice guys finished last.

LATER THAT AFTERNOON, Mercy was so excited about her new job that she could barely focus as her mother pinned the hem of Dilly's cowgirl miniskirt. This was the final fitting and Dilly's face was a study in thunder. Darkness whirled across her sweet features as her grandmother tugged the material and used sharp straight pins to stab through the gathered flounce that flashed with sequins. This was Mercy's last chance to save Dilly from this next round of pageants. But, she'd promised not to argue with Hope in front of Dilly. She'd have to wait until after her niece went home with Clay before she tackled Hope.

Mercy felt helpless in the face of her mom's flawless imitation of a stone wall. There was nothing Mercy could do to stop Hope from flying Dilly to New Mexico for the upcoming pageant. She'd wracked her brain but had come up with no ideas for stalling.

She hoped Clay had reconsidered giving Dilly a couple months' break. She heard a man's footsteps in the kitchen and Clay rounded the corner into the living room.

"Hey there, Punk," Clay said. He braced for Dilly's usual slam into his knees.

But her face crumpled. "Daddy, I'm not allowed to move," she wailed with a sniff.

Hope sat back and released her. "I didn't want to stick you with a pin. You know that." She cast her eyes skyward.

"Did you have a fun day?" Clay asked Dilly.

She nodded and settled her head in the crook of his neck. "Yah-huh. Did you?"

"Yes, I did. I saw your Aunt Mercy on a date at the bakery."

Mercy quickly broke in before her mother could speak. "I would have told you before, but you're not speaking to me much these days," she said to Hope while pinning Clay with a glare. "I got a job working for Logan Hughes. Clay saw us working out the details while we had coffee in the bakery. His office is overhead. It was *not* a date."

Hope sniffed. "I know where he's situated, Mercy. But I don't know what all you could do for him. You have no skills, and no experience working in an office. Besides, you're . . ." She trailed off and then bit her lip.

"Besides what?"

"Your agent will call any day now. I don't see the point—"

Clay cleared his throat to indicate how close they'd come to another argument. Mercy hoped he was finished stirring the pot. As soon as they were alone, she'd tell him to stay out of her business.

"Hope," he said, "I've got a handful of bare skin here along Dilly's waist. Why?" He smoothed his hand along the expanse of flesh exposed by Dilly's cropped vest and low-slung miniskirt. "Get down, Punk. I want to get a better look at you."

Dilly pirouetted for her father, then did a bump and grind in a flourish that tightened the skin around his eyes.

"That's enough, Punk. I've seen enough." His gaze cut to Hope and then on to Mercy, who shook her head.

"I have nothing to do with this," she said. She pinched her lips closed. Clay and Hope knew how she felt about Dilly's pageants. She didn't need to repeat herself.

"You go get your regular clothes on, Punk. I want to talk to your grandmother."

The formal title brought Hope to her feet. "Clay," she said, as soon as Dilly was out of earshot. "All she needs is a couple of trophies and she'll be having the time of her life."

His gaze burned hellfire. "And dressing her like some pop star on crack and making her grind her hips is the way to win?"

Hope's mouth hung suspended for a second too long. "She's a child and I resent what you're implying." She blinked furiously.

Mercy stood. "I'll help her get changed. There are pins in the skirt." She walked to the sewing room where she found Dilly yanking off the vest. She helped her slide the skirt down and off. After pulling on her top, jeans, and sneakers, she took her niece's hand. When they stepped into the hall, Clay was waiting for them. "You said I could join you at the park," she said. "Let's go."

"Aunt Mercy's coming with us," he told Dilly. "You okay with that?"

"Yay!" Dilly skipped ahead down the hall and then waited for the adults to catch up. "Wanna come to our place for supper? Dad's gots hamburgers."

Clay shrugged and looked sheepish. "She loves them. I use one of those tabletop grills when the weather's too bad for outside grilling, but we should be fine tonight."

He must have forgotten that his original invitation had been to go to the play park, not for dinner. Dinner at his place. Her belly fluttered the way it had in his truck yesterday.

And the way it had in the bakery earlier when he'd whispered in her ear. Heat suffused her chest and neck at the idea of being with Clay in his home. "I'll get my purse," she said without quibbling about the exact invitation she'd received.

While she was in her room she took a moment to run a comb through her hair and slick on some lip-gloss. *What the hell she might as well go for broke.* She leaned over, reached into her top and scooped her breasts into her bra cups to their best advantage. The girls looked better and Mercy wanted to skip along the hall the way Dilly had.

Chapter Eight

MERCY STOOD BESIDE Clay at the foot of the slide in the play park as Dilly settled at the top. "She's having fun. Do you come all the time?"

"Most nights, but when she's having a tantrum I don't reward her with play time. We go straight home to wind down." He ran his fingers through his hair. "I wish I knew the best way to handle her. Sometimes I'm okay, but when she launches into a tantrum I wonder what the hell I know about raising kids."

Dilly slid to the bottom with both hands on the edges of the slide. She squealed with delight. Mercy clapped along with Clay. "Whee!" When Dilly ran back for her next turn, Mercy decided to ask the pertinent question.

"After I left the den, what did you and Mom decide about her cowgirl costume?" She held her breath, hoping he'd put a stop to the pageants for a time.

He firmed his lips. "No bump and grind."

"But the costume stays as is?"

"She'll add a couple of inches to the vest and skirt," he said.

"And she's not taking a break from the circuit?"

"No." His flat tone brooked no argument.

Dilly slid to the bottom of the slide with her hands in the air this time, like the bigger kids. She wanted to tell her to hold on tight, but Clay didn't notice that Dilly loved the thrill of sliding hands-free.

"Yes. Your mom has her reasons and now I see where she's coming from. So I'm in as long as the costumes and dances are appropriate. Hope and I agree on that now."

She leaned in and spoke quietly. "My mother agreeing with anyone is amazing, especially when it comes to what she says is best." She'd make certain her mom fixed the length of the costume as promised.

He turned his serious gaze on her. Up close like this, Clay Foster took her breath away. "All I want is to raise Dilly in a happy environment. For that, I need your mom's help."

"You have excellent instincts, Clay. I wish you'd have more faith in yourself." Janna had quickly soured on answering her newborn's demands and had leaned on Clay for most of Dilly's care within weeks.

He patted Dilly's head as she raced past to climb the steps back to the top again. "Two more times, Dilly." He held up two fingers as she held the handrail and climbed to the top to wait her turn behind a younger child who needed some coaxing. Long seconds passed and Mercy held her breath waiting to see if Dilly would grow impatient.

"She's doing well waiting for her turn," he said to Mercy. "Good girl, Dilly, you wait for the boy to slide first."

Dilly giggled and clapped her hands. "You go, boy," she said.

The mother tossed them a grateful look and encouraged her son with outstretched hands.

"She's learning patience," Mercy said. She'd heard him voice his doubts about his parenting skills before but she saw no evidence of Dilly being unhappy anywhere but after her dance classes. But she had to keep quiet for now. Hope had turned Clay's mind and only time would make him see reason. She saw no point arguing.

For now, here in the sunny play park while Dilly was giggly, she had to let the subject drop. They were having fun and Dilly was happy. "I'm looking forward to seeing your new home and having you cook for me," she said to Clay.

"Grilling burgers isn't cooking and I'm hoping you'll help with the Punk."

"I'll do more if you've got salad greens," she offered with a smile. "Deal."

He switched conversational gears. "Hughes looked happy today. Does he understand that when your agent calls you'll leave? From what I hear, his business is just getting established. Losing you could be a problem." He sounded relaxed, his focus on Dilly, where it should be.

"My mother's wrong. My agent won't call." Thank God Logan had believed in Mercy enough to give her a chance. "I won't leave Logan on a whim. He deserves better. I'm grateful for this chance and I hope my mother doesn't poison Logan against me or make him believe he made a mistake hiring me."

Clay toed the dirt and waited for Dilly's next slide into his arms.

"There's nothing for me in L.A. No parts, no work, no classes, no interest from my agent. My career is a bust."

"Is that what you told Logan?"

"Of course. It's the truth." She laughed at Dilly's giggles. "Maybe in a month or two, I'll have enough money to get my own place." If anyone could find her a well-priced rental, it was Logan.

Dilly climbed to the top of the slide again and held up one finger. "One more time, Daddy."

"That's right, Punk." He mirrored her hand and then crouched at the bottom of the slide with his arms open wide to scoop her up. She giggled and held her arms out to him, too. When she slid into him, he held her close, landed on his back and pretended that she'd knocked him over. "Ow! Oh, no."

Her delighted screeches echoed around the play equipment. Then she went still and patted his cheeks with grubby hands. "Daddy, I hurted you?" She gave his face a serious inspection.

"No, Punk, I'm fine." He scrambled to his feet and allowed Dilly to run ahead toward his car. "Not too fast, Dilly, Aunt Mercy's a slowpoke."

Her giggles drifted behind her as she picked up speed. "Will she run out into the parking lot?" Mercy geared up to catch her niece if necessary.

"No, I taught her to touch the headlight if I'm not holding her hand."

She relaxed at his words and settled into a stroll beside him. Clay bumped his shoulder gently against hers and she didn't step away. One stretch of her fingers would allow him to hold her hand, but with Dilly being yards away it seemed wrong.

Aunties and daddies shouldn't hold hands in the park. But still, she bumped his shoulder back.

He ducked his head. "You'll stick around? Even if your agent calls?"

She was saved from answering by a call from across the park.

"Hi ya, Doctor Foster," a boy of about nine called. He trotted closer with a tiny dog on a leash. A well-built blonde followed close behind. One look at her gaze said her smile was for Clay and Clay alone.

She gave Mercy a dismissive glance Mercy remembered well. Shandy Armstrong. "Hello, Shandy," she said. "You're not Armstrong now, though. You married one of the Camden brothers."

"Married and divorced. Slumming, Mercy?" She cocked her hip in another familiar gesture. Shandy still knew how to use body language. She was a natural at expressing boredom, sexuality, benign indifference and more with subtle shifts of her lips, eyes, and hips.

"No," Mercy responded blandly to Shandy's rude question while Clay chatted with the boy. "This is your son? He looks like his dad," she said after a moment.

"Yes." Shandy sauntered closer, crossed her arms under her heavy breasts and spoke again. "Clay is my vet. He takes wonderful care of us." The implication was clear. Clay gave a guilty start at her tone.

"I'm sure he does." Mercy kept her voice cool and vaguely disinterested. She looked past Shandy toward her niece and waved.

Dilly stood in front of Clay's car with her palm on the headlamp. "Daddy, Auntie Mercy, I'm touching the glass. It's time to go-oh."

"Nice to see you, Shandy. I'm sure we'll bump into each other again." She waved to Dilly to let her see she wouldn't have long to wait.

Shandy stepped to her son's side. She clasped Clay's forearm. "Clay, I thought I'd seen you here before. Good timing. Your daughter's delightful."

"Dad-dee!"

Mercy headed for the car and her impatient niece. "I'll get her, Clay," she said and gave Shandy a pleasant nod and smile. Mercy knew when to back off and Shandy's message had been clear.

Of course, Clay would have interested women. He was free to see whomever he chose. He could sleep with half a dozen women in a month if he wanted. He probably had, would and could. He might be arranging a rendezvous right now with nothing more than a smoldering look.

She would not glance back to check.

She would *not*.

When she made it to the car and took hold of Dilly's hand, releasing her from the safety of the headlamp, it was natural to face the park to wait. Clay stood in conversation with Shandy's son. He ruffled the boy's hair and then jogged toward the parking lot.

Clay neared and Dilly ran to him. Scooping her into his arms, he didn't look like a man who'd scored a date. He still had the dark look of a loner in his eyes sometimes. Except now, with Dilly, that loner was not in evidence. He looked like a man besotted with one sweet girl, a man whose heart was filled to the brim.

Janna used to complain that when she and Clay argued, her husband was cold as the polar vortex. Janna had hated that she could never tell what he was thinking. She'd told Mercy that she never got through to him, never broke his iron control. And for the first time, Mercy wondered why her sister would want to infuriate her husband.

He picked up Dilly and swung her around. "Wait here for a second," he said to Mercy. After he buckled Dilly into her car seat, he closed her door and then came to stand with Mercy beside the car, out of Dilly's hearing. "You didn't get a chance to answer my question. Will you be staying now that you've got a job?"

She shifted to allow him room to lean on the hood. He slid into her personal space as if it was his, too. They stood with their shoulders touching, hips inches apart, looking out across the playground.

"I'm staying," she said, convinced that her agent would never call. "But I need to get my own place, figure out what I want to do with the rest of my life. By my age, most people have settled into careers or families. I'm starting fresh."

"Some people would love a fresh start." He looked out across the field, a muscle jumping in his jaw.

"How about you? Are you happy with how your life's going?" She stopped, suddenly aware that she'd jammed her foot into her mouth and tried desperately to find a way to pull it back out. Her heart raced as he turned his head to stare at her with truthful intensity.

For the life of her, she couldn't understand how Janna could find this man cold. He bristled with energy, intensity, honesty, and damn it, plain old sex appeal.

He cleared his throat and nodded a couple of times. "You need to hear me now," he said in a hoarse whisper. "Janna wouldn't be with us, even if she was alive. Nothing was working for her anymore. Not me and not Dilly. Our life was not what she wanted." The bald confession seemed torn from him.

Reeling, Mercy needed a second to process what he'd said. She took that second to look through the windshield to check on Dilly. She was singing quietly and playing with a toy horse. Mercy blinked and then turned back to find Clay still staring intently into her eyes. "You said she was leaving you that night," she whispered back. She didn't understand how her sister could run out into the night, jump in the car, and tear down the road away from her baby. Away from Clay.

He nodded. "I was relieved if you want the truth. I saw my future with Dilly but not with Janna. We fought all the time. It was exactly what I didn't want for my kid and I didn't have the skills to fix it."

Stunned, Mercy could barely pull up a coherent thought. "You're saying your life is better without my sister?"

"The way we were was bad for everyone. No one was happy. Could we have changed things? Maybe. But not without years of work and the Punk would have witnessed a lot of—"

She put up her hand to stop him. "I get it, I do. In a perfect world, Janna would have come around. She'd have sobered up and been the mother Dilly needed. But this world is far from perfect. And so was my sister, but that doesn't mean we didn't all love her." Including Hope.

"I did love her," he said. "Early on she was the woman I wanted. But having Dilly changed everything about what I wanted." He smiled as if memories of his baby girl washed all the heartache away.

Babies should change everything. It hurt that her sister hadn't accepted that one life truth.

"My mother's still devastated," she said. "Janna was wrong about our mom. She loved Janna and it kills her that Janna believed otherwise. But they were caught in a vicious whirlpool that sucked the life out of any chance they had of fixing things between them." Hindsight made it clear.

He nodded. "Since you've come home I've had my eyes opened. I should thank you for that."

"Opened enough to take my advice about the pageants?" She couldn't resist bumping his shoulder again. "Sorry, I can be relentless when I want something."

"Talbot women should come with a warning: 'Caution! Bulldozer.'" He'd meant to lighten the mood and he'd succeeded.

From the play area, Shandy watched them. "You have a fan," Mercy said with a nod in the other woman's direction. Was he happy that women like Shandy were available? Did she scratch his itch?

"She's always friendly."

Mercy wouldn't ask. He had a right to his privacy and it would be rude to pry. Rude and foolish. He might wonder at her sudden interest in his love life. They were in-laws, linked by love for a child. That was all.

The important thing was that Dilly was happy and loved and, aside from some tense moments between Hope and Mercy, family strife was a distant memory. "I wish Janna had left that night with a clear mind. She might—the accident might not have happened."

He shook his head. "She loved the drama of fighting with me. Arguing meant she needn't take responsibility for her actions. She had plenty of chances to leave with a cool head. She could have left Dilly with your mom, and walked away. She could have gone out for a case of beer one night and never come back. But she didn't." He looked across the field again and his jaw tightened. "But simply walking out wasn't exciting enough. Janna needed the heat of an argument to propel her out the door."

Another piece of the puzzle fell into place. Mercy understood why he'd stayed removed from the heat in their arguments. He knew what Janna had been up to. Given her own conversations with Janna, Clay's version had the ring of truth. If Janna had left in the cold light of day, she'd have had to face the truth that she was abandoning her child. She needed someone to blame for her decision to run. Who better to blame than Clay?

It was all too difficult to process and nothing either of them said now could change what had happened. They had to think of Dilly.

Mercy touched Clay's forearm and faced him square on. "Dilly doesn't have to be like that. She won't embrace the drama if we handle things right. But we have to act quickly."

He gave her a wry glance. "You don't let up, do you? I won't talk about the pageants yet. I'm still considering those, but I sure as hell won't have my child dressed like a hooker at an army base. If that means she loses, then so be it."

"In my mom's defense, she's right about times changing on the circuit. Things are different now." She shrugged. "I don't believe Dilly will ever enjoy herself."

"Not even if she wins?"

Mercy shook her head. "Not even then."

"Daddy, I'm hungry." The call came from inside and both adults laughed and took their seats inside the SUV.

In the back, Dilly stuck out her tummy, pulled up her T-shirt and patted her belly. "Look, I gots a hole."

Clay laughed. "Don't worry Punk. We'll fill it up with a burger when we get home."

"Auntie Mercy too?"

Mercy raised her T-shirt to expose her navel. "My empty belly needs to be filled too," she said. She buckled her seatbelt and waited for Clay to reverse out of the spot, but his gaze was glued to her still-exposed belly.

"Have mercy," he muttered while Dilly's squeals and giggles filled the space with warmth and affection.

CLAY GRITTED HIS TEETH at the sight of Mercy's smooth, toned stomach. When she noticed, she pulled her top down to hide her flesh, but it was too late, and they both knew it. He'd been flat-out ogling her. What red-blooded man wouldn't?

At the exit to the park, Dilly piped up from the back seat, "Auntie Mercy read me my story, 'kay?" Which meant Dilly wanted her aunt, and not him, for her bedtime routine.

"If Auntie Mercy reads your story then she has to stay 'til bedtime." And he'd be alone with her after their diminutive chaperone fell asleep. "We'll have to get you home," he said to Mercy. "But once she's in bed, I'm in for the night. I can't leave her to drive you back." Her eyes widened and for a flash, he wondered if she thought he was inviting her to spend the night. And that took him down a path to a place he couldn't go.

"I'd love to help put her to bed," she said after a quick breath. "Stop by my parents' place and I'll borrow a vehicle. Then I can get myself home." On the last word, she sounded breezy. She turned to Dilly. "Would you like it if I kissed you good night, too?"

"Yes." His daughter's voice came tinged with the reverence only afforded her favorite dreams-come-true.

A hard knot formed and made swallowing impossible. Dilly wanted Mercy to stay as much as he did. Damn it, the thing he swore he didn't want to happen already had. Dilly had fallen under Mercy's spell and there was no going back.

Still, when he pulled to a stop in front of the Talbot place, he wasn't sure if Mercy would actually show up for dinner.

"I'll be along soon," she said, both aggravating and relieving him. "Fire up the grill." She hustled up the driveway to the house. He watched her lithe strides and recalled her looking much the same in high school: untouchable, cool, and poised. He shook his head to wake up his common sense, but it had gone dormant at the idea of being alone with her after Dilly went to bed.

Nate's truck sat beside Hope's minivan in the driveway and it dawned on him that Mercy would have to leave immediately after putting Dilly down for the night. There would be no time for more than a brief conversation because she lived with her parents. They'd be waiting up, aware of Dilly's bedtime.

He chuckled at the familiarity. How many times had he chafed that Janna lived under the watchful eye of these same people?

Life had a way of laughing at Clay, and tonight he had to laugh along with it.

Dilly started singing her new favorite song. He chimed in, hoping to get the memory of Mercy's fine swaying butt out of his mind. It worked until he stepped into his house and pictured that same butt heading up the staircase in front of him. He bit off a groan.

It was a mistake to have her at the house. More than a mistake—it was a tragedy in the making.

"Auntie Mercy's coming! Auntie Mercy's coming!" Dilly squealed and ran in circles in the living room, her excitement a stark reminder of how rarely they had company. For a moment he was struck by how limited their family life was.

For him, it was work, home, and the rescue.

For Dilly, life was classes she hated, practice, travel, and pageants. And standing still while her grandmother tried not to stick her with pins.

Dilly wound down after five minutes and went to stand by the front window to watch the driveway.

Forty-five minutes later, he decided Mercy had changed her mind. Which was fine by him, except Dilly was disappointed and Mercy should know better than to break promises to a child.

He looked at the clock again. It was a fifteen-minute drive from the Talbot home. Dilly set a place at the table for her aunt. By climbing onto the dining chair and kneeling, she was able to slide the dinner plate onto the placemat. He wasn't sure how to properly arrange the cutlery. Fancy place settings were beyond his limited experience, and he had a pang of guilt about all the things he wasn't able to teach his daughter.

"Dilly, I'm searching for how to set a table. Want to help?"

"I'm busy," she said.

He smiled as she moved her booster seat to the chair next to Mercy's. Normally, Dilly sat beside him so he could cut her meat for her. Tonight's dinner loomed large for Dilly and she wanted to make a good impression.

He frowned, reminded again how much potential there was for hurt when Mercy left to return to her career. No matter what she said, or how she saw her career going, Mercy was a huge talent and one that deserved recognition. He'd seen that much when Janna had played a couple of old VHS tapes of her sister's pageants.

Janna had provided a snarky play-by-play, but Clay had been impressed. When he'd said as much, the evening had turned into a full-on screaming match with Clay trying to follow Janna's drunken logic.

He hadn't understood his wife then and he sure as hell didn't see his wife's logic now. Mercy had been doing what she loved to do but Janna hated her for it. Sibling rivalry at its worst.

He found what he'd searched for on the Internet and called Dilly to come sit on his knee to watch the video on how to set a casual table. "Knives go on the right," he said, "with the sharp edge facing the plate. But I'll put the knives out, Punk."

"'Kay."

A few minutes later the doorbell rang and Dilly screeched off to answer with Clay following close behind. "Auntie Mercy," she said when she tugged the door open. "Come see where you sit." She clasped Mercy's hand and pulled her to the table where her aunt made the appropriately excited comments.

Clay kept his eyes on the pair while he pulled the burgers out of the fridge and put the makings of a salad on the counter. Mercy's perfect profile matched her sister's and from what he could see, Dilly's would be much the same. After some explanations on where and why they were sitting next to each other, Dilly dragged Mercy off to see her room.

Clay frowned as he tore and washed lettuce. Dilly hadn't taken anyone to her room before because Clay never invited guests. This was another thing he needed to rectify. She needed to experience social gatherings and have people visit them.

She needed a regular life with a real family. His stomach sank with all the things he'd done wrong.

He fell two steps behind everyone else when it came to giving his girl what she needed. Other men were naturals at being fathers. Clay could barely remember his own father without a beer in his hand and several empties on the table.

He shut the memory away.

Mercy and Dilly returned to the great room. "I'll make the salad. It's the least I can do." Her eyes warmed. "Oh, I forgot. I picked up an apple pie on the way out here. I'll go get it. I can't believe I ignored the smell of apple pie inside the truck. That should've been enough of a reminder." The pie accounted for the lag time in the trip to his place. He felt like an ass for believing Mercy could blow off an invitation issued by her own niece.

She turned to leave but Dilly grabbed her hand. "I wanna come!" Dilly frowned and thunder crossed her features as if she expected to be denied.

"Of course you'll come," Mercy said and swung her hand to make Dilly giggle.

Dilly's mood shifted back to joyful in a nanosecond. They returned with Dilly holding one side of the pie box and Mercy the other.

"That must have taken some negotiation," he said with a nod at the way they shared the effort.

Mercy smiled a heart-stopper and helped Dilly set the pie on the counter. Clay pulled a package of buns out of the breadbox on the counter.

Mercy nudged him away from the salad fixings and took the chopping knife from his hand. "I'll do this. You can start the burgers. Dilly, please go wash your hands for supper."

Dilly dashed off and a moment later he heard the water running in the main-floor bathroom sink.

"That was easy. She often puts up a fuss about washing her hands." He collected the plate of meat patties to take out to the grill.

"She's trying to make a good impression." The way Mercy cut tomatoes fascinated him. Her hands were quick and sure and she cut the tomatoes into perfect cubes. He could watch her all night.

"The day after Janna died, your mom showed up with some new clothes for Dilly. Then she went through the fridge and cupboards and gave me instructions on a proper diet for a baby. That's when I learned my way around a kitchen. If I'd been left to my own devices, we'd be living on takeout and frozen pizza." He wasn't used to sharing his kitchen workspace, but he found pleasure in it with Mercy.

"You have good reasons to be grateful to my mom," she said quietly. She glanced at him over her shoulder as he stepped out to put the meat on the grill. The automatic actions gave him a moment to think.

The Mercy he was coming to know was deeper than he'd expected and more thoughtful than Janna let on. She already understood him better than his wife ever had.

Dangerous territory.

The door opened behind him and Mercy joined him beside the grill. She took an appreciative sniff. "These smell great. Dilly said it was time for her show and she turned on the television."

"She watches fifteen minutes of TV whenever I'm cooking. I probably shouldn't use the TV as a babysitter, but I worry she might touch the stove or spill something hot on herself if she tries to help me or gets underfoot."

Mercy nodded. "Better safe than sorry, and a few minutes a day should be fine. She's singing along with the program. And single parents don't have an extra pair of hands or eyes to help with supervision."

A single parent. He supposed he was. He'd never labeled his life in that way. Instead of wondering what it would be like to have a partner, he focused on cooking the burgers.

"Your home is lovely, Clay. It's not at all like I—well—not what I expected. Janna never said much about how you lived."

"I'm sure she told you about the arguments. About how cold I was." He replayed several choice terms she'd used for him. One of her favorites was *icy bastard.*

"She was my sister. We shared some things but not all." She was hedging and they both knew it.

"I knew you were diplomatic when you got Dilly to share carrying the pie. Usually, she fights tooth and nail when she wants to do something."

"I told her if she dropped it I wouldn't get another and no one would get any pie."

He flipped the burgers. "Dilly knows all my weaknesses," he said with a laugh. "And knows exactly when I'll cave and when I won't. But she hasn't figured you out yet."

He focused on the grill for a moment. When Mercy didn't speak, he filled in the silence with a question. "I started to build this place before Janna died. She didn't tell you about it?"

"She told me she hated living at the back of the lot in the trailer. And then the conversation went downhill. Not one of our finest." She studied her fingernails, giving him a *don't ask* signal. "But, no, not about the building plans."

Janna hadn't cared enough to offer suggestions or ideas on the house. The time he'd spent on the plans had been another bone of contention. In retrospect, she'd been right. Adding a house construction to their already-strained marriage had proven to be too much and had caused more arguments. "Janna wouldn't recognize this place now. Not the yard or the house. And if it's all the same to you, I'd prefer we not talk about her this evening."

"Agreed," she said with a soft glance. She turned away and walked the perimeter of the deck and gazed toward the ring of trees that bisected the backyard. The roof of their old trailer was barely visible through the leafy shield. "Great property for a dog. You could bring Beau here and let him run free."

"As much as we love him, he's settled at Karen's place and he has a job to do. Here, he'd be lonely all day." He peered at the underside of a burger and decided it was almost cooked. "And now you have a job, too." With Logan Hughes.

"Yes, I do. I hope it'll work out well. Logan needs another person to handle calls when he can't."

Clay shrugged. "I'm surprised he's that busy already. He hasn't been open long."

"He tells me the business is on track. There are opportunities looming and he can't afford to miss out on them. That's where I come in. I told him I'd keep business clothes with me at all times. I can switch gears from pooper scooper to assistant in minutes." She chewed her lip. "Do you think Karen would mind if I used her shower in a pinch?"

He chuckled. "Not if it meant you keeping your job." Karen had a good heart. "I'm glad she let go of whatever grudge she harbored."

"Me, too."

"I've got beer in the fridge if you'd like one."

"No, thanks, I have to drive home. But I can get you one."

"I'd rather have an iced tea," he said. "I don't hold beer or liquor in the same high regard I used to."

Her eyes clouded. "Of course. Two iced teas coming up," she said.

"Put them on the table. The burgers are done," he said and piled them on a clean plate.

After they enjoyed their burgers and salad, Dilly grabbed Mercy's hand and hauled her around the house again while Clay cleared the table and loaded the dishwasher. Dilly wanted to show off the whole place and Mercy tagged along like a barge behind a tugboat.

When Mercy stood at the upstairs loft railing with a *help me* expression, Clay laughed. "She's trying to avoid bedtime. She wants to stay up because you're here." Another reminder of how isolated they'd become. He had to change that.

He needed to make friends with other parents with children. Maybe it was time to put Dilly into nursery school or daycare where she could make friends with other kids her age. He doubted Hope would go for it, though. She was a hands-on grandmother, and until Mercy had come back, the arrangement with Hope had worked.

Bath time was another adventure in Dilly-land and Mercy ended up soaked from her shoulders to her thighs. Dilly wanted to show her aunt how she could swim like a seal. She flipped and flopped and giggled when waves splashed over the side of the tub.

Mercy took it all in stride and made fish faces that sent Dilly into giggles.

His mouth went dry as he saw the joy on both their faces. Dilly's laughter ran clear and true and Mercy's eyes filled with love at the sound. Dilly climbed out, got dried off then screeched with laughter as she ran naked to her room.

Clay gave chase with her nightie held up like a shield. She squealed and dived under the covers, which meant a full minute of tickling before she popped out again with her thumb in her mouth. He slipped her nightie over her head and settled her back.

"The thumb is the signal that she's ready to sleep," he said to Mercy, who'd watched the whole procedure in happy bemusement.

"Then I guess it's time for me to leave." She leaned over the bed and kissed Dilly's forehead. "Do you still want me to read your story?"

"Ya-huh." Dilly slid contentedly to her sleep position but stretched her pudgy fingers out to clasp Mercy's hand.

Clay handed her the storybook. "She's already gone past her bedtime." He bent to his daughter for their goodnight kiss and held up one finger to reinforce his instructions. "One time, Dilly."

"'Kay." As she agreed, her eyelids drooped and Clay doubted she'd make it through to the end of her friendly bear tale.

Clay left Mercy to read and went downstairs to the great room to wait. She'd be leaving shortly, although he'd give a lot to have her stay. Too bad it was too warm for the fire. Lit, the fireplace lent a soft glow to the room.

He heard a door close and watched Mercy tiptoe along the loft hall and down the stairs. Her damp blouse still clung to her, outlining her chest. He walked toward the kitchen rather than watch the dip and sway of her breasts.

"She's marvelous, Clay."

"The love of my life," he said. "Ice cream?" They'd had some of the pie Mercy had brought but ice cream was an indulgence, the more outrageous the flavor the better. He held up a container with a moose face on it. "In spite of the name I can pretty much guarantee there's no moose poop in here."

"I should . . . go," she said, the last word no more than a whisper, "as much as I'd enjoy a dish of ice cream." Then one side of her mouth lifted in a vulnerable cant. "My mother will be watching what time I get home." She looked at the ceiling. "Can you believe I just said that? That I would *have* to say that?"

"We're getting past the living-with-the-parents stage. You must be feeling it." It'd been a long time since he'd dated anyone who lived with her parents. *The same parents.*

"Dating must be difficult with Dilly. Any single parent would have a hard time," she said with a dash of sympathy.

He shook his head. "I've pretty much kept to myself since Janna died." He stuck a spoon in his ice cream.

"No dates, *at all*?" Her eyes gave away her shock. He'd just admitted to being celibate.

It was his turn to glance at the ceiling. Might as well say it. "Don't look surprised. I'm still that rotten Foster kid, the one who destroyed Janna Talbot's life. I'm still the one who lives on the edge of town. The loner. Hell, even my sister deserted me. Elle didn't come home for my wife's funeral."

"To be honest, I didn't notice. I was too wrapped up in myself, I guess. And my parents." Her eyes softened in sympathy. "I'm sure Elle had her reasons."

He figured they were both remembering the bar brawl Janna and Elle were busted for. "She had important family stuff happening at the time. She couldn't leave her kids and couldn't afford to bring them."

"I wasn't aware she had a family. Janna never said."

"She has three children." Obviously, she was okay with the idea of parenting in spite of the example their parents had set. That's what he needed: a dose of Elle's confidence. "She's on her own now. She didn't make the smartest choices with men."

Mercy blinked. "Three children? On her own?"

"Whenever I tell myself I can't handle Dilly, I think of Elle." When he'd decided to keep their old trailer, it was with Elle in mind. "The trailer's out back for her if she needs it."

Clay waited in silence for Mercy to move away, or run for the door, or slap his face for the thoughts he was having.

"Well, um, thanks for the burgers. They were delicious." Her eyes tracked the spoon from the ice cream to his mouth and something rose in his gut. Fast. Hard.

"Don't look like that," he said as he set his dish down.

"Like what?" A telltale pink stood out in her cheeks.

"As if you want something stupid to happen." He put great effort into setting his spoon on the counter beside the dish.

She blinked and stared at the spoon as if the answers to life's questions rested there. "I should go."

"Yes, you should." But his hand reached for hers. Their fingers laced and he tugged her close. "Once," he said. "Just this once." The damp from her blouse felt cool against his chest but her lips were warm, soft.

Tasty.

And then she opened them.

Chapter Nine

ICE CREAM. CLAY'S MOUTH tasted of tracks of chocolate and vanilla that made her smile as Mercy molded her lips to his. She let her tongue reflect the dance he brought to her mouth. He crushed her to his chest with a fierce yearning that she answered in full.

Yes, yes. This.

This was what she craved. And more. She shifted her hips closer to his. He pressed back and she gloried in his hard length against her.

He grabbed the cheeks of her butt and dug his fingers into her flesh to hold her still. To bring her near and to push her away. They went fluid as each sought to press against the other. She rocked against him, drowning, falling, needing.

Clay closed in, stormed her, enveloped her, and then made her want to pull him in. She lifted to fit against him better, and to give him more, to give him everything.

She moaned and hit bottom, wanting to beg, but he pulled back, leaving her stunned.

She covered her lips with her fingers. Never had she felt such raging need. Before this, before *Clay*, she'd doubted she was capable of this response. She swallowed, needing air, needing control.

He was close and hot. Heat flowed between them, bringing their desire to fire-glow.

"Now we know," he said, his eyes sinking shut as he took one step back and then another.

She pulled on her ragged edges of control. Those edges slipped away. "What do we know?" she rasped.

"We—I—don't have to wonder anymore." His eyes cooled, and a mask slid into place to cover his desire.

The loner part of him stood before her. Her skin could melt right off and slide into a puddle on the floor and he wouldn't care. She blinked, gasping to comprehend. "Are you kidding me? You kissed me like that out of curiosity?" She grabbed at his elbow to stop his retreat. "I can't imagine the fireworks if you meant it."

"I meant it, Mercy. God, I meant it. But if all we had to consider was you and me, fine. We could have a great time until this burns out. But we can't go there, not with Dilly tagging along. My daughter's already attached to you. You've seen the way she looks at you; as if you're hers and no one else's.

"If we get tangled up in a mess, where will that leave her?" He swallowed hard. "She'll never understand if things go cold between us."

Her mind froze. He was ending things before they began. And he was right, of course. Dilly had to come first. She couldn't string words together so she said nothing.

He began to look desperate as seconds ticked by. "You must see that you're more vital to her well-being than you are to mine," he said. "I can't trample on her heart. I won't." He looked past her as if he couldn't bear to look at her. "I don't think you can do that, either."

She closed her eyes, hearing him, feeling him. She nodded, wishing her closed eyes meant she was asleep, that none of this had happened for real. But it had. Kissing him had been a dreadful mistake because he was right. Now they knew.

It would be good, so fucking good.

"It would kill me if she wasn't part of my life just because you and I messed up." She felt her heart swell with love for her niece. "I'll always want to be involved with her and be in her life."

"Even from L.A.?"

Familiar disappointment rose. Did no one want to believe she was a failure? "You sound like my mother." She turned and took three steps away. *No.* She had to get this out in the open. "I was in an indie film last year. I had a nice role that was pivotal to the plot. But it was short. Very little screen time. This year nothing. I'm broke and broken." No way would she tell him about her last humiliating experience in a producer's office. The meeting that proved how low she'd sunk.

"What was it called? I don't recall hearing about it."

"*Roger's Lie* and you don't recall it because no one saw it. The movie had a limited release that went nowhere. The plot was one of those action things that morphs into a comment on society. A weird blend of genres that won't excite anyone."

"Artsy?"

She shrugged. "I suppose."

He nodded but made no move toward her.

"There's nothing for me in Hollywood, Clay. But Dilly's here and I love her more than I could have dreamed."

"I'm glad." He jammed his hands into his pockets. "You'd better leave."

She nodded and walked to the hall table where she'd left her purse. Clutching it, she turned to him. "I'm glad we sorted this out. Now we can just be in-laws, the way we should be." She needed to walk out the door, but her damn legs wouldn't obey. Not yet.

Not. Quite. Yet.

She tried not to beg him with her eyes, but she lost that battle, too.

He stood immobile, but his eyes heated the space between them until her vision blurred and she knew he wouldn't take the few steps to reach her. He would never take those steps. "See you around," he said.

She left.

YOU'RE MORE VITAL TO her well-being than you are to mine. Clay's words whispered through her mind on the drive home. The words whispered, then spoke, then rose to a shout by the time she parked in her parents' driveway. She understood what he meant. They were adults and grasped the implications of their having a relationship. They couldn't risk hurting a child just so they could—what had he said?—have a great time.

He was right to call it getting tangled up. Tangles were difficult to undo. Messy. Painful. Even Dilly knew how painful it could be to untangle knots in her hair.

She turned off the ignition but her hand stayed on the key while she sat immobile, caught in a tangle of her own.

Getting involved with Clay would be the single most selfish act of her lifetime. She'd done some selfish things when it came to her career but that's what acting was: the selfish pursuit of a dream that was all about Mercy.

She could not bring that level of selfishness to bear on a child. She would not.

The key warmed under her fingers until she pulled it out and clasped it in her palm. Her dad would hate it if she messed up with Dilly. He'd never speak of it, but she'd see the unspoken pain in his eyes for the rest of her life.

She wouldn't be that lucky with her mother. Hope would never let it go.

And Clay? She'd bet her life savings if she had any that he still believed she'd return to Hollywood. A person would be Guinness-world-record stupid to tangle with someone who could leave them high and dry on the strength of a phone call. And Clay had never been stupid.

She rested her forehead on the steering wheel.

In spite of all the reasons not to kiss him again, Mercy's heart raced and she clenched the key. She could go back to his place.

Clay would let her in. He'd drag her into his arms and kiss her without stopping. They could share tonight, get it out of their systems, and never speak of it again.

He'd been celibate for two years.

It was wrong to be the first woman after her own sister.

Did that matter? Was she that selfish?

The key burned in her palm as desire burned in her belly. Dilly was asleep. She'd never know if Mercy returned to the house and was gone by morning.

She put the key back in the ignition.

Ten minutes later, she walked into her childhood home. Guilt made her creep as silently as she could. A teenaged habit leftover from when she had missed curfew or was with a boy her mother wouldn't like. This time it was her guilt-ridden conscience that made her move like a thief.

She'd almost turned the key. Had *almost* gone to Clay.

Want and selfish desire had warred to the death with her better half, the half of her that had Dilly's best interests at heart.

The sound of muted gunfire and dramatic music told her where to find her dad. She pulled her mind away from Clay and strode into the family room. Her dad sat alone watching an action movie. He loved spy thrillers.

"Did you put her to bed?" he asked.

"Read her a story and everything." She took a seat on the sofa across from him. Humphrey jumped into her lap for a cuddle. "How did Dilly become precious to me so fast?"

Dilly had been a baby like anyone else's baby when she'd been born. Of course, Mercy had felt more than mild curiosity at the first sight of her, but the visit had been too short and her mind had been on the indie flick that had just begun filming. All her life, her mind had been on something else.

At least she had the good sense now to make up for her distracted interest then.

Her father turned down the volume when the movie broke for a commercial. "Took us all of a second to fall for her. Your mother cried and I choked up looking at her red face all scrunched up as Janna held her in her arms. Janna never looked so beautiful."

They shared a moment of silence broken by the mechanical drone of her mother's treadmill. "When did Mom dust off the gym equipment?"

He shrugged. "Helps her deal with stress, she says."

"She was furious when I wanted to borrow your truck." When Hope had learned where Mercy was going, she'd stalked into the sewing room and slammed the door. Her Dad had tossed her his keys. "By the way, I used the cash you hid in my purse for gas," she said. "Thanks, but I got that job with Logan Hughes today. I won't need any more charity."

"It's a sad day when a man can't give his daughter walking-around money," he grumbled and then brightened. "That's great about the job. Hughes is a good man. I've been hearing about how he runs his business. He's dependable and honest."

"I guess." That sounded like the Logan she remembered: dependable and honest, but not exciting in the way of a loner with a dark, brooding attitude.

Rather than remember the battle she'd waged in the truck, and the burn of Clay's kiss that still stung her lips, she explained the responsibilities and the part-time hours of her new job. She deserved an acting statuette for her performance. Her dad would never guess she still wanted to run back to Clay.

One of my best performances ever and it's to an audience of one in a dark family room lit by a TV. I'll never get a best actress nomination now. Another dream gone.

"When Logan gets a couple of these contracts he's waiting on, I'll have to work more."

"Is he involved with those new homes out near the highway?"

"He hopes to sell them." The sales trailer would be going up any day and the developer had promised Logan the business. New home sales contracts often went to larger real estate companies, but Logan and the developer were old friends. Still, Logan felt the pressure to produce results. "For the first weeks, they'll sell from plans, but Logan says the show homes will be built before the end of the summer."

With luck, she'd have enough work hours to support herself by then. "I should be able to move out by Christmas."

His movie came back onscreen, but he kept the volume low. "I love having you here, Mercy. We don't want you to move out."

She patted his shoulder. "I missed you, too, Dad. But I need my own place." She needed to live like an adult. But if she lived alone, she might have given in to temptation and returned to Clay. "It's good that I'm here now, though." Until this mad desire for Clay disappeared, living with her parents was best for everyone.

AFTER MERCY LEFT HIM with the taste of her etched into his lips, Clay sat at his desk to spend time on patient file updates. It was habit, a way to sort out his day and plan for the next. But tonight he couldn't settle to the task.

Mercy had shaken his well-ordered life like pepper from a mill; hard nuggets had been ground into flakes and sprinkled like dust motes in the air, light and formless grains of need found nooks and cracks to fill inside him.

He missed his life before Mercy. He wanted that settled feeling back.

He wanted not to have to wonder about how he was raising Dilly. He wanted to leave her in Hope's hands and not worry that she'd rebel the way her mother had.

Damn Mercy Talbot for turning him upside down, for making Dilly love her, for pointing out that his child was *his* responsibility, not Hope's.

He'd failed Dilly every day since Janna died.

Every fucking day.

What he wouldn't give for a drink. The urge to open the liquor cabinet slammed into him. He had a good Scotch in there, a gift from a grateful cat owner. A drink or two, maybe three, would take the edge off. He'd be able to sleep, be able to face himself in the mirror.

Fuck.

He pressed the heels of his palms into his eye sockets. At least he'd had the good sense to send her home.

If he hadn't he'd be hip deep in Mercy right now. He rose in a fury of self-disgust.

"Fuck." He took the stairs to the second floor two at a time. He'd been celibate too long—and damn Mercy for pointing that out, too—and another long shower in a torrent of long showers that made up his sex life wouldn't cut it anymore.

CLAY'S KISS STILL BURNED three days later as Mercy settled behind Logan's monstrosity of a desk. She smoothed the broad expanse, stretching her fingers out to the opposite corners. Just as soon as sales took off at the subdivision it would be covered in papers and files. She looked forward to seeing it strewn with paperwork. Logan had told her to make herself at home and to open the company mail. There wasn't much, most invoices came electronically. She stacked a few office-equipment store flyers on the corner of the desk.

Her duties were flexible day-to-day. If Logan was here, she didn't need to come in, but if he was called away, then she dropped everything she was doing as soon as he called.

He never said much about the situations that arose, but he usually returned tense and distracted and she was glad to be of help. She'd handled a few calls without needing to check with him for the answers.

She called Karen and explained that she'd be late getting to the kennels today. She hadn't seen Clay there since the day she'd gained Ethel's trust. After that kiss, he must be avoiding her.

Avoidance was wise, all things considered. She still saw Dilly most days and Hope had finished work on the cowgirl costume. It was now more appropriate for a child. Dilly still fought against dance classes and learning how to curtsy.

The phone rang on the desk. "Hughes Realty." She'd given up on the longer greeting. Everyone was in such a hurry.

"Mercy," Logan said. "I'll be in the office in thirty minutes. Do you have time to run downstairs and pick up a coffee and a bagel for me?"

"Sure, Logan. Everything okay?" she asked, but he kept his family issues to himself.

"See you in a few."

She headed down to the street, but since he wasn't due to arrive for half an hour, Mercy decided to check out the community board in front of the post office. She read the usual notices about missing pets, used appliances for sale and babysitting services offered and was about to turn away when something caught her eye. It was a flyer with the comedy and tragedy masks watermarked on the paper.

The masks meant theater was alive and well in Welcome. She smiled at the notion of working on Broadway. Stage work. Another dream bit the dust.

The flyer was a call for auditions. A Tennessee Williams play. She memorized the phone number and turned back toward the bakery, a ludicrous idea forming. The more she turned it over in her mind, the more radical it felt and the more it made her smile.

Three steps closer and she slowed to an amble. Clay stood outside his clinic farther along the street. He was with a woman.

A woman who laughed in the sunshine and flicked her hair over her shoulder. Blond hair. Big boobs.

Shandy.

Fine, he was moving on. Most people would say they made a lovely pair. Clay with his dark, handsome features and Shandy with her mud-brown eyes and brassy hair. Two single parents had a lot in common. They could share their concerns, their children could be friends, and their beds would be warmed. Most people in Welcome would say it was past time for Clay to find a new mommy for Dilly. That it felt like a scalpel to her heart would mean nothing to the good people of Welcome.

They'd laugh if they knew how she felt about Clay. For the first time in her life, she appreciated her mother's concern for what people thought. She ducked her head when Clay looked along the street. He'd assume she was spying. Thank God she was abreast of the bakery. She slipped inside, determined not to be caught looking.

SHANDY SMILED INTO Clay's eyes with an invitation he tried not to ignore. *Ask her for coffee.* She made it seem coincidental that she was here as he made his usual walk to the post office. He tended to go at the same time every day. He was either mailing off samples to a lab or picking up something. He went because Sybil said she couldn't leave the phones. His tech could go, but Clay needed the fresh air and enjoyed stretching his legs. And sometimes he stopped for coffee. *Ask her to join you.*

"The new school year will start soon," she was saying. "And with Josh in activities most afternoons, I'll have more free time. I'm not sure how I'll fill that time without my son." Her wide eyes turned flirtatious.

A couple of heartbeats later and: *Here it is, Foster, an open invitation to heat the sheets with her and you've got nothing.* "I'm sure you'll find something to do."

He glanced up the street toward his goal of getting to the post office and caught sight of Mercy walking into the bakery. Then Logan Hughes pulled his Cadillac into a spot by his office and followed her inside. *Damn.* He shouldn't notice the eager grin on Hughes's face.

"I was on my way to pick up a package," he said to Shandy. "Care to take a few minutes for coffee with me in the bakery? I like their bagels." He motioned for her to walk with him. "If you have time now, that is."

Shandy's face lit up in delight and he caught a glimpse of the pretty girl she'd been in school. "I always have time for you, Clay."

Which gave him no kick at all.

In the short block to the bakery, he learned Shandy owned Laundromats in several nearby towns. Aside from maintenance calls and bookkeeping, she had fewer demands on her time than most business owners. She chatted happily along the way. "My father left me set," she explained as he held the bakery door open for her. Clay counted the ways she should be the right one to spend time with.

The list began with the fact that she wasn't his dead wife's sister and rounded off with she'd have time for Dilly.

And she wasn't his dead wife's *sister*. That, he reminded himself, was the biggie.

She stepped inside ahead of him and nearly collided with a man on the way out. "Logan, sorry," she said and sidestepped. Clay held the door for Hughes. As he brushed past, Clay took stock: beard stubble, red-rimmed eyes, and his shirt looked like he'd partied in it. Clay recognized the signs of hard living. "Hughes," he said with a nod. "Rough night?"

Hughes gave him a *back off* look.

Mercy came through the door right behind Hughes, smelling of flowers and happiness. Until she saw Clay. Her eyes cooled as he watched and she moved past him with the barest nod. "Clay."

"Mercy."

"Clay?" Shandy said. "Let's get a booth in the back." She reached to take his free hand and Clay let her.

Mercy hitched a step, but raised her chin and kept moving.

Damn. He had to list his reasons for killing time with Shandy again. She was not his dead wife's *sister*. She was not his dead wife's *sister*.

His head was fine with the list. It was his gut that refused to pay attention.

Chapter Ten

AFTER HAVING COFFEE with Shandy, he walked her to her car. "Care to take the kids out for pizza sometime?" She asked when she held her door open.

"Sure." He nodded and shoved his hands in his pocket. "Tonight? We could go out to the pizza joint near the highway. I've heard they have a good children's menu."

"And crayons for Dilly and Josh," Shandy said with a grin.

"Great. We'll meet you there." They agreed on a time and he told himself he'd see where this friendship could lead.

After leaving Shandy, he picked up his package of new business cards from the post office. When he stepped back outside, he looked toward his clinic and saw a frantic couple trying to unload a blanket-wrapped dog from the back seat of their car. The dog heaved and wriggled and his head popped up from the blanket that covered him. A collie. He ran to help, dodging other pedestrians on the way.

"What have you got there?" he called as he ran toward them.

"We hit him with our car out by the new housing subdivision by the highway. He dashed out into the road." The couple struggled to contain the determined dog.

"He must have been chasing something," the woman said with a sharp look at her husband. The collie groaned.

"Is there any blood?" Clay asked.

"No," the man said. "I think it was a thump to his hip. He wasn't bleeding, but he kept trying to stand. I sat in back with him."

"I feel terrible. I was reading the billboard, and distracted my husband," the woman said with a throb in her voice. "We're thinking of moving into Springhill Meadows," she explained as she closed the car door and followed the men to the clinic door. "We're the Morrisons."

"I'm the vet," he said and gave them his name. "We'll take a good look. Could be nothing worse than a bad bruise." He looked at the collie's face and into his eyes. "He's alert."

"We don't know who owns him," the man said. "But we'll cover the costs."

By now they were inside and Sybil, used to desperate expressions, jumped up to hold the door to the surgery for them. Clay instructed the couple on how best to lay the dog on the table and then waved them out of the room.

His tech arrived to muzzle the dog, although the collie was more interested in jumping off the table than being handled. Overall, the injury was minor. The man was correct to say this was no more than a thump and bruising.

Still, he gave the dog a thorough examination.

Ten minutes in and Sybil buzzed through to tell him she'd called Nate to say Clay would be late picking up Dilly. He hoped he'd still be able to avoid seeing Mercy. That woman was spinning him in circles and he had to make it stop.

He was so hot for Mercy he couldn't warm up to a suitable, available woman like Shandy. That's why he needed the pizza date. He needed to convince himself to see reason. Shandy represented the logical choice, the best choice for his daughter.

Why the hell didn't Mercy go back to Hollywood and leave him in peace?

It still bit his ass that she'd been sharing coffee and baked goods in those tight quarters Hughes called an office. He knew it was just the two of them up there.

And Hughes had a good rep around town; had been known forever as a nice guy. A nice fucking guy.

He looked at the collie's x-rays. No fractures. Nothing that would indicate anything more than a slam to his soft tissue. "You are one lucky dog," he said as he was rewarded with a good tail wag.

His tech found a tattoo in his ear. One of theirs. "Tell Sybil to call the owners. I'll talk to the people who brought him in." They hadn't left the waiting room.

They lowered the dog to the floor and he continued to wag his tail stiffly. He snuffled Clay's hand in thanks. Clay attached a leash and took him out to the waiting couple. "I wanted you to see him on his feet," he said. "A couple days on a mild pain med if he needs it and he'll be good. When his owners get here, I'll have a word with them about allowing him to roam. The construction across the road has disturbed a lot of wildlife. He likely caught sight of a hare or gopher."

"He came out of nowhere and I couldn't stop in time," the woman said, still fretful. "We'll wait for the owners if it's all the same to you."

Clay nodded, checked the time and went into his office to change clothes. Maybe he could get Dilly before Mercy got there after all. His good feeling about the collie vanished when he arrived at the Talbot home. Both vehicles were in the drive, which meant Mercy was home.

He parked behind Nate's truck and headed inside. As he strolled through the empty kitchen he heard the unmistakable sound of Hope and Mercy going at each other again. His back went up.

Mercy had told him that night at his place that the women had managed to be civil when Dilly was with them. He slowed to listen, hoping she'd kept to her word.

"You're going and that's that," Mercy said in a tone he'd never heard from her before. But he'd heard the same icy inflection from Janna lots of times. It sounded as if Mercy was determined to get her way. The question was who was she talking to? He stalled, waiting to hear more.

Hope responded with a brusque: "I don't have time for your nonsense. There's a pageant in Seattle next weekend. And at the end of the month, there's another in New Mexico. Both Dilly's costumes need work, and I'm waiting for a new wig that'll need styling because they never look right and—"

"Cancel the Seattle pageant," Mercy cut off her mother's excuses midstream.

He felt the hiss and steam of a brewing argument between the women. He walked into the family room to scoop up his daughter, but she wasn't there. Mercy had her back to him so Hope saw him first.

"We'll let Clay decide *right now* what's best for Dilly." Hope's gaze crackled into his.

"Where is she?" he asked, keeping his voice calm.

Mercy tossed him the information over her shoulder. "Outside with Dad. I made sure she wasn't in the house to hear this."

He rubbed his chin. "I appreciate that." And he also appreciated the view he had of Mercy dressed in a tight black skirt and heels. Her blouse was silky looking and white as snow. Not her shit-shoveling clothes. And not the time to dream about running his hands up her thighs. He reined in his wayward thoughts. "What's going on?"

Hope came to stand directly in front of him, elbowing aside her daughter to get there. "Mercy's got the mistaken impression I should audition for a part in a play. As if I've got time for that, what with all I have to do to keep Dilly on track." She huffed in a breath and wound up for more.

Mercy turned to face them both, eyes narrowed at the back of her mother's head. How Hope didn't feel the burn, he'd never know.

"What play?" he asked, not sure he heard right.

"Cat on a Hot Tin Roof," Mercy replied.

"You could play Maggie," he said to lighten the tension. He had a vague notion Maggie was the younger woman in the play.

Hope blinked. "Maggie?" Her lips lifted in a self-satisfied smile. "You think so?" She straightened her back and squared her shoulders. "I could dye my hair black like Liz Taylor's."

Mercy rolled her eyes. "Or you could let the director decide which part you'd be suited for. It's local theater. I'm sure it would be fun." Then she mouthed the words *Big Mama* to him, a role she no doubt believed Hope could pull off. He pinned his lips into a thin line, not wanting to give anything away.

"You want to distract me from the pageants," Hope said.

Mercy stepped up to her mother and set her hands on each arm. Hope looked directly into her daughter's eyes. "Please hear me. I want you to use your dramatic flair to have some fun. Aside from all the business involved in acting, there's fun, too. Haven't you ever wondered what it feels like to pretend to be someone else?"

"Of course I have," his mother-in-law said. "You inherited your talent from someone, after all." She shrugged off Mercy's hands.

"Then go to the audition. Dilly can miss the Seattle pageant while you prepare. I'll coach you."

Hope's gaze softened. "Maggie, huh?" She directed the question to Clay.

He nodded. "Maggie."

Hope smiled, rolled her shoulders and pivoted on one leg. With an exaggerated roll of her hips, she sashayed toward the door leading to the garden. "I'll get Dilly, shall I?" she said in a Southern drawl.

Mercy bit her lip and Clay shoved his hands in his pockets and stared at the floor in case she made him laugh out loud.

"Save me from these Talbot women," he muttered.

Hope continued her version of a seductive stroll outside to where Nate stood looking at her like she'd lost her mind.

Mercy burst into giggles. "Well, I do declare, a star is born."

Clay shook his head, determined not to be charmed. "This audition is on the weekend. Do you think she'll go?"

"Not yet, but I'll convince her." She had an ace up her sleeve. "She actually called my agent's office to bully his assistant. Esme doesn't want to hear another word from my mother." Mercy shrugged as if to shift out from under the embarrassment. "The auditions are on Saturday and they'll make their final decisions Monday afternoon."

"I'm okay with her missing a pageant," he admitted.

"Good. Thank you," Mercy said with a grin. "We need this week to prepare Mom. Dilly may have to miss some dance classes."

She was pushing her luck. "I can't see Hope giving Dilly that much slack."

"You're right." Mercy shrugged. "Even if nothing comes of this, it's a good idea for Mom to see what it's like onstage. Maybe she'll get some perspective on what Dilly faces."

And what Mercy had dealt with and Janna had bailed out on, he thought. Dilly barreled in through the door from the garden. Clay braced for her slam into his legs. "Daddy, I gots a bat and a ball."

Sure enough, Nate brought in a wide plastic bat and a softball-sized plastic ball. "There's a tee, too," he said to Clay.

Nate frowned at Mercy. "What got into your mother? She looks like she's got a broken hip." He exaggerated the sway, making Dilly squeal in delight.

Hope came in with the tee in her hands and a glare for her husband. "Here, take it," she said and set the tee beside Clay. "She's *not* learning to play baseball. Not on my watch."

Clay raised an eyebrow and looked at his daughter. "Would you like to play ball, Dilly?"

"Ya-huh." She twirled an errant curl around her finger.

"Fine, I'll start by teaching you to throw and catch the ball. This ball," he said, taking the virtually harmless plastic one from Nate. "See? It won't hurt if it bangs your nose." He touched the tip of her nose with the ball. She giggled.

"'Kay." She hopped around like a bunny. "Daddy, let's go."

"Tomorrow, we'll practice your dance for the pageant, Dilly. And we'll try on your new wig, too," Hope said. "It should arrive in the morning." She glared daggers at Mercy.

"Aren't you practicing for your audition this weekend?" Mercy prodded.

"Don't be ridiculous," Hope snapped. "I'm not cut out for the stage, a fact your father made abundantly clear." She looked mutinous and Clay saw one of Dilly's rebellious expressions in Hope's face. He now called it the Talbot face.

Mercy crossed her arms, set her chin and gave Hope the same expression. "I've already told them you'd be there." She raised a hand to hold off her mother's next argument. "Besides, you're my mother. Of course, you're cut out for the stage." She made a walking gesture with two fingers. "What was that Maggie impression if not acting?"

"A bit of fun, that's all. Your father told me I'd lost my mind so I camped it up."

Mercy shook her head. "That phony attempt at coyness won't work, Mom. You will not embarrass me by being a no-show. What would people think?"

Clay ducked his head at that one. She had Hope cornered. No way would his mother-in-law allow people to snicker about a missed audition.

Hope went to speak again, but closed her mouth and set her lips. Her gaze flashed to Dilly and she shifted in an angry huff, clearly trying to stem the tide of disagreement. After a moment, she looked resigned. "I'll think about it." Her voice held less bluster. "But I'm not promising anything."

Mercy did a victory fist bump and then offered him a high-five, which he returned. Hope blew out a huff of indignant air at their antics. Dilly giggled.

The slap of Mercy's palm buzzed along his arm. The brief touch reminded him of when they'd bumped shoulders in the park and how much he wanted those companionable moments to happen again.

Instead of dwelling on Mercy, he drew thoughts of Shandy into his head. *Shandy is not my dead wife's sister. She's nice and available and comes with no messed-up memories or guilt. And she is* not *my sister-in-law.*

It was time to give his daughter a fresh perspective. "Hey, Punk, we're going out for pizza tonight."

"Auntie Mercy too?"

"Not this time. We're going with—" Too late, he realized his mistake. He should have kept this quiet until they were alone.

"A date?" Hope asked with an avid expression in her eyes.

"A group thing," he said. Not exactly a lie. Shandy and Josh joining him and Dilly made a group. "It's Shandy Camden and her boy, Josh. Shandy and I knew each other from school."

Hope looked surprised. "Single mothers come with baggage."

"No less than I do," he ground out. "Josh is a good kid."

He noted that Mercy focused on the window overlooking the garden and then turned to give her *perfectly perfect* smile. Brittle and phony and fake. Hope saw it, too.

"Have fun, Dilly," Mercy said and kissed her forehead before walking out of the room. "I'm late for the rescue kennels," she said on the way down the hall. "Ethel's waiting."

Which meant she hadn't been to Karen's yet. That was why she was still wearing her skirt and blouse. Her legs looked great in those heels. He gritted his teeth at the memory of how her ass fit in his palms.

If she were headed to the kennels, they'd see each other once more before this day was done.

He shouldn't be looking forward to seeing her, but he was.

AFTER MERCY CHANGED clothes to go to the kennels she found her mother on the treadmill. "Esme called me," she said, watching for Hope's reaction. "You shouldn't have pestered her, Mom."

"I thought you were late for the kennels." Her mom glanced outside to where her dad was leashing Humphrey for his walk. She turned off the machine and slowed to a stop. "I'll join them," she said.

Typical of her mother to ignore the Esme warning but Mercy couldn't let her get away with it. "I hope you finally understand that there is *nothing* for me in Hollywood. I'm finished." She set her teeth for this next part, but she had to say it. "Also, you embarrassed me by calling Mr. Chastain. If a miracle happened and he thought of me for a part, do you believe he'd call me after you bullied Esme?"

"'Bully' is an ugly term. I was being pro-active." Her mother looked chastened. "I'm sorry if Esme felt I went too far."

Mercy sighed. "You meant well, but it's time to accept the end of my career. I have."

Hope stepped down and faced her. "What can I do to make it up to you?"

"Go on the audition."

"If I go, will it help smooth things over between us? I hate that we're crossing swords all the time. It's not like us." Her mother reached out.

Mercy took her offered hands. "It's not like us to fight. But the audition will do a lot of good. You'll see what it's like to be onstage being judged. If you hate it, maybe you'll see how Dilly feels."

Hope's eyes widened and then she blinked. "All right. I'll do it for you so we can stop our bickering. But this has nothing to do with Dilly."

Mercy had won a small victory. She would force herself to patience and see what the weekend brought. For now, she was heading to the kennels and, with any luck, she'd see Clay.

ETHEL SCAMPERED AROUND her feet as Mercy fed the other dogs. Beau had kissed them both with his usual enthusiasm and Ethel was taken with him. Beau's steadying influence calmed her, just as Clay said it would.

Karen had done most of the feeding by the time she arrived and Mercy noticed the effort the older woman made to pretend her knees weren't aching. "What does your doctor say about the pain you're in?"

"Knee replacements." She held on to the chain-link for balance as she stood. She leaned heavily and grimaced.

"When are you scheduled? Maybe I can round up some help out here for when you're recuperating." Her father would come to assist for sure. Maybe Logan would too if he had time.

"Around about the fifteenth of Neverary. I can't keep this up." She shook her head and her fingers clenched around the metal. "The fundraising, hefting the supplies, and hell, the disappointments are enough to stop a Marine in his tracks. I kind of fell into it because I already had the kennels and Clay needed somewhere to put the fighting dogs and pups." She shook her head. "That was a day out of hell, I'll tell ya."

"It must have been."

Karen looked at her in her steady, measuring way. "Made me ashamed of my own species."

Mercy nodded, touched by the kindness she'd shown and the sacrifices Karen made to care for her charges. She bent to pet Ethel's scruffy head. Beau immediately nudged Ethel out of the way to get his share. "You greedy boy."

He grinned up at her and then closed his eyes in ecstasy as she gave him a good, deep scratch behind his ears. He moaned in appreciation. "He's vocal. Always has something to say."

"Pit bulls generally do. I'm sure you've heard him say haroo. I swear it's 'hello.'"

"I have heard him say that." She rubbed his ear deeper. He looked blissed out.

"Clay's here," Karen said as his SUV rolled to a stop. Beau bolted toward Clay and got in a couple of good licks before Clay could get Dilly out of her car seat.

He set Dilly on the ground, still clutching the plastic softball. She rolled it toward Ethel, but the dog ran behind Mercy's legs to hide. Dilly ran to get the ball herself. "Silly Ethel."

Karen glanced from Mercy to Clay and back again. "Haven't seen you two at the same time in days. I've got more dogs to feed." She ambled off and snapped her fingers so Beau would follow.

Ethel ran into her kennel to get away from Dilly. "Okay, girl," Mercy said to the dog. "I get the hint." She latched the gate. "I'm not sure she's used to children."

"Probably not," Clay said. "Dilly's good with dogs, but her squeals can upset nervous ones. We're working on her modulating her tone, but it's tough for her to remember."

"I tries to benember," Dilly said solemnly.

Mercy dropped a kiss to her niece's head and then turned to leave. "Time to start shoveling." She pulled a pair of gardening gloves she'd borrowed from her father out of her back pocket. She slapped them against her palm. "See you," she said. There was nothing more to say if they were to stay on strictly friendly terms.

She took three steps and Clay cleared his throat. "That was a good idea you had about your mother's audition." He caught Dilly's ball in one hand and rolled it back to her. "Did you convince Hope to give the acting a try?"

"I coerced her into auditioning. "

"Nothing too harsh, I hope?"

"No. Neither of us wants to bicker. Believe it or not, we don't usually have disagreements. Not ongoing ones, at any rate." Mercy shrugged. "I hoped Dilly could have the weekend off. That way you could have more group time."

Even to her own ears, she sounded snide. "Sorry, that was uncalled for," she said gently. "Of course, you should have family outings. Shandy and her boy, right?" She softened her tone and tried to look contrite. She wasn't sure it worked.

Clay's eyes narrowed. "The other night, with you, I realized it's time to move on. Dilly deserves—"

She raised her hand so he'd stop referring to the kiss that had blown her mind. "No need to explain. You made your thoughts perfectly clear. I'm not . . . upset or hurt. I totally agree with you." She wasn't mommy material—hell, she was barely an aunt. "It's time Dilly had more in her life."

She indicated her niece who was wrapped up in chasing the ball and throwing it to her dad as hard as she could. Mercy gave him her most-practiced smile and he scowled when he saw it.

"Shandy's a nice woman," he said. "Her boy, Josh, is a good kid. His dad left for a job in California."

She shrugged. "Again, I don't need an explanation." And she didn't want to think about Shandy in his house. Not in his kitchen or in that gorgeous great room by the fire or in his bed. She caught her breath when she wondered if together, Shandy and Clay would add another child to their joint family.

Would the Talbots be welcome in that new family's life? Surely they'd work it all out so that Hope and Nate wouldn't lose contact with Dilly. "I have to stop talking about this now, Clay." Before it broke her heart. And yes, she would rather shovel shit than accept Shandy getting her hooks into Janna's husband and raising Janna's daughter.

She picked up the shovel and bucket and moved off on stiff legs.

"Auntie Mercy, can I come?"

She didn't stop or turn, just kept walking. "No, sweetling, this is my job and I have to do it alone."

Being broke in Hollywood was a piece of cake compared to life in Welcome.

AT THE PIZZA JOINT later that evening, Clay wiped Dilly's face and hands after they'd all had pizza. "Maybe you'd like to come out to the house?"

"That would be great," Shandy agreed.

Josh nodded. "Cool," he said. "Do you have any games?"

"Not for boys your age, but you could stream TV shows." Clay cocked an eyebrow at Shandy. She gave him a nod.

Josh had helped Dilly color their placemats with the crayons the server had provided.

"Dilly's tired. We should get her home."

Dilly squirmed to get down. They all followed her lead and headed outside to their cars. Shandy opened the car door for Dilly while Josh went to her car for the drive to Clay's place.

Dilly shook her head, stuck out her lower lip and shrugged away from Shandy's helping hands. She climbed into her car seat on her own. When she settled, she stuck her thumb into her mouth and wrapped her finger over her nose. Shandy chuckled. "That's a tired girl," she said and reached to buckle her in.

Dilly smacked at her hands and screamed. "No! No! Dad-dee!"

Shandy backed away from the open door with her hands up. "Daddy then," she said with disappointment etched on her face. She looked at Clay, at a loss. "Sorry."

"She can be determined," he said apologetically and leaned in to secure his daughter into the seat. "Dilly, no screaming. Shandy wanted to help *me,* and I appreciate it."

The Punk nodded, but he read a tumult of resistance in her eyes.

Shandy and Josh followed in their car and an hour later, with Josh installed in the great room watching a movie and Dilly in bed, Clay and Shandy sat on the deck together. It was too warm to light the gas fire pit table, but they propped their feet up on it and sipped an iced tea.

"I love your home and this backyard is perfect." She kicked off her sneakers and stretched her toes with a sigh. "I love this time of night. Josh is wound down, fed and engaged elsewhere while I get a few minutes to unwind."

Clay nodded. "Bedtime is the most wonderful time of the day." They clinked their glasses of iced tea in a shared toast.

"This was good, Clay," she said. "Going out with the kids and seeing them interact was nice."

"Josh is a good kid. Does he see his dad much?"

She pressed her lips together and nodded. "Not as much as he would if Dan lived closer. I give Dan points for trying, though." She smiled. "He's a better father than he was a husband."

He detected no bitterness in her face or voice. More proof of her kind nature. He stood and leaned against the deck rail to face the yard. She joined him and stood close, touching her shoulder to his.

In a reflex, he jerked away. She noticed. Her lips turned down, but she filled the awkward moments that followed with chitchat designed to put him at ease.

He tried, but he felt like his home had been invaded by strangers. She didn't belong here. As much as he wanted to join in the conversation, to make a worthwhile effort, he soon fell into monosyllabic responses that discouraged them both.

"The air's getting chillier," she said as night fell and crickets sang. "That's my cue to leave." She straightened and looked at him. Her gaze softened, accepting and sad.

"I'm sorry I wasn't better company," he offered.

"Me, too." She looked steadily at him, making him feel small. "You should have been. There's no reason we couldn't make this work, at least for a while."

"You're worth more than short term," he said. "That's not what you need. And not what Josh needs. You should have it all, Shandy, and I can't give it to you." Logic and common sense said they had solid reasons to make a go of it. But he'd never followed logic when it came to women. He wasn't convinced many men did.

She blinked and patted his cheek. "Well, to paraphrase, we'll always have that night by the lake."

He allowed a grin and a nod. "Yes, we will." Teens, beer, and hormones had been a potent mix. But that behavior was better lived in the moment. Best not to muddy the memory with adult mistakes when they should know better.

"I hope you find the one who makes you happy, Clay." She tilted her head and then pushed off from the railing. "Because it wasn't Janna."

Which made Shandy Camden way more perceptive than he'd thought.

Chapter Eleven

ON FRIDAY MORNING IN the office, Mercy held her first paycheck in her hand. "This is too much, Logan. I haven't worked this many hours." She wondered if this was a pay-off. "You're not firing me, are you?"

He raised his hands. Today was a good day and he looked refreshed and healthy. "You've done way more than I expected. You've stepped in and stepped up when I couldn't." He flashed a wide smile and shoved his hands into his slacks pockets. His shirt was freshly ironed, his eyes clear. "You're handling calls on your own and when I get in, this place is in perfect order. I couldn't ask for a better assistant. You deserve every dollar and more."

She folded the check in two and slipped it into the side pocket of her purse, warmth suffusing her at his generosity. He must have figured out how broke she was.

"Thank you," she said. "I've enjoyed the time. I had no idea I could have fun acting as if I know what I'm doing."

"There are exciting developments on the horizon." He waved her into the visitor's chair. "My buddy Zach is building out at Springhill Meadows. The sales trailer is now in place."

He unrolled a poster-sized sheet of paper and held it up for her to see. "These are the floor plans. We can start selling now." His enthusiasm infected her and she felt a rush of anticipation for a challenge different from all the other challenges she'd faced.

"Wonderful," she said. "I'll get those enlarged and laminated. We'll put them on the walls." She'd have to study them to see the differences between the models.

"Larger ones will be on the sales office wall. We'll move an office into one of the model homes as soon as it's built," he said. "We'll also have options for finishes available. Different countertops, cabinetry, and plumbing fixtures."

"We'll need to be in constant touch about client names so we can work together. If I know what model the caller is interested in they'll have more faith that we're both aware of what's happening with them."

"Right," he said. "We may be a new office, with next-to-no staff but that can work to our advantage." He nodded. "Teamwork will make this project a success."

She felt needed and appreciated, and in all her career, she'd never had that happen. Excitement about the future with Logan crowded out the pleasure of receiving her paycheck. There would be more checks coming her way. She'd be moving to her own place before she knew it. "What's next?"

"Advertising. Zach's got a marketing team and with our various and different contacts around town, we can get word-of-mouth started." He laughed. "Just between us, his marketing team is his wife. Sarah is also his designer and decorator. She's got a knack for knowing what appeals to today's new homebuyer. My personal experience is more in the resale market, but I'm happy to sell whatever they create."

She studied the floor plans, trying to make sense of the boxes, lines, and dimensions she read. "Will there be any stores or schools out that way? I ask because these home plans look perfect for growing families. I would imagine they'd enjoy walking the neighborhood. Some stores or cafes, maybe medical offices and the like would be a draw. Playgrounds, too." She'd seen lots of moms with strollers at the play park when she'd been there with Dilly and Clay.

Logan unrolled another, much larger sheet of heavy paper and covered the desk with it. "This is the neighborhood plan. This center square is set aside for a playground and this edge here"—he pointed to a deep swath on the edge of the lots—"is a strip mall with room for standalone restaurants in the parking lot. Plans call for office space above the storefronts."

"Perfect." A community feel would make the homes easier to sell. "This is good for us, right?"

"And for Welcome. Growth stalled for a number of years but with the economy picking up we need the homes or people will buy in Bellingham or Blaine. This is a fantastic opportunity and we have to make the best of it. If sales don't take off in the first six months, Zach will find another sales team and we'll both be looking for work."

"You can count on me," she said firmly.

"You'll be around for that long?"

"Guaranteed." She stuck out her hand and he shook it. She barely felt the twinge of regret. She'd just committed to six more months in Welcome.

"How are you settling back into town?"

"Now that I'm working things are looking up," she said brightly. But inside she wasn't sure. With Shandy and her son on the scene, she had her worries about her family hanging together. But Logan had his own family issues and didn't need to hear about her worries. "On the family front, you'll have a chuckle about this because you know my mom."

"Okay, I'll bite. What's the joke?"

"She's trying out for a part in the local production of *Cat on a Hot Tin Roof* by Tennessee Williams." She could hardly believe Hope had taken up Mercy's challenge.

He chuckled. "I know who wrote it. What part?"

"She assumes it's for Maggie, but she'd make a perfect Big Mama."

"Your mother as Big Mama?" He exaggerated a considering expression by tapping his finger against his chin. "That may hit close to home."

She burst into laughter.

One short rap on the door brought the shared laugh to a halt as the door opened with a sharp *whoosh*.

"Am I interrupting?" Clay asked with his eyes sharply focused on Logan. He shifted his icy gaze to Mercy. "This is family stuff and I wondered if I could steal Mercy for a few minutes." He bent his head in expectation.

"Sure thing," Logan said with a wink for her. "While you're out you can run to the bank."

She smiled at him and patted her purse where it lay on the desk. She picked it up and slung it over her shoulder. "Thanks, I will."

Maybe Clay's date with Shandy had gone well and he wanted Dilly to go Seattle next weekend after all. Maybe he wanted private time with Shandy. Mercy's stomach curled. "Walk with me to the credit union, Clay. We can talk on the way."

He held the door open for her and touched the small of her back as she strode past him. The intimate feel of his fingertips sent shivers to places they didn't belong. The door closed behind them and they were alone in the hallway. In the first two steps Clay's hand slid from her back to her upper arm and he pulled her to a stop, dragging her close to his chest.

She looked up. His jaw clenched until a muscle jumped. "Are you all right? Is it Dilly? Did—"

He cut her off with a kiss that blazed so hot she swore she heard fire alarms. He turned her back to the wall and raised her hands over her head as he took more kisses and set her heart to jackhammer speed. *Yes.* She wanted to say it out loud, but she dared not in case he stopped.

Instead, she kissed him back, lust rising like a wave between them. He pressed against her full length and sought more contact. Thigh to thigh, belly to belly, they heated the air around them and the wall at her back.

She tugged her hands-free of his grip and clasped the back of his head and kissed him deeply. Their tongues danced and twined while she moved against him. From somewhere nearby, she heard a slight scraping sound.

He lifted his face, his lips damp and his blue eyes aflame.

Next to her head, a picture swayed against the wall. They'd been grinding each other so hard and fast they'd rocked it sideways. Clay straightened the frame. For a brief moment, she wondered if they'd made the walls in Logan's office shake.

"Well, you certainly got my attention," she said. She kept her voice down. Shaken and trembling, she said, "Is this what you came for?" Clearly, he hadn't come to tell her he'd had a great time with Shandy. Her heart did a cheer.

"I didn't think I came for a kiss." He blew out a breath. He followed her cue and whispered, "But it turns out I'm not prepared to be a good father. I'm selfish and I want to give us a shot."

She set two fingertips to his lips. "You're a great father, Clay Foster, and I won't hear you say anything different. But I agree with what you said the other night. Dilly can't be affected by whatever happens to us. She can't know that I'm anything more than her auntie." She closed her eyes and held her breath. She had more reasons not to let this happen but they wouldn't come to mind. "Let's not forget what my mother would say about it."

He lifted one side of his mouth in an off-kilter grin. "You want to sneak around?"

She frowned, but the idea had merit. And as adults, when it ended, they could set aside their residual feelings and move ahead for Dilly's sake. "Maybe," she said and watched his eyes light with interest. "I hate to say it, but yes, we should keep this quiet."

He considered her suggestion for all of two seconds. "Sounds hot. I'm in." He straightened away from her and she felt the distance.

"No kissing in public."

"Right," he said.

"No holding hands, either."

"Agreed." But his eyes heated. "If we're sneaking around, there's a motel not far from here."

She swatted him lightly and felt a thrill race to her vitals. "I bet you do."

"It's across the border."

She shook her head. "The line-ups can be too long." The border crossing at Blaine was twenty minutes away, but if they couldn't get back on time, people, namely her parents, would notice. "Logan needs me to be available on short notice."

"Logan. Yeah, of course." He pressed his hips against hers and she melted. "I'll find another way."

She nodded and kissed him again because she felt edgy and excited for the first time in years. "I'm aflutter, like a girl," she admitted. "Silly, right?" But he leaned close again and took her mind to places she yearned for.

"This weekend," he said.

She wanted now. Here.

The desire in his eyes said he wanted the same thing.

She groaned with the full weight of disappointment. "I'm coaching Mom all weekend to help her prep for the audition next Saturday."

He dropped his head back and looked at the ceiling. He blew out a breath and called on his patience. "Have mercy . . ."

The door to the women's services office opened and a young woman with long, thin hair stepped into the hall. She gave them a furtive glance, tucked her hair behind her ears, and then headed on light feet down the stairs.

They followed, fingers touching as they walked the narrow stairs side by side.

By the time they stepped out into the street, Mercy had smoothed her hair and touched up her lip-gloss. "Walk me to the credit union?"

"Sure, I'll go into the post office on the way back."

They strolled, not touching, and nodded to people along the street as they passed.

The credit union was a solid brick square building set back from the street. The whole edifice was meant to inspire confidence. All Mercy saw was a way to start saving money so she could move into her own place. Once she did, she and Clay would have more freedom to be together.

"I'll go to the post office and meet you back here," he said.

She touched his arm. His eyes tracked where her fingers moved, ever so slightly, in a light caress. "I want you now," she whispered. "Is there a place we can duck into?"

He shook his head and sliced the air with his hand. "You mean for a quickie? Much as I love 'em, a quickie won't do. Our first time . . . ." He trailed off, letting her imagination burn.

"We'll manage somehow." With Dilly in their lives and with her living at home, pulling off a clandestine affair was next to impossible. Her mind darted but couldn't settle on an easy solution. But they'd come up with something workable. "Once I move out it'll be easier."

"Until then, coach your mother in the day and give your nights to me." He nodded and moved his arm out from under her touch. "Tomorrow I'll take Dilly somewhere fun and tire her out. Once she falls into bed, she'll be down for the night." His eyes lit with anticipation that mirrored her own.

This could work. "I'll see you after she's asleep. I'll tell them I've made plans with old friends." Her parents thought Clay was seeing Shandy, so they wouldn't suspect she was the one visiting Clay after Dilly's bedtime. "I feel like a teenager sneaking out." She leaned close and whispered, barely controlling a giggle.

"You could wear a cheerleader's outfit if it helps." With a shrug and a nonchalant air, he left her standing on the street in front of the credit union, her mind awhirl with all they'd planned.

This was crazy wrong.

But another part of her screamed it was crazy right, too. Tomorrow night she'd be with Clay in the best sense of the phrase.

ON SATURDAY AFTERNOON, Mercy sent Hope into the kitchen for another attempt at making an entrance. "Mom, I've seen you make lots of entrances in your life. What's the problem with this one?"

"I'm in a near panic. My palms are damp and I need a shower. I shouldn't have taken this on."

Mercy smiled into the empty den. She hadn't expected this level of stage fright, but it was a gift. Finally, Hope would understand the judgment her daughter and granddaughter faced.

Still, she wanted her mother on stage, not running off of it. "You're breezing into a room full of people you love and who love you," she coaxed. "There's no one to be afraid of, no one who dislikes you or makes you uncomfortable or nervous."

Nate had taken Dilly out for the morning. He said he couldn't bear to see his wife suffer. That and she'd told him to leave.

"Right, I'm not uncomfortable or nervous," she parroted back to Mercy. "I'm in a room full of friendly, supportive faces. But I'm still hot all over as if my blood's running scared."

"You can do this, Mom." Mercy cajoled her. "Just sail in as if you own the stage. You *own* it. Just the way Liz Taylor owned the role of Maggie, so will you."

"I own it, the way Liz Taylor did," Hope droned as she blew out a breath. Hope strode into the family room with a firm smile and her arms raised in an elegant pose. "Big Daddy," she said in a lilting voice, "I'm glad you could come. And where is Brick this fine evening?" She paused as if listening to a question. "Why no, he didn't tell me he'd be late. He must have stopped somewhere to buy me roses. A dozen long-stemmed roses . . ." She trailed off after her ad lib while Mercy gathered her shocked wits.

Mercy stood and clapped and grabbed her for a strong hug. "Mom! You were perfect."

"Of course I was perfect," she said, sounding just as surprised as Mercy felt.

"How did you do it?" It was amazing because just moments before Hope had been a total basket case.

Hope got a glimmer of pride in her gaze. "You reminded me of my prom when you said Liz Taylor owned the role. I *owned* my prom night. Not a single other girl in town looked as good as I did. That time it was my mother who pushed me, not my daughter." She sighed and clapped her palms to her cheeks. "I'll just have to hold on to my inner Liz."

"Right. We'll end things here while you're feeling it," Mercy said. "Next time we'll prepare a monologue. Maybe we should also consider doing one for Big Mama."

Hope's eyes tightened. "I should?"

"Can't hurt," Mercy said with a shrug and hoped it was enough to ease her mom into considering the role of the older woman. Ego could be a delicate thing. She should know. She held her breath, but when her mother nodded in agreement, she relaxed. "You've had enough for today. You've worked hard and earned a soak in the tub."

Hope tilted her head and considered her daughter. "You look happy. What's going on?"

Clay. Just the thought of him warmed her cheeks. "Nothing much. I'm meeting with some old high-school friends tonight."

"It'll do you good to catch up with people around here. Especially if you're looking for possible buyers for that subdivision. A lot of women you graduated with are mothers now and could be looking for homes."

"Good idea."

"And if they're not, they'll likely be interested in everything to do with Logan Hughes. That man's a good catch for women who're looking. And for women who aren't looking for anything permanent, I'd say he'd be good fun."

Mercy frowned but chose to ignore the comment. "I'll get ready, then." Let her mother think whatever she wanted about her working for Logan.

"Yes, Logan would be a much better choice than Clay. That man's a wrecking ball for decent women."

"I'm not sure why you'd say that. He was faithful to Janna, and he's a good father. You need to judge him for the man he is today and not where he came from." Too late, she knew her mistake. Defending Clay might alert her mother to their mutual interest.

Hope looked flustered. "I meant that he wouldn't be an appropriate man to become interested in. Not for you."

Mercy walked away to leave her mother to stew.

CLAY FINISHED HIS SATURDAY shift and left the clinic to find Dilly at the park with Nate. Nate was the kind of grandfather who took her out: for ice cream, to the play park, for walks, for fries at the diner. Her time with Grampa was an event and Dilly was crazy about him. Nate Talbot was the best man Clay knew, and if he was ever blessed to see grandchildren, he planned to be a grandfather just like him.

Clay had learned a lot from Nate in the years he'd known him. His quiet strength in the face of the family drama that swirled around Janna had been a lifeline at times. In the early days, the battles between Hope and Janna had been epic. Back then, Clay had ignored Nate as long as he had Janna. But the older man's example in the face of all the battles had been the complete opposite of what he'd seen at home. Through Nate's stoicism and quiet forbearance, Clay had come to admire the man.

Eventually, as life moved on, he realized Janna was using him as a weapon against her parents. He'd done whatever he could to make Janna see reason. That's when the battles between Clay and Janna had escalated. Janna had accused him of taking Hope's side against her when all he'd wanted was for the screaming to end.

If Janna went a week without a drama, she created one.

By the time Clay had come to accept his unwitting part in the emotional torture of Hope and Nate, Janna had one more weapon of life destruction up her sleeve. She announced her pregnancy and Clay had been wrapped tighter in her web. He'd wanted to end the marriage, but he'd dragged his heels.

If he'd walked out when he should have . . .

Well, I have Dilly now, and I can't imagine life without her. Some days, when he looked at her, he felt that his life had begun the same day hers had. He'd hoped like a fool that Janna felt the same way.

He'd hoped that was enough to rebuild their marriage.

And now, there was Mercy. Mercy and him. Mercy and Dilly. There were too many ways this could go bad.

But brainless bastard that he was, he'd kissed her. He hadn't meant to kiss Mercy in the hallway. He'd gone to the office to see if she'd like to join him for coffee, but when he'd walked in and seen her laughing with Hughes, a haze had formed behind his eyes. In the haze sat Hughes with a smug face that said he'd won.

All he could think of to dispel the bastard's expression was to learn once and for all if there was anything worth chasing with Mercy.

He'd spend the rest of his day with her. His heart quickened. It had been a brilliant stroke to convince Hope to audition. Not just because it gave him time with Mercy, but he was reconsidering the whole pageant thing. Maybe Mercy was right and they should step back from the circuit for a few months.

Dilly's crying jags and temper had worsened. He wondered if they'd been ignoring the cause, as Mercy suggested. He pulled into a parking spot in front of the play area and waved at Nate who pushed Dilly on the swings. She loved time spent with her grandfather and never got into a temper with him. Maybe that's what grampas were for. He wouldn't know because his grandfather had died in prison before Clay had been born.

Clay climbed out of the vehicle and headed toward his daughter. "Hey, Dilly," he said. "Having fun?"

She laughed and they passed a few minutes telling each other about their day while Nate pushed her gently in the swing. Her hair blew around her head. Dilly loved setting her face into the breeze.

"If Hope was here would she let Dilly's hair blow around like that?"

Nate shook his head. "Hope doesn't bring her."

"Thanks for the bat-and-ball set. She loves it."

"That was Mercy," Nate said and stared out across the playing fields as he pushed. "She thinks dance isn't enough to tire her out or not fun enough. Something like that."

"Yes, I've heard." At the mention of Mercy's name, Clay felt a pang of conscience and wondered what Nate would think of him sneaking around with her. He respected Nate. If things went sour with Mercy, where would that leave things with Nate? All the more reason for caution.

The more he thought about this thing with Mercy, the more people he saw being affected, or hurt. All they needed was time to see what they were doing and where this was heading. If they were careful no one would know. Caution would save everyone a boatload of heartache.

"Dilly and I toss the ball around in the evenings before we eat," he said. Dilly had given up her fifteen minutes of television without a fight to play with him. "She's catching on already. Actually, she's pretty good. No fear of the ball and she grips the bat like a pro."

Nate chuckled. "Janna was a natural athlete."

"I had no idea." He hadn't known her before they'd started running around together.

"She loved running more than anything. Good marathoner."

There had been so much he and his wife had never discussed. Hopes, dreams, ambitions. She said all she wanted was Clay, but now he wondered. God, they'd been kids with no thoughts of the future. "Apparently there was a lot I didn't know about my wife."

Nate nodded. "I'm sure. Perspective comes with time. Now I see there were times I didn't step in and I should have. I kept quiet when I should have spoken up." His voice broke and pain leaked into his features.

All Clay could offer was a hand on his father-in-law's shoulder while he stared into the distance to give Nate time to collect himself. They stood for a moment, lost in their musings as Dilly swung and giggled to herself.

"Clay, don't make my mistake. If you see something you don't like or agree with in regard to Dilly and Hope, speak up. Let your thoughts be known."

Clay snorted, unconvinced that he knew what was best for anyone, let alone his daughter. "I'm not sure Hope will listen." He took his hand from Nate's shoulder. "But at least she listened to me about that cowgirl get-up."

"I'll make certain she hears you, Clay. I won't make the same mistakes I made with Janna. When those two fought, it was a pitched battle, and I'd take Mercy out with me until the dust settled. I turned my back and let it all happen." His voice firmed as he admitted his part in the mess that Janna had become.

Clay decided to let him speak without interruption. Nate had never opened up to him before, and considering his relationship with his own father, he figured a dose of honesty would go a long way. But he was blown away that Nate felt guilt over not getting between Janna and Hope. Something like that would have caused a free-for-all in his family.

Dilly's giggles were carried off on the light breeze amid her calls to go higher. She was a daredevil. Like her mother. Nate pushed a tiny bit harder and Dilly squealed with joy. "Big one!" she demanded.

"Once Hope gave up on the pageants with Janna, she turned to Mercy and found a willing student. Mercy took to the stage and loved the applause, the dresses, and the shiny sparkly stuff. It became easy to leave Janna to her own devices." Nate shook his head sadly.

"That was another mistake, another time I should have stepped in. I allowed a distance to grow between Hope and our daughter by not taking over and being involved. She wanted to play softball and it was a fine idea. Hope was angry over the pageants and she wouldn't allow Janna to sign up for ball. I asked Janna to give her mother time to get over her disappointment, but by the next year, she'd lost interest." Nate drew in a deep breath. "Or maybe she just gave up."

"She told me Hope loved Mercy more than her and once she figured that out, Janna didn't care about what she did anymore." Her rebellion had begun way before he'd hooked up with her. "And where did Mercy fit in?"

"Mercy fit into Hope's plans like a hand in a glove. Janna became sullen, but we put it down to hormones and all that." He waved a hand, a man's defense against girly differences.

Mercy must have remembered about Janna wanting to play ball. There could be no other reason for her to purchase the bat and ball. Soon he would set the ball on the tee to see if Dilly could hit it. "You want to help teach Dilly how to swing a bat? She's ready."

Nate nodded and Clay figured he'd said all he would about Janna. A relief.

"Did Mercy run marathons?"

"More of a sprinter." Nate turned his face and gave him a long, steady look. "Mercy won't be here for long, son. You might want to keep that in mind."

"Her agent called?" His belly fell while he waited for the long moment it took for Nate to respond. Of course, Hope would have told Nate about warning Clay off Mercy and naturally, Nate would back her up.

"No, they haven't called. But I have no doubt she'll be hearing from Hollywood soon and that'll be that."

"She told Logan Hughes she'd be here for at least six months."

"Did she now?" Nate put his hands on the chains that held Dilly's swing and brought it to a stop. "I need an ice cream cone. Clay, do you see a girl who might like one, too?"

Dilly squealed and laughed. "Yes, Grampa, MEEEE!"

In the midst of Dilly's happy chatter, his phone buzzed in his pocket. The phone display read "Hughes Realty." He answered and walked a few steps away for privacy. Nate was busy getting Dilly out of the swing. She ran for the slide and Nate followed her.

"The coaching session's over," Mercy said into his ear, excitement dripping from her mouth into his ear. His whole body responded.

"Is it safe to come get you?" Whatever warning he'd heard from Nate was long gone. He clenched the phone tighter, remembering the taste of her. Wanting the feel of her against him again.

She laughed. "You're with my dad and Dilly, right?"

"Right," he said and waved to Nate to go ahead and follow Dilly to the slide.

"Mom's taking a nap. She didn't sleep well and I pushed her pretty hard. "

"Nate's taking Dilly for ice cream."

"I told Mom I'm meeting with some old friends from school." She sounded breathy and excited. He felt the same way.

"Good. You can call later and tell them not to wait up."

"Great idea." Her voice sounded tense and excited in his ear. Much the way he felt.

"I've had some experience sneaking girls out of the Talbot house." Hell, this was happening. Tonight. His mind went electric with possibilities. Synapses blew, sparklers went off and focus narrowed to one thing and it wasn't anywhere near the brain.

She chuckled low and sexy. Her focus had narrowed too.

He was about to click off when he heard her voice again. "Wait," she said. "What about Shandy? Is there anything I should know?"

"I wouldn't have kissed you if there was anyone in the way."

She said nothing for a full three seconds. He was about to ask if she was still there when her voice came again. "Thanks, Clay. And, um, same here."

So Logan was just her boss, nothing more. *Nice guys do finish last.*

He hung up. "You two go on without me, I've got an errand to run." The pharmacy for protection and the flower shop for roses.

Nate gave him a slow and considering stare but said nothing.

Avoiding Nate's gaze, Clay looked at his daughter. "I'll catch up before you're finished," he promised.

"'Kay, see ya later. Grampa, can I gets chocolate?" as she headed up the ladder for one more slide.

A mere father could not compete with chocolate ice cream, he decided as he jogged across the park to his car. Hallelujah.

Six months. They had six months to see if this would go anywhere. Six months of sneaking around like kids. This was the craziest scheme. But maybe they *could* pull it off because it was crazy.

He wondered if Hughes believed Mercy would stay for the full six months. Hughes was no fool; he knew damn well if Mercy got a part, she'd leave Hughes Realty as fast as she could. Obviously, Logan Hughes wanted her for as long as he could have her, just the way Clay did.

Chapter Twelve

CLAY CHANGED HIS SHEETS while Mercy read a bedtime story to Dilly. He lit a couple of scented candles and changed his mind. *Too desperate.* He blew them out. The smell of burnt matches filled the room. He opened a window and flapped the curtains to help draw out the smoky air.

He looked down the hall toward his daughter's room. Through the open door, he saw Mercy lean over and kiss Dilly on the forehead. His cue. Nerves jumped under his skin as he strode into Dilly's room to kiss her goodnight.

Her eyes were already closed and the sweet scent of her freshly shampooed hair filled his nose as he pressed his lips to her cheek. "'Night, Punk."

She sucked her thumb harder in response. For a moment all he could do was watch her. "How can such a little thing hold my heart so tight? Sometimes I could hug her right into my chest."

"How can such a sweet imp be so dramatic?" Mercy said.

He glanced over his shoulder and felt her wry look across the room. "Drama from a Talbot female? Hard to believe."

"Isn't it just?" Mercy chuckled and held out her hand. He took it and together they closed Dilly's door and walked into the hall. "I hoped she'd be asleep before I got here." That had been the plan, but when Mercy had arrived Dilly had still been in the bath. He'd called out to Mercy that the door was unlocked. At first sight, Dilly demanded Mercy read her bedtime story. "Will she say I was here?"

"If she does we can say she was remembering the last time you visited."

Near the top of the stairs, he tugged Mercy close for a quick kiss. "Wine? Or something stronger?"

She flattened a hand to her belly. "A cup of tea would calm my nerves."

"Nerves? Why would you have nerves?"

She rolled her eyes. "I tend to feel nervous when I'm about to jump off a cliff."

"You described my feelings exactly."

She glanced toward his bedroom door. "Maybe we should slow down." She licked her lips.

He pulled her close, set his lips to her ear. "We'll go slow or fast, or hard, or not at all. Whatever you want, but I hope you don't choose the last option."

She released a slow breath and her expression read as trepidation. "Most of the time I get swept up in the moment and then things progress as they will. I meet someone I'm attracted to and either the chemistry is right or it isn't. With you, it's all *important*."

"There's more at stake than where this is going or not going. It's bigger than wondering if we'll share breakfast or skip out before work. This is like nothing else we've ever done."

"Or people we've ever done," she quipped and immediately looked contrite. "Don't misunderstand. Hookups are not my thing. I don't take sex lightly. But this—this is too much to wrap my head around."

"There's a lot at stake. But if we don't see this out, it'll be like a burr under the skin."

She tilted her forehead to his. "Yes, it will. It'll never go away unless we kill it."

"Most relationships start off hopeful," he said with a grimace. "Words like 'kill' and 'burr' sound fatalistic."

"Would you prefer that we say we're going into this with our eyes open?"

"Better."

Her soft smile drew him close. He kissed her again and this time, her lips molded to his and opened to invite his tongue. His heart beat a tattoo and blood rushed in time with it, pulsing and strong. He pulled back before he overreached her boundaries. He grasped for control.

"It's been a long time." His voice was a husky rasp of need.

She kissed his chin, and then each corner of his mouth with butterfly wings for lips. "Mercy, I'm—" He bit off the words because he was hard already. Hard everywhere. Muscles tensed from his scalp to his soles. Still, she didn't stop kissing him.

She set her lips to his Adam's apple, his collarbones, his neck and then reached to tug at his ear. She nipped him and he groaned against her temple. "Forget the tea, Clay. Show me your room. Take me there, take me anywhere."

"Have mercy," he groaned and took her mouth, sweeping his tongue inside. Her breasts mashed against his chest. All that softness and fluid heat. He shook with need as he imagined her wet heat, her smooth thighs, and her sweet kisses. He needed more kisses even as he pressed his lips to hers. He'd never get enough and he wanted it all.

All.

He shuffled her backward to his room. She clung to him and let him guide her. "Oh, Clay. You wreck me. Just take me down to the bone and wreck me."

They reached the open door to his room and halted for another kiss. He pulled back. "Okay?" He nodded toward the bed and wondered if he should have left the candles burning.

She looked around the room and paled. "That's not Janna's—"

"Bed? No. There's nothing left of her now. Not in this room, or in this house, or in here." He patted his chest where his heart thudded harder. If she freaked out, he'd have to find a way to slow things to a crawl. He wasn't sure he could.

"She lives in Dilly," she whispered. "The biggest, best thing my sister ever did for this world."

"The biggest and best thing," he said. He breathed deep. Mercy loved Dilly. *Loved her.* No matter what became of them, she would love his daughter for the rest of her life. His last bit of resistance melted. This felt right. He slid his hand down her arm to her hand and entwined his fingers with hers. "I'm ready to jump off this cliff, Mercy, are you?"

"Yes."

THIS IS NOT JANNA'S room *and not Janna's bed.* Thoughts bounced like ping-pong balls through a wind tunnel. *But this is Janna's husband.* She'd tried to wait this out, she really had. She didn't want to want Clay Foster. She hadn't been looking for a man when she came back to Welcome.

She wasn't sure about anything; not her acting career, not her goals, or her ambitions now that acting was out of her life. She didn't know where she'd end up or how she'd get there.

Of all the things she didn't know, she knew *this* was right. She held tight to his hand and stepped into his bedroom, her low belly fluttering and excited.

Crazy to wonder if Clay felt as if he was cheating on his wife. Her sister had never cared about fidelity or honesty between partners. Janna had slept with anyone who glanced her way before and after her marriage. Crazier still to feel guilty about owning that knowledge.

He left her to shut the window. Then he picked up a pack of matches and waved it at a couple of candles. A flash of uncertainty crossed his face. "Want to set the mood?"

She stepped over to him and closed her fingers over the pack of matches. "Let's light our own fire," she said. Blazing up the sheets was not one of her skills. "I'm not all that confident in the bedroom," she admitted.

Clay cupped her face and looked into her eyes and made her wonder what he saw there. Whatever it was made his eyes light with interest. "You're perfect." He rubbed his knuckles across her cheekbone then forked his fingers into her hair to hold her still. Her belly swooped and dove and moisture built between her legs.

Yes. He kissed her with a swiftness that threatened to carry her away and made her thoughts bounce and pop like champagne bubbles and she didn't care. Not about anything anymore.

He set to work on the buttons of her blouse while she worked to pull his polo shirt over his head. They ended up bare-chested at the same time and stopped to stare at each other. The sound of their breaths filled the space between them as they looked. Her nipples beaded and rose and his chest hair matched the crow-dark hair of his head. He had the perfect V that narrowed to follow a line to his groin. Her mouth watered. They reached for each other at the same time, breaths heaving in and out in synch. The heat of his hands covered her breasts while the hard plane of his chest and the whorls of chest hair filled her palms.

Had she ever felt this before? Had she ever wanted like this before? "You feel good," she murmured.

He blinked as if relieved to hear it. "God, Mercy. You're perfect. As perfect as any dream could be." He weighed her breasts and rubbed his thumb across her nipples.

Arrows of need shot with amazing accuracy to her womb. She flowered and opened and felt more moisture.

There may have been a whimper . . . but she didn't care if he saw how much she wanted him, or if he heard her moan, felt her thrash, scented her sex. The earthiness of everything she wanted overcame her.

This is what she was here for. To be with him in every way he wanted her. She slid her hands to his belt and unbuckled it, quick, quick. "Easy, there," he said with a sexy chuckle. "Let me help. I'm stiff—"

She touched the head of his penis before he managed to drop his jeans. Her touch made him freeze into stillness and he ended on a groan as she thumbed his tip. "You're hot as coals," she whispered.

He slid his hand into her jeans as she spoke. "Unh." The shock of his sudden move brought waves of sensation that made her sag forward. Rough fingers played and sought and touched. A man's fingers.

Clay's touch, so much better than her own. "Yes," she said and kicked off her jeans. She pushed him back toward the bed and they fell together, kissing and groping and sighing and wanting.

Wanting *so much* . . .

"This will be fast," he said.

"Yes."

"I can't go slowly."

"You don't have to."

He opened the nightstand drawer. "These are fresh," he said as he held up a condom packet. "No chances."

She nodded and took the package to open it. Her fingers shook because he kissed her belly while she worked at the foil. "Please, Clay," she begged and shifted against him, trying to open her legs, rip open the package and control her urge to buck against him at the same time.

He rolled his face into the softness of her belly, growling and nipping and kissing. "You're driving me wild," she murmured. The packet tore open and she popped the condom out into her hand. She tapped him on the shoulder to get his attention, but he ignored her and slid his head lower.

Lower still.

And took her with his mouth. She arched into him and cried out as his tongue turned her insides molten. She shuddered and shook as he growled some more. She finally understood what he meant when he said: Have mercy! "Don't stop, please, don't . . . stop . . ."

Tension wound tighter as he took her closer and closer to the pinnacle. When the tipping point came she flooded his mouth with release and she swore he laughed in triumph as she came.

After a long moment of holding her close and letting her ease back to Earth, he took the condom from her limp fingers and slipped it on. With a strong grip, he pulled her up tight and close to his crotch. She let her legs fall open in invitation, giving him full access.

The expression on his face went male and determined. Nothing would come between Clay and his goal. She closed her eyes and whispered one word over and over. "In, in, in." And she was fully *in:* in his life, in his home, his arms, maybe in his heart in some way.

The rush when he speared into her took her higher than she'd ever been. He held her, stilled her, let her body adjust and then . . . he moved.

Clay moved the bed, the room, the house, the Earth itself as he roared into her time and again. She caught his rhythm, fast, hard and rocked with him until he stopped, suspended as tension gripped him. In the stillness of his gathering strength, need coiled in her belly once more. Clay went deep, deeper, harder, faster and life hung still and clear and perfect.

Triumph took him but this time, it was hers, too. She wanted to weep for what they'd found. A single tear tracked down her temple and she wiped it away before he could see. He wouldn't understand what she cried for because she wasn't sure herself.

Moments later, he settled at her side and flung his leg over hers holding her in his heat and strength. "You okay?" his voice was ragged at the edges, his breath still returning. He slid his palm to her belly to cup her. Mild pulses still ebbed inside her as her body righted itself.

Not that life would ever go back to the way it was. Not after Clay. "I told someone once that I was no good at sex. I was wrong," she said. She was bad at faking it, that's all. "I've never had what we just had."

"Good." He bussed the tip of her nose with a quick kiss. "I'll be right back." He left her, making sure she was covered by the duvet and disappeared into the bathroom. While the water ran, she gathered her scattered composure.

Her life had changed in less than twenty minutes. But this was the month for changes—too many to comprehend at one time. Especially not now with the scent of him filling her nose and while the pulses of afterglow still warmed her.

Clay returned and slid into bed with her again. His body heated hers right away. "What is it with men? You're like furnaces."

He grinned. "It's because women have such cold feet." He rubbed his feet against hers under the cover.

"I like you, Clay Foster." Great sex and a hot foot rub. The man was made for her.

"I like you, Mercy. Even if you are a Talbot woman," he teased and then nuzzled her neck beside her ear. When she felt the slight tug of his teeth, she realized he'd liked it when she'd tried that maneuver on him.

"Nibbling? That's your idea of foreplay?" But she sent her hand south past his belly. Her breath caught as he nipped harder. When she found him growing hard again she cooed, "Oh, Mr. Foster, something's come between us."

"Damn straight," he said and launched a full frontal assault that soon had her gasping and grasping for the next tip-over into oblivion.

BY MIDNIGHT, MERCY and Clay were raiding his fridge. He wore pajama bottoms and she felt swallowed up by his robe. "I should go home soon. Or at least call to tell my parents not to wait up."

"Will you wake them?"

"Dad watches late-night talk shows."

"He looked at me funny today," he said. "He reminded me that you'll leave if your career picks up again."

She walked into his arms to press against him. "He's wrong, my career is dead."

But Clay frowned at her. "I believe he was warning me to steer clear of you. Nate was probing, nothing more." Clay nodded. "Also, he's taking on your mother about Dilly's lessons."

That surprised her. "I'll call and tell Dad that my friend had one drink too many so I drove her home and I'll be late."

"You're good."

"Acting is lying for a living, it's giving people what they want to see," she said with a shrug. "No biggie."

He nodded. "No biggie."

She got home three hours later and no one was awake. She and Clay had decimated the food supplies in the fridge, then they'd gone back to bed for more of each other.

She was sore, tired, replete and sated. And no one would ever know.

Chapter Thirteen

SUNDAY MORNING MERCY rolled to her back with a stretch. She felt deliciously tender where Clay had spent the most time pleasing her. Her tongue seemed swollen from all the attention she'd given him back. She supposed she should feel guilty, but she couldn't, not when she felt this sated. She heard someone rattling around in the kitchen and the smell of coffee and bacon wafted under her bedroom door. Another stretch, another smile and another shiver of anticipation for the next time she was alone with Clay and then she climbed out of bed.

She drew on her short silky robe and padded down the hall to follow the delicious scent of morning in the Talbot kitchen.

"Coffee," she mumbled to herself and froze as Dilly rounded the corner and charged into the room. Mercy braced her legs against the body slam.

"Auntie Mercy!"

The full weight of her niece crashed into her and Mercy stumbled backward a step. "Whoa, there, sweetie." She kneeled to give Dilly a hug and kiss. "I didn't know you'd be here this morning."

"Daddy and Grampa want to play," she said in a solemn voice. "They teach me."

She looked up to see Clay grinning at her from the far side of the sandwich bar. He held up Dilly's plastic bat and tee. "Softball. She's learning to swing a bat." He got an eyeful of Mercy in her nightie and open robe as she rose to her full height.

"Sounds like a great way to spend the morning." His heated gaze said how much he'd enjoyed the great way they'd spent last night.

Heat rose from her neck to her scalp at the look he gave her. "Can I get you a coffee?"

"Sure, thanks." To Dilly, he said, "Let's go outside to show Grampa and Grammy what we brought." He hooked a thumb to indicate that both her parents were in the garden.

While she poured mugs of coffee for both of them, he delivered Dilly and her toys to Nate and Hope.

She heard him return to the house. He was a blur as he swept her into his arms for a blistering kiss. "Miss me?" he asked after he'd thoroughly woken her aching lady parts.

"Not as much as you obviously missed me," she quipped with a smile. "You're a terrible tease," she said against his lips. His hands wandered down her back to her ass and he cupped her with a gentle squeeze. "Sore?" he asked.

She smiled. "A smidge, but it's worth it." They heard the sliding door slide in its track and pulled apart. She handed him his mug and they separated, she with her back to the fridge, he with his butt against the counter.

Hope rounded the corner. She raised an eyebrow at Mercy's still-open robe. "I made bacon sandwiches for breakfast. There's enough for you both if you'd like."

"I'm in," Clay said with a grin. He drained his coffee while Mercy tied her robe closed.

"I'll go shower and change," she said. "I'll be right back."

CLAY SLID AROUND THE breakfast bar and took a stool. "Dilly's having fun?" he asked Hope.

"Nate's warming her up by tossing her the ball. He says when you're ready you can join him to show her how to hold the bat."

"Great," he said awkwardly. They weren't often alone, but since Hope's visit to his place, he'd hoped some of the ice between them had broken. Maybe not.

She slid a couple of pieces of bread into the toaster and set it. "Mercy assumes that if I get this role I'll abandon my ambitions for Dilly."

"She's only three and a bit. I'm wondering if we shouldn't let her be a kid a while longer." There, he said it. Since Hope was ready to converse instead of making pronouncements, he opened up.

"Dancing is hard, pageants are tough and she needs to learn dedication. Without those things, I fear she'll go Janna's way and I refuse to allow it." And here they were back again in pronouncement land.

"I hoped all these classes would help her be more like Mercy," he said. "But now I see that may have been wrong."

"Dilly needs discipline, Clay. She needs to learn to listen to her teachers and apply her talent."

Maybe she doesn't have any talent for dance. He suspected that possibility had never entered Hope's mind. Not back in the day with Janna and not with Dilly.

"You're a father now, Clay. You'll understand when I say that I gave my everything to my girls. I did my best." She patted her chest over her heart. "But no one knew the trials I had with Janna. She defied me at every turn."

"I remember," he said and slid his mug from one hand to the other. She was getting emotional and he feared another bout of tears like that time on his deck. "And when Janna forced your hand you turned to Mercy."

"After all the battles with Janna, Mercy was a bright spot." She sighed. "Giving up on Dilly feels wrong. It feels as if I'm making the same mistake I did with Janna.

"I know what people thought when Janna died," she went on. "They thought '*Good riddance.*' When a troubled child dies, there's no real sympathy, no understanding. There are platitudes to your face and sniggers behind your back."

Clay had wondered the same thing about people when the word got out that Janna had been drunk when her car hit that tree. He hung his head, overcome with the memories.

"Oh, Clay, I didn't mean you felt that way. You loved my daughter and you're a good father to Dilly. I know you want what's best for her."

From the backyard, he heard Dilly's delighted squeals and Nate's low voice encouraging her. Mercy wanted what was best for Dilly, too, but it was too soon to give up on the pageants and lessons. "Would Mercy step in while she's here? She had all the lessons. Maybe Dilly would take instruction from her more easily than from her teachers."

Hope straightened away from buttering the toast, set the knife down and then turned to him. "If she'd do that, Dilly wouldn't lose what she's learned."

"If the lessons are tough on her, Dilly might respond better with less pressure."

Hope smiled and her eyes lit. "Clay, you're a master negotiator. I'm sure Mercy will help."

"Help with what?" Mercy said as she strolled back into the kitchen. Her face was freshly scrubbed and she looked good enough to eat. *Mind out of the gutter, Foster.* Her hair was still damp from her shower and she was dressed in a pair of pants that hugged her shapely legs and butt. Her V-necked T-shirt exposed just enough of her cleavage to draw his eye. Now that he'd nuzzled her there and knew how responsive she was, he could barely think.

"I'll let you ask her, Clay. Mercy responds better to you than to me these days," Hope said. "The bacon and toast are ready for sandwiches. I'll go check on Dilly."

He made certain that Hope had left the house before speaking again. His throat felt dry and his jeans felt tight. He shifted, trying to settle. "I suggested to your mother you might step in to coach Dilly rather than have her continue at the dance school."

Mercy's hand froze in midair with the half-full coffee pot.

"Should I duck?" he asked. Janna had tossed a few kitchen utensils at him over the years, so he was prepared for anything now. But all Mercy did was frown. She didn't look angry exactly, just a bit surprised.

"You think the dance teacher is causing her tantrums."

He put his hands up like a robber who'd just been caught. "With help from your mom. But maybe with you more involved, Dilly would have a buffer."

She poured a fresh mug of coffee for him and herself, nodding all the while. "I'll do it if my mother cancels Dilly's classes. And I'll work with her in short, fun bursts. If you find us twirling around in her room at bedtime, don't come in."

"Doesn't sound like the discipline Hope says she needs, but I'll take it."

"The trick to having discipline is to want it for yourself. Dilly needs to *want* to dance and if I make it fun for a while, maybe the discipline will come later."

"So you'll be her fun dance coach."

He'd swear the sun had come out in the Talbot's kitchen. Mercy's smile was just that bright. "Come here," she said softly.

After a quick glance to see if anyone was watching from the garden, Clay left his seat and kissed her long, slow, and hard. "I want you at my place again tonight."

"And I want to be there."

THE AFTERNOON BEFORE the audition, Mercy cleaned out the last dog enclosure for the day. She'd added a walk with Ethel into her daily routine when her chores were done. When Mercy unclipped a leash from the kennel chain-link for her favorite inmate, Ethel danced on her hind legs in anticipation.

"Okay girl, we've both earned a few moments to stretch out the kinks." Mercy led the dog to the back area of the lot where volunteers had created walking paths through the woods. She crisscrossed the area, giving Ethel lots of time to sniff her favorite spots.

Birds twittered overhead and a squirrel chastised them from a tree limb. "This area is for us, my friend, not you," she told the indignant squirrel. Ethel cocked her head at the squirrel's antics and stalled until Mercy gave the leash a gentle tug. "Will you let me talk?" she asked the dog.

Ethel hopped into gear and they continued. "Talking to a dog is weird, but I need to talk out my problems. Saying them aloud helps me," she said.

Ethel peed.

"Yeah, thanks for that undying interest," she said on a dry note. "I haven't heard a peep from Esme so that indie role's long gone. I didn't want it anyway. Who wants to end their career looking like a hag?"

Ethel grabbed a twig and gave it a shake. The energetic head wag looked like an emphatic no.

"Glad you agree," Mercy continued. "All week Clay and I have hardly said more than two words to each other in front of my parents." And they spoke of nothing more important than the weather because whenever she glanced at him his eyes screamed horny. It was best not to look, and certainly not within sight of Hope.

"I keep my distance, too," she continued. Except at night. She'd worried by Wednesday that her parents would get curious about her whereabouts so she'd stayed in with them. It had been the longest evening of her life.

Otherwise, she and Clay stayed at least three feet apart whenever he was at the house with Dilly. They were careful to have no accidental brushes of fingers. No sidelong glances. No secret smiles.

"But on the phone, I need a fan. That man knows how to keep the fires burning."

Before Janna died she'd been fully functional in the sex drive department. She'd never felt deprived or lacking in desire but grief had tamped back that side of her and she'd barely missed it. But Clay made every womanly desire she'd ever had flood back as if her drought had never happened.

"As for my mom, I've coached her as best I can. Tomorrow morning will be the test. I believe she's got talent, but she's nervous." She recognized the mercurial signs of devastating fear of failure coupled with secret hope. Feelings roiled like hurricane-driven waves and no amount of coaching would ease the storm. "She has her heart set on being Maggie, but she's just not right for the part." She'd tried a few times to hint that Big Mama could be the role for her, but Hope had steadfastly ignored her.

Ethel snuffled at the base of a poplar.

"All I want is to get home and wash the dog poop off so I can meet Clay and Dilly at the park." But Karen needed help with the laundry because her knees were more painful all the time. "As soon as the laundry's done, I'm out of here."

Ethel yipped as if she wanted out of here, too. "I know, girl. When I get a place of my own, you'll have a home with me." Mercy wasn't sure when she'd accepted Ethel as hers, but it felt right. Ethel yipped again and wagged her stub of a tail as if she could fly like a helicopter.

MERCY THREW A LOAD of towels into Karen's washer and set the machine for a heavy load. They bathed all the new arrivals. That meant lots of laundry.

Karen sat in her kitchen with a cup of coffee and her feet up on a chair while Mercy tended to the wash. Karen's knees were giving her hell today. Mercy was happy to see her sit down for a bit. "Have a coffee when you're done," Karen said and waved at another chair across from her.

Mercy didn't want to take the time, but since it was the first time Karen had been this hospitable, she helped herself to a mug. She took the chair opposite Karen at the table.

"So how are you settling in? You've been home a month or more now. Got that job. Got a man and your mother's stopped telling everyone your business. How'd you work that out? I've never known Hope Talbot to keep her gob shut about you."

Mercy snagged on the "got a man" comment. She squeezed the handle of her coffee mug until her knuckles went white. They'd been careful.

Karen couldn't know about her and Clay. They hadn't been at the kennels at the same time this week. Karen was fishing. Mercy took a sip of coffee and then set her mug down. She shrugged with her features schooled into nonchalance. Focus on what Karen had said about Hope, she told herself. "My mother is coming around to the idea that I may not return to my career. My dreams haven't panned out."

"Dreams are for fools," Karen said with a smug look. "I don't know anyone who's ever chased a dream and had it come true."

"I know a few who've succeeded in their life's dream," Mercy offered. "Clay for one." But Karen's expression closed.

"Since I came home my life's been on hold. There's nothing happening anywhere. I find that difficult when I'm used to a busier schedule and a hectic pace." Acting classes, auditions, waitressing and pestering her agent had meant next to no free time. "At work, Logan's focused on the new subdivision and I'm helping as much as I can." Coaching her mom this week and her short bursts of dancing with Dilly hardly took any time. "I'm doing okay here with the dogs. But I'm used to running at high speed."

Karen nodded. "You're fine with the dogs. I appreciate the help," she said through begrudging lips.

"I'm glad to hear it." She hadn't heard any snarky comments for a few days. She grinned but wasn't fooled. Karen hid her curiosity behind a veil of idle conversation.

"Logan's business is doing all right?"

The question seemed innocuous. Maybe she should let Karen assume she was involved with Logan. She rejected the idea. Logan didn't need rumors flying around.

"Hughes Realty is about to take off," she replied smoothly. Not that she'd tell Karen any of her personal observations, but Logan seemed concerned. They hadn't had an inquiry yet and the lag grated on their nerves. Logan had so much riding on this project that he was antsy. Once they got the first offer in and put to bed, he'd feel better. But Mercy would be damned if she shared any of this with Karen.

Whatever disasters were befalling Logan's family came more frequently than before. He was ragged with exhaustion and had installed a cot in the office for catnaps. They were on tenterhooks as days dragged on without that first auspicious inquiry.

Mercy had to get off this train of thought. Failing at her career was one thing, but she didn't want to see Logan's future fall apart, too. "How's your daughter?" she asked, to turn the conversation Karen's way.

"Brianna's good. She's coming for a visit soon." Karen massaged liniment into her knee. "Who's the man?"

Mercy blinked. "What man?"

"Someone put that sway in your hips and that mush in your eyes."

Mercy lifted the mug to her lips and looked down toward the rim to hide her gaze. "No one you know."

"So there is a man." Karen laughed a *gotcha* kind of laugh.

"I should have seen your agenda when you offered me coffee. You've never been this nice to me before." Her cell phone vibrated. "Wait, that's the job phone." Excitement gathered like a knot in her stomach. She held up a hand for silence and cleared her throat before answering. "Hughes Realty, how may I help you?"

Karen watched with expectant eyes.

"Yeah, uh, my wife and I want to check out that new subdivision. The sign said you people have the information."

Oh. No. Logan had forwarded this call, which meant this first inquiry was—*no! no! no!*—up to her. The knot of excitement inside her developed a case of hives. She stood because she could *not* remain seated.

"Yes, we have lots of plans," she used her most businesslike tone, while she flapped one hand in excitement. "All kinds of plans."

Karen made a slowing motion with her hands and Mercy drew a calming breath.

"Would you care to meet with me at the office?" she asked in an encouraging tone. "I'd love to show you the floor plans and neighborhood plan."

"Sure thing."

She gave him the address.

"Is that down the street from the vet clinic?"

"Yes, over the bakery."

"We'll be there."

"Thank you." She disconnected. This was it. She had to step up and be clear and focused and professional. The comment about the clinic brought Clay to mind. She wanted to call him; wanted to hear his voice cheering her on.

Just plain wanted to hear his voice.

Karen rose slowly to stand beside her. She nodded at Karen and ended the call. Then she let out a short squeal. Karen laughed.

"I have forty-five minutes to shower, change and get to the office. This is it, Karen, what Logan's been waiting for." And it was up to her to make a good impression on these people. Her stomach clenched.

"Bathroom's down the hall," Karen said. "Go shower. And why the hell isn't Logan taking care of this?"

"He's been called away."

"Must be his brother again," Karen said with a sly nod.

Karen was clearly the conduit through which all knowledge flowed in Welcome. The conduit waved her on. "Get going, I won't say anything about Logan's troubles. I keep my damn mouth shut."

Mercy narrowed her gaze but stayed mum on the topic of Logan Hughes. She barely recalled Logan's younger brother, Jamie, the football jock. Maybe he was ill and needed care from family members. It would be just like Logan to dedicate his time to his family if they needed him.

But right now, Logan needed *her*, and she had to deliver on her promise to do her best. She hurried out to her dad's truck to get her office clothes to change into. When she ran through the kitchen again on the way to shower, she heard Karen call from the laundry room, "Break a leg."

THE MORRISONS WERE interested in the largest model. Since they were older than the demographic the subdivision was aimed at, Mercy grew curious about their circumstances, especially when they showed particular interest in the location of the school.

Mr. Morrison seemed less willing to show enthusiasm than his wife, but Mercy knew which of them would make the final decision. And it wasn't Mr. Morrison. His wife gushed about the kitchen, mentioned that their grandchildren would be living with them and when the tour of the model home concluded, Mercy knew the truth.

The Morrisons would be raising their grandchildren. For whatever reason, the children's parents were unable to be in their children's lives. Mercy's heart ached for this family.

"We had planned on retiring and downsizing to a smaller home, but now . . . well, this one will do nicely," Mrs. Morrison said. "The children need a fresh start, with new friends and a nice new school."

Mercy set her hand on the woman's arm and caught her gaze. She hoped her eyes conveyed her understanding and sympathy. "Then a fresh start is what they'll get here." She waved her hand across the community plan.

Mrs. Morrison gave her a grateful smile. "Do you think so?"

She felt the pressure to live up to these people's expectations. For the first time, something she was doing could make a difference in a family's life. Mercy had no doubt the Morrison family would thrive if they took this deal.

"This will be a complete community. Your grandchildren will have everything they need," she promised. The pressure inside lifted with her words.

She'd just done something good and it was for a family of strangers, a family in need of a hopeful future.

She directed her next comment to the husband. "And getting into the neighborhood early will be less expensive and the builder's offering some free upgrades for the first buyers."

For the first time, he gave her a happy grin. "Now we're talking," he said. "How soon will the models be ready to walk through? I'm interested, but buying from plans without seeing a structure goes against the grain."

"HELPING THE MORRISONS make their decision to buy makes me feel as if I've done something real," Mercy told Clay as she stretched out beside him on his king sized bed later that night. "As real as it gets for someone like me, who's never actually helped anyone, let alone total strangers."

Clay rose to his elbow to lean over her. His eyes took on a glow as they searched hers. He smelled of sex and man, his body warm and oh-so-right next to hers. Cocooned in him, she waited while he gathered his thoughts, wondering if she sounded needy. She'd sunk to fishing for compliments.

"You've gained Ethel's trust," he said with a teasing twinkle. But he softened the comment with a kiss on the tip of her nose.

She chuckled. "You are aware Ethel's a dog, right? Not a person? All it took to earn her trust was some kibble, a kind voice, and a few belly rubs." He didn't understand how her life had always been about her. Acting demanded everything. Chasing that Hollywood dream had stunted her emotional life. After Janna had died, she'd kept on with her auditions and classes while ignoring the pain of her loss.

For two years she'd blanked out her parents' grief and ignored her sister's baby girl until she was forced back home. Swamped with all she'd avoided up to now, she swallowed hard and blew out a long breath.

"I'm such a rotten person, Clay. You have no idea how rotten."

"Mercy." He lifted her chin with a fingertip, making her focus on him. "You can't believe the Morrisons are the only people to have benefitted from your return to Welcome." He shook his head. "You're making me say this?"

"What?" He'd confused her and she had no idea what he'd say next.

"Dilly's a different child than she was. She's happier with you around. Your mother's taking to the stage and I'm allowing for the idea that Dilly needs a break. That's huge."

She warmed at his words and slid her hand down his arm to settle at his waist. "Honest? You're considering giving her a break?"

He kissed her nose and nodded. "And me? I'm damn grateful you're here with me."

As sweet as his words were, she felt a twinge. "Don't be grateful. We may have made a terrible mistake by being together. If we break up, Dilly will know something bad happened." She clasped his cheeks between her palms. "We both understand how unlikely this is to work out. Dilly's bright and observant. She'll know in a heartbeat if things change. Neither of us is that good an actor that we can hide a broken relationship." She'd messed up and was dragging Clay down with her. And where Clay went Dilly went. Disaster loomed. "It hurts to think about how much damage we could do to her."

He cupped her breast. "You're a tad late with this." He bent and kissed her nipple. "And you're taking all the blame. Don't." She closed her eyes, afraid to hope that everything they'd done wouldn't blow three lives apart. "We're in this now, and I, for one, want to stay in for as long as you're here."

Her eyes filled because it hurt that he still doubted her. "I'm here, Clay. I'm not going anywhere."

He looked as if he wanted to say something, but he hesitated. "We won't let anything hurt Dilly. You won't and I won't." His voice was firm and full of conviction she wanted to share but couldn't.

"My mother suspects something's going on, even if it's just a conspiracy to get Dilly off the circuit. And Karen grilled me on the man in my life. She tells me I've got a man-glow."

"A man-glow. I like it." But then Clay frowned. "Karen's fishing, and we're careful around your mother. She may suspect, but she can't be certain."

"I'm avoiding my mom as much as possible, aside from giving her acting tips. That's a safe area."

She didn't mention how Karen had fished for information about Logan. Talking about him while she was in bed with Clay didn't feel right. Clay needed to be more secure about her feelings before she could casually discuss her good-guy boss.

Who was she kidding? She needed to be more secure in her feelings for Clay too. Right now, everything was a jumble of desire, attraction, and, if she was completely honest, shock, because she'd come to believe that he being her sister's husband wasn't a biggie.

She needed to get her head on straight. Not to mention her heart. But the more time she spent with Clay, the deeper and more confused her feelings became. "When I said I'm not going back to Hollywood, I meant it."

He shook his head, already denying what she was about to say without hearing it.

"You need to hear this, Clay." And more, she needed to say it. "I'll begin at the moment when I accepted that everything I'd dreamed of had turned to ash. Don't stop me until I'm done. I can't say this twice."

"Okay, shoot. I'm listening."

"I was in a second-floor office on Hollywood Boulevard, about a block from Vine. There was a contract on the desk in front of me. My palms were sweating, the clock ticking, my breath felt as if it had stopped. I wanted to sign, but the ballpoint was cheap and the ink gathered at the tip. I couldn't take my eyes off that blob of ink as I stared at the contract and thought of what it meant. But mostly I thought about the money.

"I needed the money, Clay. More than anything, I *needed* the money."

He soothed her with a kiss to her shoulder.

"I told myself to sign. Signing meant rent money. Food money." She closed her eyes to find the fortitude to continue.

Food money. Rent money. The air drew close and too warm. A voice shouted from the street below: a homeless guy named Ernie yelling obscenities. She'd given him the change she'd found in her sofa cushions that morning. He said he was waiting for his big break. *Sure, aren't we all?*

If she didn't sign at the *X* she'd be as good as done. Like Ernie the homeless guy.

Still, she let the ink congeal, blue and sticky, on the ball tip.

Cheap pen.

Cheap office.

"We'll make you a star, honey," J.D. had said. His voice turned silky.

Cheap man.

She swallowed, impatient with her stupid self. Her whole life had been about making it, and now she didn't have the guts to do this one thing?

"We'll start filming right away." J.D. had looked past Mercy to his waiting secretary and gave the woman a sharp nod. "It's easier to jump right in."

"I'm sure it is," Mercy muttered.

J.D.'s gaze sharpened on hers. "You're not the first actress to have second thoughts. But they don't pay the bills, right, honey?"

The secretary leaned down to Mercy's ear. "It's not like you haven't done any of this before."

She slid her gaze to the other woman's. Cheap mascara clumped her lashes that rimmed impossibly green contact lenses, while stale perfume wafted from her cavernous cleavage. The scent of old cigarettes clung to her hair and clothes.

"Sorry," Mercy murmured. "But I'm not good at it."

J.D.'s eyes looked harder with each passing second. "You got something better to do? Go do it."

"Better? No," she said and set the pen down on the desk. His secretary patted her shoulder, her red-tipped fingers like talons. "Not better, but at least it won't make me sick."

J.D. frowned and chewed on the end of his cigar. That had to be unhealthy.

Mercy stood and walked out of the office, its walls lined with the publicity photos of the other women the porn producer called stars.

On the way out she heard him say, "I toldja she was too old. Twenty-eight if she's a day. At eighteen, we'd'a had her."

They'd pretended to believe she was twenty-three the first time she'd walked in. They still believed it, her ego said, no matter their bitchy comments as she left.

Her grin slid off her face as she took her seat on the next bus. She was down to her last hundred bucks and with the restaurant where she waitressed closing for major renovations, she was out of a rent-paying job for three weeks, maybe more.

She could sofa surf with friends. Make the rounds for a few nights at a time, if anyone was willing. But to have a friend she needed to be a friend and as her career had stuttered to a stall, she'd isolated herself from those who'd reached out to her. She squeezed her eyes shut. No one would offer her a place. No one.

"Mercy, I had no idea things ever got that bad." Clay cuddled her closer, startling her. She'd been so deep in the memory she'd almost forgotten where she was as she'd relived her deepest humiliation.

"No one knew I hit rock bottom. I couldn't tell my parents or anyone. I can't believe I walked into that place and thought I could pull it off." She made a face, determined to play it down.

"I blamed my isolation on my faltering career and refused to believe that Janna's death had anything to do with it." She blinked wetness out of her eyes. "I denied my grief for two years while it ate me up." She left the bed and went into the bathroom to wash her face.

Once in there, the flood of memories continued as she stared in the mirror, her face a billboard for grief, doubt and loss. She wasn't that woman anymore. She was the new, improved Mercy Talbot.

But the memories still came. As the bus pulled away from the stop, she'd dug out her cell phone and tried her agent's office number. He'd been ducking her calls, but still, she'd hoped something had come up. She wouldn't tell him about her near miss with J.D. That had been a stupid idea anyway. "Hi, Esme," she said when her call was picked up. "This is Mercy Talbot, is he in?"

"Sorry, honey, he's not." But Mercy heard her agent's voice in the background before Esme muffled the mouthpiece. Mr. Chastain hadn't taken a call from her in months.

"It's okay, Esme," Mercy responded gently to the lie. It wasn't Esme's fault she worked for a jerk. "Just tell him I've decided to leave town for a few days. My cell won't work where I'm going," she lied. "I'll be unavailable if he calls." She was down to the last few minutes on her pay-as-you-go card. And she had one more call to make.

"Sure thing, honey, I'll tell him." Esme was a kind woman at heart and recognized Mercy's pathetic attempt to save face.

"Okay then. I'll, um, check in?" Oh, God, she'd actually made that a question, as if she didn't have the right to call. She closed her eyes and sagged into her seat.

But Esme, bless her heart, didn't miss a beat. "There's a part in an indie I heard about just this morning."

"You're serious?" She straightened, unable to keep the hope out of her voice. *Pathetic.*

"It may not be right for you, but I'll see what I can do."

She wasn't sure Esme was supposed to talk about possibilities. She wasn't an agent, just an assistant, but still, in spite of knowing better, hope blossomed. "I'll call in a couple days, then," she said.

"There is one thing," Esme said, then took a deep breath.

Mercy braced for the worst.

"It's for an older mother. One with a hard life."

"A washed-out hag?" From "We can make you a star!" to "washed-out hag" in five minutes. A record. But that was Hollywood, defined.

"Not exactly a hag, honey. Just call."

An indie production. No one would see it and the pay would suck just like the indie she'd done before but she was out of options now that she'd walked out of J.D.'s office. She couldn't face rebuilding that burnt bridge. She wasn't good enough at sex to be filmed.

Clay tapped on the bathroom door. "You okay? I hear sniffling."

She opened the door. "I'm lousy at sex," she said, dabbing at her eyes. She had been sniffling. At heart, she was still the pathetic failed actress. She tamped down her emotions.

"If you believe what we've been doing is lousy, wait until I bring my A-game." He laughed at her. "You're one messed-up bag of beautiful, Mercy Talbot."

She moved into his welcoming arms with a frown. What they'd shared had been spectacular. "I'm glad you see me as beautiful and there's nothing wrong with the game you're bringing. I just haven't had a lot of fireworks, the way I've had with you. I figured it was me."

"Fireworks describes it for me, too." He enveloped her against his warm chest and coaxed her back to bed. "You need to get this all out. Now, start where you left off."

She settled against him, their legs entwining. "Where was I?"

"You were on the bus leaving that asshole's office."

She smiled at the apt description. "Right. Esme asked me if I was okay and called me 'honey.'"

Esme had pulled her out of her numbed shock after telling her she could find work as a washed-out hag. "You don't sound like yourself," Esme had said.

"I was used to brusque questions from Esme. But when she called me 'honey' I took it as more evidence of my pathetic state. I told her I wasn't okay but I would be. Just as soon as I figure out what a washed-up thirty-year-old does with the ashes of her dreams." She'd ended the call, wondering why everyone in that godforsaken town thought using the word "honey" made them sound friendly.

"My sort-of boyfriend dumped me. He was superstitious and said winners hung out with winners."

"Another asshole." Clay hugged her and patted her shoulder. "You were surrounded."

"He said my run of bad luck tainted his chances. Before Janna's accident, I probably would have felt the same way. I told you I was a rotten person."

"From what I can gather, actors have to make their own luck and you were sidelined by grief that you didn't acknowledge. A grief counselor explained that to me once."

"You're probably right," she fudged. But Mercy had no one else to blame for her circumstances. Not Janna, for dying and leaving a baby, not her mother, and not her ex. Her failure was all on her.

She recalled the way the glare from the noon sun shot through the bus window in spite of the dark-tinted glass. She sank her chin into her hand and then skimmed the sidewalk. Maybe she'd see someone to help her out with a role or an audition or maybe a quick loan. As the bus cruised down Sunset, she saw a couple of directors she'd worked for, but they ducked into a coffee shop. If she jumped off the bus she couldn't afford to get back on. She stayed in her seat.

"When I was on the bus, I realized I didn't have to leap off and chase down two directors I saw walking by. I didn't have to pretend it was a chance meeting." She rose up on her elbow and kissed Clay's forehead. "My heart lightened because I accepted that there would be no more chasing parts, no more acting classes, no more dieting, or power yoga. No more disappointment. No more rejection. No more wondering if a nip or tuck or injection for the settled lines on my forehead would help." Her lips lifted in a gentle, unpracticed smile. "No more shattered dreams."

"Forehead lines? You're kidding."

"I'm thirty. And in Hollywood that's ancient." She shook her head. "The thing is I have no way to replace the dreams I've lost. It's not as if I can scoop the ashes into an urn to set it on a mantel. I can't point and say, 'There they are, all the years I worked and trained and suffered for my craft.' No, there's nothing to show for all the effort. Nothing, zippo, nada."

"Starting from nothing means having a clean slate," he said softly.

"Yes, a clean slate." Bare, empty: a wide-open world where she could start fresh. *Big effing deal.* She'd told herself the same thing whenever she failed but here she was: broke and living with her parents. More than broke, she felt broken.

"I used to be an optimist, but all those rejections kicked that shit out of my head."

He frowned and looked disturbed by her story. "How do you see yourself now if not as an optimist?"

She considered her last couple of years and set aside the word pessimist, which she tried hard not to be.

"A realist." She nodded. "That feels right. I'm a realist who believes the world is impartial. God, or the universe or the collective unconscious, whatever you want to call it, doesn't care one whit how hard a person works, how determined they are to succeed or how bad or mean they are."

Life happened as it happened and no matter what a person did, impartiality or indifference ruled.

Ugh.

She hated the idea, but realism demanded acceptance of that one ugly truth. She closed her eyes, rested her head on Clay's shoulder and let the broken truth lay waste.

Chapter Fourteen

ON THE SATURDAY MORNING of the audition, Mercy swore it was the character Maggie who showered, Maggie who dressed and Maggie who climbed into the back seat and allowed Mercy to drive her to the theater for the audition. When they arrived, the parking lot only had a few spots left.

A smidgen of Hope's fear leaked into her voice. "There are a lot of people here." She slipped her sunglasses on and then covered her hair with a kerchief. It looked like 1956 in the car.

"You're right, but try to remember what you said before about owning this," Mercy responded. "Own it the way you owned your prom." She patted her mother's cold hand.

Hope flapped Mercy's hand away and shifted to sit straighter in her seat. "You be certain to stay out here, Mercy. As agreed."

As if.

Hope climbed out her door, smoothed her pencil skirt and strode with purpose toward the door of the theater. She threaded her way through the other parked cars and held her head high.

Watching her, Mercy couldn't help but be proud. Her mom was scared but determined and as prepared as she could be. As soon as she disappeared inside the building, Mercy got out of the mini-van and followed her. No way would she miss this.

Mercy stood in the back of the theater in the shadows. When they called her mom, Hope stepped into the spotlight and Mercy held her breath. She'd taught her as much as she could in a short time. She hoped it was enough. But still, this entire exercise was about teaching Hope what it was like to be judged onstage, not about getting the part.

Over time, Mercy had developed a thick skin, but Hope was far more fragile. *More like Janna.*

"Mrs. Talbot." It was a woman's voice that Mercy didn't recognize. But her mother did because she could see Hope raise her chin. Haughty to the end. "Please read the pages handed to you. We understand you haven't had any experience so just be yourself." The voice fell flat on the word *yourself.*

Hope skimmed the pages and gasped. "But this isn't Maggie, it's Big Mama."

"What was that, Hope? We didn't hear you." This time it was a man's voice. Whoever it was wanted to see her mother fail.

"Well, if you want Big Mama, I'll damn well give you Big Mama." Hope's voice came strong and sure. And suddenly Big Mama stood on that stage and took control of the scene, the dialogue, and the character.

At the end of the audition, there was silence as Mercy dashed off back to the car, her pride about to fly out of her chest. Her mom had rocked it!

Back in the car, Mercy asked how it went as if she hadn't a clue. "It was all a blur," Hope responded vaguely. She didn't say another word all the way home.

HOPE HAD STAYED SILENT and had rebuffed Mercy's attempts at conversation. Mercy sat at the kitchen counter as Hope made busywork at the sink and staring blindly out the window.

"Your father's home," Hope said, sounding breathless. Mercy stayed seated so she could hear her mom's answers when her dad asked questions. Hope gave her a sidelong glance that Mercy ignored.

Nate came into the kitchen. "Hi," he said with a quick buss on Hope's cheek and an inquisitive glance at Mercy. "How did the audition go?"

"It's a bit hazy." Hope turned toward him. "Melanie James and Simon Phipps ran the thing. They'll have the final say."

Melanie James had been the snide one. Mercy remembered the name but couldn't put a face to her. It was Simon Phipps she'd talked to about her mother's audition. He'd seemed open and receptive, but Mercy had been fooled by casting people before.

"Either way, I won't be in the play." Hope plastered a phony smile on her face. "I have too much to do with Dilly."

"Dilly's fine. You should take the part if they offer it." Her dad smiled to encourage her, but Hope turned back to the spotless sink and gave it another wipe.

Mercy sat in silence but crossed her fingers for luck as she watched her mother straighten and turn back to face Nate.

"I didn't read for Maggie," she said. "I read for Big Mama."

"You don't say." He ran his hand over his hair. "You'd make a great Big Mama. It's a good role. As for Maggie, it's likely they have their favorites anyway."

"Maybe. But what a waste of time and effort. I canceled Dilly's appearance at the Seattle pageant for this."

Her father cleared his throat. "I can't see that as a tragedy." His voice was level and firm.

Boom. There it was: real support for Mercy's cause.

Her mom sighed and looked up at him. "You too? *You* want Dilly to take a break?" She turned enraged eyes toward Mercy as if it was all her fault.

Which, of course, it was.

"This smells like a conspiracy." She pulled out of Nate's arms, fury rising in her eyes and stance. Embattled, Hope opened her mouth to say more, but her father put two fingers to her lips.

"You're a beautiful woman, Hope. And I say you'd make the most attractive Big Mama ever."

She reared back. "I wouldn't accept the part if Melanie James and Simon Phipps *beg* me to."

"How did it feel to be up there, Mom, on that stage reading for a role? That's what I'm interested in," Mercy said.

"Frightening, that's how. I don't know how you've managed all this time, Mercy. The staring, the judgment . . ." She trailed off and when no one spoke, she rallied. "That's what you wanted, wasn't it? For me to be in your shoes?"

"And Dilly's."

The starch went out of Hope's back and she seemed to fold in on herself. She covered her face with her hands. Nate gathered her close and patted her back. He looked warningly at Mercy over Hope's head. Mercy bit her lip and waited.

It didn't take long for Hope to sniffle against his shoulder. With a long sigh she said, "If you say the word, I'll let Dilly take a break from the pageants."

"Dilly needs time off, Hope," her dad responded and hugged her tighter. "I believe Clay would agree."

"Do you believe I'm wrong in what I want for Dilly?" Ignoring Mercy, she looked up into Nate's eyes.

"You want what's best for her. We all want her happy, productive, and well-rounded with school and sports and dance. Dilly will learn discipline, and kindness, and everything that's important. But I'm not convinced forcing her into pageants is the way to make all that happen."

Mercy froze in her seat. If she moved or spoke, she was afraid she'd interrupt and ruin everything. Hope was, at long last, seeing the truth.

"We should *listen* to Dilly, Hope. Whenever you say she's like her mother, she fights it. We've got her convinced that being like Janna means she's a bad girl. Why else would she scream that she's good?"

Her mother's sharp intake of breath spoke of painful realization. "How many times have I ignored her when she's said that?" Her voice came out hollow, strained.

"I don't know, but I didn't listen to her either. You need to step back." Nate cleared his throat. "Why not focus on yourself for a while? Let Clay decide what's best for Dilly."

With a sniff for emphasis, Hope nodded. "She's the one who matters."

Two hours later Simon Phipps called and Hope accepted the part. "Take *that*, Melanie James," she said as she hung up after the call.

AFTER HIS MORNING AT work, Clay drove up the street to the Talbot house, still processing Mercy's midnight confession. He saw her in a whole new light. Far from having it easy, Mercy had suffered and worked her butt off and still ended up back in Welcome, living in her parents' home. Shocking as it was, and as sorry as he felt that she'd hit bottom, there was a part of him that accepted she had no plans to return to her career.

He admired the way she'd picked herself up and kept going. All those measly jobs she'd gone after, all the rejection and unkind remarks from people in glorious Welcome hadn't stopped her from trying.

She must feel grateful to Logan for giving her a chance. And there it was: a childish response to her working with Hughes. It shouldn't feel like a jab to his ego, but Clay had to admit it did.

Was he that guy? The jealous, possessive guy who didn't want his woman to succeed at a job she liked? His woman—*whoa*—did he feel as if Mercy was his?

Holy shit, he did. He wanted her. He'd claimed her for his with their first kiss. No wonder the job with Hughes had irritated him.

But did Mercy feel the same way about him? If Hughes made a play for her, how would she react?

Of course, Hughes would jump on Mercy if he could. But after hearing about her close call in the porn producer's office, Clay knew her self-respect was intact. She wouldn't sleep with her boss to keep her job. She liked Logan, remembered him fondly, but she had no deeper feelings for him.

He hoped she saved all the deeper stuff for Clay. And her attachment to Dilly was unshakeable.

Mercy enjoyed her job with Hughes. Surprised by her success in connecting with people, she found it satisfying and fulfilling, two responses he understood.

He'd gone around in his mind for a week, wondering what to do about Mercy. If they stepped into the light with their relationship, there'd be hell to pay from Hope.

Nate would likely reserve judgment until he saw how Dilly was affected.

But Dilly would pay the highest price if things went wrong. He still couldn't trust that wouldn't happen.

Any relationship could fail, and he and Mercy had a few more things to deal with than the average couple. Like Janna's memory and Janna's daughter.

Clay still wasn't convinced he could raise Dilly to be the confident, self-respecting woman her aunt had turned out to be.

As he pulled up to park, he saw Hope's minivan approach, but Nate hailed him from the open garage. "Hey, Clay. Got a minute?"

He answered by walking into the garage. "Need a hand?"

Nate gave him a steady look that sent a ripple through his gut.

"You can come up with an explanation for why my truck's been at your place several times this week."

Nate nodded as their minivan pulled into the driveway. The nod said the question had come from Hope.

Shit, Clay should have told Mercy to pull the truck around back instead of leaving it at the front of the house where anyone driving by could see it.

"Sure thing," he nodded. "It's not a mystery. Mercy's been watching Dilly." It was half true. The other night he'd made a grocery run while Mercy put Dilly to bed. He looked just as steadily back at his father-in-law, his face set to impassive. He may want to tell them Dilly needed a break, but he couldn't get into it about Mercy. Not yet.

Hope helped Dilly get out of the van. "Run along inside now, Dilly, I'll be right there," she said. "You can watch your show."

Clay waited for his chance to speak. When Dilly was out of earshot, he said, "Before you ask about Mercy being at my place, I'm seeing someone and I don't want Dilly to know yet. I don't want her to get attached." The lie had come to him like a whisper from Janna. She'd always been a good liar.

Nate grinned and offered his hand. "Well, that's great news, son. Great news." He rubbed his jaw. "Best to play your cards close in a town this size."

Hope looked startled. "Who is it?" she asked.

Nate shook his head. "There's no point pushing, Hope. Leave things be, for once."

She settled on her heels and pinched her lips together. "It's not Shandy. I already heard she's seeing someone else."

Clay said nothing.

After a long, assessing moment, Hope caved. "As long as she's a decent woman. She'll be an influence on Dilly. Naturally, we'll want to know more about her." But her eyes went moist and Clay saw that it frightened her that Dilly might someday have a stepmom.

He was misleading them, but there was no reason to be cruel. "She understands that you'll be there for Dilly, Hope. You don't have to worry that you'll lose your granddaughter."

She glanced with relief at Nate. "Okay, then. We'll look forward to hearing more about her. If things work out." She opened the door into the house and entered.

The men followed. Dilly was in the family room, singing along with her show. "I've made a decision." He turned toward Hope in the kitchen. "Dilly will take a break from classes and pageants until you're finished with the play. I don't want her to go to New Mexico."

"You've already heard I got the part?" Hope asked in a curious tone.

"I haven't fired Sybil, so of course I've heard," he teased. It wasn't quite a lie because Sybil had told him after Mercy had.

"Humph. That Sybil can't hold her tongue about anything. Never could."

"While you put your energy into the play," Clay said with a glance at a smiling Nate, "Dilly will take some time off. Everyone will have a fresh perspective when life returns to normal."

"Great idea," Nate said. "We'll still have Dilly with us, but Hope will enjoy her evening rehearsals more without having had a battle in the afternoon."

Hope glared at Nate. "As long as Mercy continues with Dilly's coaching. I don't want Dilly to fall behind."

"I LIED TO YOUR FATHER," Clay told Mercy at the play park half an hour after the discussion with Nate and Hope. "I lied to a man I respect and admire," Clay said, his tone filled with guilt and regret.

She watched as Dilly climbed the slide's short ladder. "Did he believe I sit with Dilly while you date someone?" She kept her voice low to keep the conversation away from the ears of other parents supervising their children, although the squeals and laughter drowned out a lot.

"Yes, he believed me and I feel like shit."

"I don't know what to say. We're in the same position we were when we started. It all comes down to Dilly." Her stomach clamped into a knot. She crossed her arms over her waist and hugged herself lightly.

Someone caught his eye across the park and he nodded curtly. Mercy tracked his gaze. Shandy. Mercy fully expected the other woman to approach, but when she turned her back to them, Mercy had to wonder why.

"Shandy's not coming over to say hello? Has she given you up?"

"Yes. She knows I'm a lost cause. Sybil and your mother told me she's seeing someone new."

Mercy got the feeling Shandy knew something was brewing between them. "Maybe I should stop meeting you here. It's too public."

"You want to give up playtime with Dilly?" He cocked an eyebrow.

"No." Not ever.

"Then it's settled." He clapped his hands once. "Time for home, Punk," Clay called. He stepped to the bottom of the slide and caught Dilly up in his arms when she came down. "I have news for you."

She pressed his cheeks together and he blew a raspberry. Dilly giggled. "You know Grammy is acting in a play?"

"She goes to 'hearse."

Mercy and Clay burst into laughter. "We'll keep talk of a hearse out of her hearing," Mercy managed to say.

"Fine by me," Clay said. "Dilly, while Grammy is busy with *rehearsals* I've decided that for a *while* you don't have to go to any classes." Dilly shrieked in delight and then gave him a smacker of a kiss on the lips. When he set her back on her feet to walk to the car, he shook his head. "Auntie Mercy will continue to help you with your dancing and other things."

"Yay, yay, yaaaay!" She hopped and jumped along beside him, clearly happy with her newfound freedom.

"You've made her day. Let's go home and set up that tee in the yard. Dilly can take some practice swings while we get dinner ready." Had she just laid claim to his house as home? She bit her lip, wondering if he'd noticed. But he didn't seem to mind her remark.

Maybe her confession last week had cleared the way for a stronger relationship than the secret fling they'd been enjoying. What they shared was hot, fun, and sexy as hell, but it wasn't real.

But she had to wonder if it could be.

Once at the house, Mercy parked the truck out of sight in Clay's garage. They'd decided to step up their vigilance on keeping their private lives private. Neither of them wanted any more gossip about where she was spending her time.

When she stepped into the house through the mudroom, she heard Clay talking in a manner that said it wasn't Dilly to whom he was speaking. In the kitchen, she saw him on the phone. He waved her to a seat at the island. She checked on Dilly in the living room and settled in to wait while Clay was on the phone.

"Elle, the trailer's ready. Just say the word and I'll have it cleaned and the utilities turned on. It's yours." He listened for a moment. "When did that happen?" He sounded shocked but went silent as his sister responded. His brows knit. "You'll need a double-wide."

Mercy heard muffled protests from the phone. "No sweat. It'll be done. I'll see you when I see you." He hung up and a muscle jumped in his jaw. "Elle's coming home."

"To live?"

He nodded. "With four children."

"You said she had three."

"Because the last time I heard she did."

"She's on her own?" *With four children?*

"That's right."

Clearly, Elle's life had taken a winding path since leaving Welcome. "I know how it feels when life kicks you in the head. We'll make her feel at home." And now she was using *we*. Clay appeared not to have noticed.

"She needs a helping hand. We all do at some point." His gaze clouded as his thoughts turned inward.

She warmed to see Clay wanting to be there for his sister and her children. Their relationship was clearly different from the one she'd shared with Janna. Half friendly, half hateful she and Janna's rivalries never ended. All of those difficult emotions made her grief more complicated. With Janna gone, there was no way to mend fences or become better sisters to each other.

All Mercy could do was be involved in Dilly's life. If she did nothing else right, she'd keep that promise.

"Welcome's wagging tongues will burn with this news," she said. "There's a whole tribe of Fosters on the way back to town. However will the townspeople cope?"

"With pitchforks and burning torches," Clay suggested.

She slid off her stool, checked to see that Dilly wasn't watching and stepped into Clay's waiting arms. He tugged her backward, out of viewing range behind the kitchen wall. "I love that you're ready to take all this on." She kissed him lightly on the lips.

He replied with a kiss to her nose. "And I love that you didn't blink at the news."

"Of course I blinked." She softened her words with a quick kiss. "I'm wondering how Elle's return will affect us. It'll be harder to be here with you."

"Only if we're still sneaking around." He responded with a kiss of his own.

In spite of her fresh concern about going public, a trill of desire sang in her belly, but with Dilly close by she gave him a sigh of frustration and left his arms. He clasped her elbow. "Sometime soon this will get away from us and Dilly will notice," he said. "We should decide what we'll do when that time comes."

"Dilly will be distracted with a crowd of new cousins to play with. But Elle is a different story. Having her here will be awkward." She didn't have a lot of memories of Elle Foster, other than her in-your-face attitude whenever Clay needed back-up in school. And most of those memories were filtered through Janna's comments. "Elle didn't much care for Janna. It's intimidating to meet her."

His eyes warmed. "We'll deal with that when she arrives. I'll handle Elle. You don't have a thing to worry about." He leaned in close to whisper. "She'll see right away that you're not Janna. You're nothing like her."

"Meantime, you'll have a lot to do to get the houses switched out."

He tugged her close again and nuzzled her neck. "Which means I'll need you here more often to watch Dilly."

"That was quick thinking with my parents. Did they believe you?"

"They believed enough and that's all I care about for now."

"Daddee! I wanna help," Dilly called. Her footsteps gained speed and Mercy stepped away. "Auntie Mercy, help me help." She barreled around the corner into the kitchen work area. By then Mercy was at the cupboard that held the dishes.

"Here you go, Dilly," she said and passed her the unbreakable plates they'd taken to using with her. She flashed Clay a look of longing and set about helping Dilly set the table.

The L word had come up. Not in the *I love you* context, but close enough. She did love that he was open to having his sister crash back into his life with her children in tow. It was the truth. How could there be any harm in saying so?

What had floored her was that he said it back. This felt like more than a fling. At least for her. She cast Clay a sidelong glance as he pulled fresh vegetables out of the crisper in the fridge.

"Stir fry," he said. "That's quick."

"And 'lishus. Yay!"

Clay laughed. "She likes to hear the sizzle from the wok."

"You're a great dad," Mercy said with conviction because he tried hard to be everything Dilly needed.

He froze, and after a moment of consideration, his jaw went tight. She could see him struggle with words, but in the end, he said nothing.

She couldn't understand why Clay had a hard time accepting a compliment on his parenting, but she left him to his thoughts and focused on chopping vegetables for the wok. Dilly stayed out of the way of the knives and waited patiently, chattering to herself.

After the vegetables were prepared, Mercy heard her phone ring. Assuming it was Logan, she dashed to her purse to answer, but it was her mom. "You have to call your agent. That Esme woman left a message. Then she hung up before I could get any information out of her. She's rude."

"Esme called? She's brusque, Mom, and insanely busy." Before she could take the phone into Clay's office and close the door, Dilly called to her for help with something.

"Are you at Clay's?" her mom asked. "Is that Dilly I hear?"

"Yes, Clay's going out and I'm here to be with Dilly," she said through a niggle of guilt.

Silence, but Mercy refused to break it. Then a huff came to her ear. "Let me know what this call from the agency is about right away," her mom demanded.

"It's likely nothing important, but I'll let you know."

"Right away." The tone pushed for a vow.

"Yes, I promise, Mom." She lifted the phone away from her mouth. "Dilly, it's time to wash your hands. Sorry, Mom, I have to go. She needs my help."

Chapter Fifteen

MERCY MADE THE CALL to Esme from Clay's den at the front of the house. "Esme, it's Mercy Talbot."

"I'm glad you called. There's some news. *Roger's Lie* got a best-picture nom at the World Film Festival in Barcelona."

"That's wonderful!" Everyone involved in *Roger's Lie* deserved recognition and she cheered inside for all they'd accomplished on a shoestring.

"There's more. You got a best-supporting-actress nomination." Her raspy voice warmed in Mercy's ear but she could barely hear over the buzzing of a thousand bees in her head. She fell heavily into Clay's leather recliner.

"What?"

"The list was just announced. You're on it, honey."

The rest of the conversation blurred and Mercy only caught half of it. Esme was listing all the people who'd called asking about her. She heard the names of casting directors, producers, and A-list actors. She couldn't sort all the news because her brain shut down.

"I'm sorry. I have to go. People are waiting and Dilly's hungry and—"

"It's a lot to take in." Esme chuckled. Esme *never* chuckled. "We'll talk tomorrow after all this sinks in. But Mercy, don't talk to anyone without checking with me first. We'll be in touch about our next move."

Next move. It had been so long since she'd had a next move to contemplate, she wasn't sure she remembered how. But she still understood that it was Esme she'd be talking to. She doubted Mr. Chastain would bother.

Exhilaration, validation, glorious joy, ran over fear, disbelief, and ended in dread. The maelstrom boiled and rolled and brought on waves of nausea. This was it. This was her dream come true.

Then why the dread?

She didn't know, couldn't understand. Didn't want it. But the dread grew with each moment.

After several minutes and a few swipes at her wet eyes, Mercy pulled to her feet. She had to return to the kitchen looking normal.

She couldn't let Dilly or Clay see the turmoil the phone call had brought. She had to keep it together until she could think clearly.

After Dilly went to bed, she'd tell Clay her life had taken another weird turn. She wanted nothing more than to run out to the table and blurt the news. She wanted to feel unadulterated joy, but she couldn't.

Her decisions going forward had to be thought through. Running back to Hollywood on impulse was what the old Mercy would do. Today, the new Mercy was in charge and she was a better person.

She'd developed obligations and responsibilities to others in her personal life and in her work life. Mercy Talbot was needed by other people for the first time.

And she loved it. She loved them. She loved Dilly and Clay, even Logan for giving her a chance. She appreciated Karen, struggling to get through every day for the love of her dogs. She'd found new depths to her father and she'd come to see the sacrifices her mother had made over the years. She'd come to grips with her grief over Janna.

But this news could open doors and bring her dead dreams back to life.

She'd choose her moment to tell Clay about the phone call. She'd gauge his response and then decide how much more she should share. Esme had blown her composure to atomic particles and there was no way to put everything back to the way it was.

But she couldn't see the right, best path to her future. A voice inside her head spoke of caution. Just because she was nominated, didn't mean she'd win. And while it was a thrill, an international film festival in Spain didn't mean she'd have smooth sailing from here on.

HALF AN HOUR AFTER Dilly's bedtime ritual, Clay climbed into his soaker tub with her and settled behind her. She sighed and leaned back against his chest, feeling the slippery slide of his wet flesh at her back. Tugging his arms around her, she let the warm bath do its magic on her sore muscles.

"There was a lot of action at the kennels today. Three new dogs came in but four were adopted," she said.

"Karen told me." He skimmed his hands up her arms to her shoulders and began to knead her there. "Will you tell me what that phone call was about? When you got back to the kitchen your color was high and you looked ready to dance out of your shoes."

She stilled. Too bad they weren't facing each other because she'd love to read his eyes as she told him her news. "My agency called."

He stopped kneading but kept his palms on her shoulders. The silence from him prompted her to break into a sweat.

"I had a meaty part in an indie last year. I played a kidnap victim who went from pleading for her life to making a clever plan to escape and then being brave enough to make it work. Unfortunately, my character ran out into the street to get help and was killed by a car.

The kidnappers murdered the driver and took my body. The rest of the movie was about keeping up the pretense that their victim was still alive."

"Sounds great. And?"

"It was a pivotal role. I got to prove I had range. I showed fear, courage, and daring. Screen time was short but the whole movie hinged on me being able to engage the audience and make them care that I'd died."

She felt him nod. "What does this mean for the woman whose dreams were dead?" He stiffened up with every word, his voice going distant.

She spoke carefully because he was scaring her with his stillness. "The movie's been nominated for best picture in a small but prestigious film festival. Indie films can take a long time to catch on if they do at all. It's a miracle anyone saw me, let alone caught my name."

"People noticed? What people?"

"I was nominated for best supporting actress in an action film. It's not that big a deal." She was still reeling from all the names of actors and directors who'd been calling Chastain's office. But Clay's reaction made her cautious. She didn't say any more.

Never mind that indie role *this* was the best performance of her life. Thank God he couldn't see her face. His distant voice, his lack of interest all pointed to disappointment.

She turned her head to watch his expression. "You don't look pleased," she said.

"Sure I am." He gave her a quick smile, but the nod that came with it was terse. He wasn't sure how to react.

"I can see you're surprised by all this. Believe me, I am too."

"It must be gratifying to get some validation for all your work and study."

"Yes, it is," she whispered because she was afraid to tell him the rest. The water shifted around them as she faced forward again. She tensed and the warm bathwater suddenly felt chill.

"I can't stay tonight," she said. "My mom knows about the call, and if I don't get home and put out that fire she'll go ballistic." She climbed out of the tub.

He didn't move to join her, just sat with a face carved from granite. She wrapped her body in a towel and escaped from the bathroom. When she was dressed she didn't bother to return to the bathroom for a kiss goodbye. "I'll call you later," she called through the doorway as she left the room fighting tears.

THE BEGINNING OF THE end. That's what this was, Clay decided. Mercy had the news she'd been waiting for. What more would she need to hear before she headed back to the life she wanted?

He slipped between the sheets that smelled of her, rolled to his back and cupped his head in his palms. Staring at the slow-moving fan overhead, he waited for his heart to slow and his mind to clear. She'd be leaving soon.

He'd almost believed that she'd stay. Her confession last week had nearly convinced him that she had no more interest in pursuing her career.

Thank God Elle was coming back. He'd have his hands full getting her trailer swapped out for a bigger one. He'd fill more time getting to know her kids. He'd be too busy to miss Mercy. Way too busy.

Dilly would miss her like hell.

He rolled to his side and punched his pillow into shape. He'd make damn sure Mercy stayed in his daughter's life. As soon as the thought came, he softened. Mercy would never walk away from Dilly.

She loved his daughter like her own; it was in her eyes, her voice, and in her easy affection with Dilly. Mercy had taken on Hope in a fierce battle to protect Dilly from the rejections and hard knocks Janna had faced.

He wasn't pissed off for Dilly; he was pissed because he was the one who'd miss Mercy. He'd miss her in his house, his bed, his life. He'd miss thinking about her—how her day went, how she came home from the kennels smelling of dog and not caring that her hands were scratched and her nails ragged. Who'd have believed a woman who'd spent her life being perfection on two legs would wade into rescue work like she was born to it?

Sleep evaded him until he climbed out of bed and went down to his office. He had checks to write and other business items to see to.

"DADDY, ARE YOU IN THERE?" Dilly's fingers threatened to blind him as she tried pulling open his eyelids. His head was at a weird angle and his pillow as hard as wood. He clasped Dilly's hand. "Yes, Punk, I'm awake." He lifted his head. He'd fallen asleep at his desk. His mouth tasted like brine. He swore his eyeballs had been rolled in a sandbox.

Dilly looked fresh and sweet. Her hair was a cloud of soft waves and her eyes looked solemn. "How come you slept here?"

"I didn't mean to. I was working and got sleepy." He stood and stretched. "Let's get you some breakfast. While you eat it, I'll take a quick shower."

She promised not to do anything but sit at the table and eat, but still, he dashed upstairs, took the fastest shower he could and dressed quickly. When he was done, he looked over the railing from the gallery and saw her waiting. "You can put your dishes on the counter now," he said as he combed his hair. "Then come upstairs to get dressed. Auntie Mercy got your clothes out for you."

"I want my purple pants."

"They're dirty. Remember you fell in the puddle?"

"I want my purple paaaaants!" She threw her dishes into the sink with a clatter.

Thank God Mercy had found some unbreakable ones for Dilly. She said it would do Dilly good to help more and be responsible for her own dishes. Mercy was right—as long as Dilly didn't use the dishes as a weapon.

"I'll brush my teeth and when I'm finished I'm coming to your room," he said. "When I get there, I want to see you getting dressed." He didn't give a rat's ass what pants she wore, but he couldn't allow a challenge to go unanswered.

Dilly put on her angriest face and marched across the living room to the stairs. Every step up was a thudding commentary on her determination to get her own way. Clay controlled a smile.

As he brushed his teeth, he hoped he could keep his sense of humor when Mercy told him the rest of whatever that phone call was about because, in the darkest hours of the night, he realized she hadn't told him everything. He'd spent the next hours wondering what it would mean to an actor to have a nomination like hers.

He braced himself and headed to Dilly's room to see what clothes she'd put on.

"MERCY, THIS WILL MEAN you can write your own ticket. Casting agents will be crawling all over you," Hope's voice rose in excitement over breakfast. "I can barely eat, I'm so thrilled."

Mercy gave her father a *help me* look, but he looked as addled as Hope did.

"This was voted on by the judges at the festival?" Nate asked.

"Of course it was," her mother answered. "Mercy, that entertainment magazine will soon start collecting votes. Let's hope they take notice of your nomination and put you on the list."

"No, Mom, not likely." Her eggs tasted like chalk. "Those awards are about big-budget Hollywood movies, not quiet films like *Roger's Lie*." They'd filmed on a tight budget and focused on the disintegration of the men in the kidnapping gang more than wild action.

"It would be fabulous if they did though."

Her dad chimed in again. "That would mean regular people voting, kiddo. Not the types that criticize and schmooze with the A-list actors. Regular people have a say in those nominations."

"That's right," Mercy said with a nod. "But let's not get ahead of ourselves. Esme will keep in touch." She paused until she had their full attention. "In the meantime, we can't talk to the press."

Hope gasped. "I knew this day would come. You're having your own press conference." Her eyes gleamed with ambition fulfilled.

"Mom, stop. Being nominated is an honor, but it's unlikely to take my career where you think it should." She'd kept a lot of last night's conversation to herself. Phone calls and inquiries from casting directors didn't mean much unless there was money involved. Esme would call if anything firm came in.

Life in Hollywood had taught her to be realistic. Getting her hopes up now was a fool's game.

While she wanted to keep the lid on her parents' excitement, her mind turned constantly to Clay and Dilly. What must he think of her after she ran out last night? It must have been obvious she was escaping more questions.

Questions like the ones her parents kept asking. "Look, I'll call Esme as soon as the office opens and I'll get more details," she promised. "But I am not rushing back to L.A." Again, she waited until her mother looked her in the eyes. "I don't want what I used to want." She didn't. No more wasted ambitions on a business that could kill her soul. She was no wide-eyed ingénue with huge dreams. Not anymore.

And that was the unvarnished truth. A truth that rocked her to her core.

She didn't want her old dreams resurrected. She wanted new dreams and a new life. She wanted Clay and Dilly.

Hope was the first to sputter to life after the shock wore off. "If you don't want your acting career, then what do you want? For the love of God, Mercy, what *do* you *want*?"

"In Hollywood? I don't know." No matter that she'd been nominated, no matter that some casting directors had taken note of her name, no matter that the film role was opening some previously shut doors, she didn't care. "I'd like to pick and choose my next roles and work in films I feel strongly about." A pipe dream for someone like her. The mega-famous had options like that, not actors without box-office appeal.

Mercy Talbot no longer judged herself on her Hollywood successes. Today, she knew who she was: Clay Foster's woman and Dilly Foster's auntie and Logan Hughes's assistant. But she was still Hope Talbot's daughter, and that meant that she *had* to see what all this attention would bring. She'd worked hard for so long that surely it couldn't hurt to ride out this wave to see where she landed.

Her dad cleared his throat. "I suggest you take time to consider your options. You don't want to commit to something, even verbally, if it isn't what you want." His gaze searched hers until heat rose in her cheeks. "Not in any area of your life."

Her business phone rang and she hurried to her purse to answer. She sounded breathy but businesslike as she took the call. "Sorry to call this early, Mercy," Logan said, "but I have to go out of town until tomorrow. Can you handle my ten o'clock? The Morrisons need their hands held through some color choices and upgrade decisions."

"Of course. I'll be there," she said. "What model did they decide on?"

"The Excelsior. The wife wants top-of-the-line and he wants to keep her spending in check."

"I've met them. He'll need to believe he's made a good deal. Don't worry, we'll sort it out." *Compromise.* Mid-range prices would suit Mr. Morrison on flooring and cabinetry while higher-end appliances would appeal to Mrs. Morrison. "You can count on me," she promised.

"I know. You've been great, Mercy. You should consider getting your license. You'd do well."

"You think?" Praise rained down from all quarters after a long drought. She grinned.

"Absolutely," Logan said. "I'll check in later and see how you're doing." He disconnected. This was his first overnight absence and she'd picked up a sense of relief in his tone. But she couldn't ponder Logan's family problems right now.

She faced her waiting parents. "There's an appointment I have to take care of. I need to go now. I'll call Esme later after I've had time to think."

She made certain to take both cell phones with her when she left the room to get ready for work. The Morrisons weren't due at the office until ten, but Mercy couldn't bear any more scrutiny from her parents.

When she gained the privacy of her bedroom, she called Clay. "I need to see you today. Can you swing by the office around noon? I should be finished my meeting by then."

"Sure, but I'll be dropping Dilly off shortly."

Mercy twined her hair around her finger in agitation. "I want to talk to you alone, without distractions. And please, don't engage with my mother before you see me. She's all mixed up about that call last night. She's excited."

There was a long pause. "Okay."

She heard some high-pitched yowls in the background. "Do I hear Dilly?"

"In fine form. She's mad because I'm making her wait to put on her purple pants."

"Weren't they in the dirty laundry? I laid out a sundress for her today."

"And it's a pretty one, but she's not wearing dresses anymore. Nice of her to inform me."

Mercy chuckled. "So you washed the pants?"

"Kind of. I scrubbed the knees by hand to get the worst of the mud out and now we're waiting for the dryer to finish."

"Compromise. But why is she still mad?"

"This lovely display of temper you hear in the background is about the lime-green T-shirt that doesn't fit her anymore."

"Okay," she said with another chuckle. "Well, then, good luck, and I'll see you later." She still got a tiny bit breathless at the idea of seeing him alone. She hung up and held onto the giddy reaction for as long as she could.

"THANK YOU, MR. AND Mrs. Morrison," Mercy said as she waved the couple out of the office. "It's been a pleasure," she said. "I'm sure you'll both be happy with your choices."

Just as she'd thought, compromise was the best course. The wife got the upgrades she couldn't live without while her husband saved money where he could.

She accepted their thanks and said goodbye, all the while hoping Clay would arrive on time. She peered intently through the window, searching the street for any sign of him. The door opened from the hall and she turned to see the object of her hunt slip inside the office. He closed the door at his back and smiled in that way he had that spun her in circles. He looked tired around the eyes and his lips couldn't hold the grin for long.

"ARE YOU PLANNING TO seduce me, Ms. Talbot?" Clay did his best to keep up the pretense that he hadn't been up half the night thinking. "Because I'll confess I've had my fantasies about stretching you out on top of that desk." He nodded toward Logan's substantial antique oak workspace.

Mercy went along and laughed as she was meant to. "Is that your way of saying you want to prove you're top dog?"

He cocked an eyebrow. "You could be onto something." He could afford to be magnanimous about Hughes, the nice guy who'd lost. "I've been an ass about Logan on occasion."

She shrugged. "You have nothing to worry about as far as Logan and me."

"What else do I need to be concerned about?"

She bit her lip and moved toward him. He opened his arms and kissed her lightly on the lips. "Tell me, Mercy. There's more to that phone call than what you said last night. You ran out like a coward and that's just not you."

"I needed time to think. And . . . you didn't follow me." She rolled her eyes. "I had to fill my mother in last night or she'd have hunted me down."

"How does this nomination change things for you? What's the next move?" She had him on tenterhooks, but he stilled to listen.

MERCY SAW CLAY GO STILL. "The next move is I wait and keep quiet." She couldn't control the thrills inside as she admitted the reality of what had once been a dream. "My agency has been getting calls from people."

"You need to be more specific, Mercy. This isn't my world so I don't know who you mean by 'people.'" His expression was impossible to read.

She leaned back to better see his face. "Casting agents, directors, even an A-lister looking for a new face to pair with." His eyelids dropped as she spoke. Her belly contracted to cold stone. "Clay?"

His face turned diamond hard and when he lifted his gaze to hers she could see clear down to his soul. Icy. Distant.

Gone.

"You're scaring me, Clay. Say something," she whispered.

He set her away from him. "You have to go back." His hands dropped from her forearms, his body rigid, his jaw clenched. "To Hollywood. That's where you belong."

She tilted her head to better see his eyes. "No, I don't. I belong here." He wouldn't look her in the eye.

"Taking calls for a one-man office?" His voice turned to gravel, raw and sharp-edged.

"That's not what I mean and you know it. I belong with you and Dilly." Fear gripped her heart as she understood what her sister had lived with. Clay Foster could turn to ice before a woman's eyes. There was no getting through the arctic chill in his gaze. No chipping away at the glacial façade.

She wanted to pummel him. She wanted to heat him with kisses. She wanted—oh, God—she wanted to plead.

"You'll never be happy here now," he said in a voice laden with regret. "We'll never be enough for you, not when all you've worked for is right there, within reach." He lifted a hand as if holding an invisible ball. "If you let this chance go, you'll regret it for the rest of your life."

She stood immobile, unable to speak in her defense.

He turned the door handle at his back and opened the door. "It's best we end things now before it blows up in our faces. We kept everything to ourselves. Dilly will miss you, but you'll still be in her life. You'll always be her auntie, Mercy." His voice had gone hoarse, but his eyes grew colder if that were possible.

"You can't be serious. You want to end things? Completely?" She wasn't sure she understood.

Clay was tossing her away like a fast-food wrapper. She was litter in his life, easy to dispose of, immediately forgotten. Words choked her throat but refused to come until pride came to her rescue. She smoothed her hands down her skirt. "Yes, well, I suppose this is for the best, then."

He ducked out the door as if he couldn't get away from her fast enough.

It wasn't until she heard the downstairs door slam against the frame that she knew he'd left and wouldn't climb the stairs to retract his killing words. Clay wouldn't change his mind. Wouldn't love her back.

Pride evaporated as she crumpled and sobbed against the wall.

She'd hit bottom in J.D.'s office, but that was nothing compared to being in love with a man who wanted her gone.

Chapter Sixteen

AFTER CLAY WALKED OUT on her and she'd collapsed into a puddle of self-pity, Mercy took a few minutes to pull herself together and regain her feet. Sitting in a big old pile of loss and heartbreak would not make things better.

She locked the Hughes Realty office door so no one could come in without warning. She needed time alone.

She'd been rejected before, she'd failed before, and she'd been dumped by text before. But nothing had prepared her for the emotional devastation of Clay Foster. How was she to behave normally around Dilly now? She had to find a way. She smeared her wet cheeks until they dried and then she pulled her makeup bag out of her purse for a touch-up.

As she stared at her reflection in the office washroom mirror, she recalled the role of the washed-up hag that Esme had mentioned. She'd be perfect. Wan, empty eyes, sallow cheeks, quivering lower lip; she looked beaten down by life.

She straightened, forced her lip to still and leaned in to reapply concealer, blush, and lipstick. No one but *no one* would see her laid to waste. A glimpse of her mother's haughtiness danced across her face. Everything Hope had taught her about presenting the right image filled her mind. Thank God for her mother's training.

After adding notes to the Morrison file about her meeting with them she checked the company email, saw nothing that couldn't wait until the morning, and closed up shop for the day.

By the time she arrived home, she felt stronger about facing her parents. Her mother would be distracted by all the good news.

It was her father who might see past the makeup. She put on a happy expression and prepared to do her best.

"I expected you to be packed by now and heading to Los Angeles," her dad commented from his favorite chair in the den. Her mother sat on the sofa doing a word puzzle. Humphrey was snuggled close to her side. Mercy perched on her father's footstool.

"Logan needs me and I won't leave without giving him a few days' notice." Days when she'd have to pretend her heart was still intact. Days when she'd have to pretend her brother-in-law was just her dead sister's husband. Days when looking at Dilly would make her want to sob.

But of course, she could share none of that. "Esme says we'll wait to see if anything else is brewing. Patience is key, she tells me." Being patient had gotten her broke, unwanted, and living back at home.

Her mother searched her face. "Nate," her mother said, "Humphrey needs a walk."

Nate nodded. "Come on, Humphrey. Walk." The dog jumped off the sofa and headed toward his leash in the mudroom.

Heaven help her, she had to face the dragon. After the day she'd had, she didn't need Hope's version of mothering.

To Hope, mothering meant telling Mercy what to do and how to feel while she was doing it. This, she didn't need. Not today. Not when her whole heart had shattered.

After her father left, Mercy made to rise from the footstool, but Hope put a hand on her forearm to stop her. She sagged back into her seat.

"What? You're going to tell me how happy I should be?" Mercy asked. "How I should be finding a hotel in L.A. to wait with my breath held for more nominations?"

"All of that, yes. Of course. But this is about more than your career. You've been happy lately. Fulfilled. I don't think it's your job, though anyone can see you like it and you're good at it. And it's not Logan, although he'd make a good husband someday."

Oh, no. Hope knew about Clay, Mercy was certain of it. "I'm concerned about Dilly," Mercy said, to forestall any questions about Clay. She rose and went to the dining room where she absently stacked her dad's empty plate on her mom's. "I'll clear the table."

"Leave it for me, my rehearsal doesn't start for an hour." Hope hesitated as seconds ticked by. "We're concerned for Dilly all the time. Our lives revolve around that child, but there's Clay, too." She drew in a breath and Mercy wondered if when it came out there'd be flames along with it.

"You've grown attached to him." Surprisingly, her mother's voice was calm and slightly consoling. "It's natural that you'd feel an affinity. He's your last connection to Janna and the father of your niece. But Clay is not the man you want him to be."

Mercy turned her eyes to Hope's. "He's the cold bastard my sister always said he was."

Hope's face sagged into despair. "Oh, Mercy, please tell me you haven't fallen for him."

Mercy straightened and decided it was easier to come clean. "Be assured, Clay doesn't want me. As soon as I've seen to my responsibilities with Logan, I plan to head back to L.A." There was nothing but heartache in Welcome. "I need to shower and change and get some things in order."

"Of course," Hope said. "Be kind to yourself. Remember all the good you've done here. Including with me," she said softly. "I see things differently now, Mercy. Thanks to you."

Mercy stood and kissed the top of her mother's head. "I knew I could out-stubborn you."

She went to her room and stripped. Before she slipped into her robe to head across the hall to the bathroom, her phone rang. "Mercy Talbot," she answered.

"Mercy, glad I caught you."

"Esme? You could have waited for the morning when you're back in the office." It was past eight. Did the woman never wind down? She heard a man's voice booming in the background. "Is that Mr. Chastain?"

"Yes, we just got home."

"You're not just his assistant? You're together?"

"Married for over twenty years. Hollywood's worst-kept secret."

It made sense now. Esme's interest and help with her career lately. Mr. Chastain hadn't had faith in Mercy, but his wife had. And Esme hadn't given up on her. "No, I didn't know. Thank you, Esme. For not giving up when I did."

"Aw, honey, I just kept my ears open. And look what's happened. We've had more calls." She named two competing action movie directors. "They love how plucky you were. Scared to death, but brave. That's what they want in their next movies."

A shiver ran over her naked flesh and Mercy groped for her robe. "I don't know what to say."

"Say nothing yet. *Nothing.* If you get calls for interviews, ignore them. We don't want you to look committed to either project just yet. There's a lot we need to discuss. Who's your PR team now?"

There it was; the reminder that she was a nobody. "You'll have to find me one."

"Fine. You'll need a business manager too."

"Will I?" She froze. Clay said this was what she was supposed to do, where she was supposed to be, but she was quickly being overwhelmed with decisions. "I've never needed one." She'd barely made enough to live without a roommate. A business manager was not for actors with her track record.

"You need to come back, honey," Esme said. "We need to talk in person about all this. I'll book a hotel for you. How soon can you get here? Or would you rather come stay with us?"

"I–I'll let you know." Stay with them? This was Esme, being maternal. "It'll be early next week." She fudged on the timing so she could wrap her mind around all that was happening.

That's how it went in Hollywood. One day they wouldn't spit on you if you were on fire, the next, you were golden.

Right now, she felt as if she were silver—tarnished, pitted silver.

"Mercy. This is important," Esme said in her usual brusque tone. "I understand your mother's been a big part of your career, but you have to make it clear she can't talk to the press. Not the locals and not anyone on the phone."

"Of course. I'll tell her."

"There's a room ready for you if you want to hide out with us. Just for the short term. We need to handle things delicately from here, sign you with the best PR and business-management people. Don't worry about a thing. Just get here." The line went dead.

She hung up with numb fingers. A tidal wave had swept her up and there was no telling where she'd land. Or if she'd survive the ride.

After a brief shower that did nothing to wash away the pain of Clay's dismissal, but hid her tears well, Mercy found her mother getting ready to leave for rehearsal. "I heard your voice on the phone. Was it Esme? Anything new?"

"A couple of things, but nothing concrete." She couldn't face more enthusiasm from her parents. They believed her whole future was now set, while Mercy couldn't be more confused. She forged ahead in a firm voice. "Esme made it clear that we have to keep mum. It's vital that no one learns I've had offers. It's all PR and planning. You understand how important secrecy is right now?"

Hope looked affronted as she stepped to the door. "Of course. Do you think that I'll run around town gossiping about you?"

"Yes, I do." Mercy crossed her arms and stood firm. "You cannot breathe a word of this."

Hope shrugged while her glance slid to the floor. "I may have mentioned the nomination at the rehearsal last night."

The nomination news was the least of Mercy's concerns. "But nothing else?"

"No. Not a word about possible offers." Hope bent to slip into her shoes and Mercy couldn't read her face, but she sounded truthful.

Her mom refusing bragging rights felt off. "Why not?"

"I wasn't sure what you'd end up deciding." As she rose to her full height, Hope's gaze slid sideways. "I can't tell what's going on with you anymore. And I didn't want to look the fool if you chose not to go."

Mercy had shaken Hope Talbot to the core. Hard to believe. "My coming home, getting a job, and volunteering with the dogs have changed me and you. Dad, too." Nate had put his foot down and argued with Hope. He'd stood up for Dilly, kept his garage for himself, and defended Clay. The quiet man had spoken loud and strong.

Hope threw her hands up. "I can't tell you what to do next. You've been seeing Clay, working your fingers to the bone with those dangerous dogs and now you're putting some part-time job before offers from Hollywood. God knows what this will do to Dilly. She's used to you putting her to bed, being there for dinner, taking her to the park. Don't think I don't know about this." Hope wrung her hands and her eyes filled.

She saw no point prevaricating anymore. "Clay and I are over, but we've been circumspect around Dilly. She sees me as her auntie, nothing more."

Hope's eyes filled with moisture. "I've been hard on Clay. And . . . and . . . I know that Janna was . . . difficult." She struggled for words. "Clay was the one who stepped up the moment Dilly was born." Her face fell into despair. "I denied it all along." She covered her face and shook her head. "But Janna, my Janna, she just didn't feel the way most women do when they have a child."

Mercy pulled her mother into her arms. "That doesn't mean we love Janna any less. We just have to accept that she was Janna, being Janna."

"I'm afraid, Mercy. Afraid for Dilly."

"You don't need to worry, Mom. Dilly loves fiercely, freely, and with her whole heart."

Hope sniffed and pulled herself together with a step back. "You think?"

"I'm positive. You should see her with Beau. She loves that dog. She's a caring child who knows her own mind. You've seen too much of her temper is all."

"I guess you're right. Sometimes she hates me and my rules. But she's blossomed with you in her life."

Mercy's heart warmed and beat faster as she accepted her mom's praise.

"Tee-ball was a great idea," Hope said. "Janna was athletic. It's good to see the same traits in her daughter. And Dilly's in good hands with Clay." Hope sniffed, but not with derision. Her admission had been sincere.

"I'm happy you've come to believe that." She held her mom's shoulders. "But Clay's the one who needs to hear it. He doubts himself."

"You'd never know it." Hope huffed out an echo of her previous attitude. Then she softened. "I'll tell him."

"You've been angry with him for years."

"You noticed, huh?" Hope gave her a tremulous smile.

But Mercy didn't question this turnaround, she welcomed it.

"Now," Hope said, "back to the matter at hand. You have to pack and get yourself on a plane to LAX. You'll need a hotel room and maybe we should put it in your father's name in case—"

"No," she interjected. "Not yet. Logan needs me and I'm not leaving him in the lurch." She'd never sounded more like Janna in her life: determined, confident, and obstinate. "I'll let you know my timing in the morning." She needed to think, to separate everything into columns titled needs, wants, wishes and dreams.

Those columns were tangled up in her mind like yarn. It would take a whole night of deep consideration before she could see her real future, not the one her mother dreamed of. "Mom," she said softly to ease the blow. "I'm not sure what I'll decide."

Hope blinked back tears. "You'll decide what's best. But I will say it's ridiculous to abandon everything you've worked hard for. Your dreams are coming true."

And that was the crux of Mercy's dilemma. She was no longer certain if she'd been pursuing her own dreams all these years—or Hope's.

THE NEXT DAY, CLAY stood in the office at the manufactured home dealer and signed off on the purchase agreement. A slightly used three-bedroom would be delivered next week. After trade-in for the older model, the price was better than Clay had expected.

But even this pleasant surprise was not enough to ease him. Mercy was leaving and taking his heart with her. How the hell was he supposed to move on from this?

He'd stupidly spun fairytale endings in his head. He could hear his old man snort at the idea that Clay might find happiness. *What makes you think you deserve a second chance? Of course, she's leaving. A woman like Mercy would never want the likes of you.*

He signed the deal for his sister's home and headed for his car. He had to calm down before driving. That's all Dilly needed, another parent dead in a car crash. He sat behind the steering wheel staring at the shards of his life.

Sybil called. He answered. "There's a dog over at Bushmill Farms. She got into a fight with something she shouldn't have. The owner says she's pretty torn up. How soon can you get here?"

"I'll be there before they are." *Torn up.* He knew the feeling. "Call Hope and let her know I'll be later than usual."

"Already done."

There were days Sybil was worth every dime he paid her. "Thanks. I'm on my way."

LONG AFTER THE CLINIC had closed, with the Bushmill's retriever stitched up and sleeping comfortably Clay called Hope's cell phone. "Would you bring Dilly out to my place?"

"Nate can," Hope said. "Are you sick?"

"No, I've had a long day and it's not over yet." He had to go through the old mobile out back to see if there was anything there he needed to remove. He'd fallen into the habit of using it for storage and now he wasn't sure what was out there.

"Nate will bring her. I'm off for rehearsal soon."

Mild surprise came as he realized Hope hadn't given him a hard time. He couldn't face seeing Mercy again after how he'd treated her yesterday. "Thanks, Hope. Tell Nate I'll be in the house out back."

"What are you doing with it?"

"Elle's coming home. She'll need a place to live. I'm moving a bigger unit onto the lot out back for her."

"She can't stay in your house? You have lots of room."

"She's got four children and they'll need more space and privacy."

"I see. Is her husband coming too? Surely they won't be with you for long?"

He closed his eyes and reminded himself again that he was grateful for all her help with Dilly. "They'll be there for as long as they need." He didn't bother mentioning his sister's single state. Hope would find out soon enough because she'd ask people until she got an answer.

"Mercy didn't mention this, Clay."

"I'm sure there's a lot she didn't mention."

"Apparently." Hope sniffed. "But all those children. Are you sure they'll be a good influence on Dilly?"

This was pure Hope Talbot wielding disapproval like an ax. She would never let him forget he was still a Foster. If there was anyone Hope hated more than Clay, it was his sister, Elle.

Hope had never forgiven Elle for the brawl Hope refused to believe Janna had started. Elle had finished it, but not until the cops had been called. He closed his eyes at the remembered humiliation. His girlfriend and his sister, fighting over him. Maybe Hope's assessment wasn't too far off after all.

When he let her question hang in silence, she huffed, "I'll tell Nate to find you out at the old trailer."

"Thanks." He hung up. As much as he loved his sister, Hope had a point. Elle must be overrun with four kids to raise and throwing Dilly into that mess of unknown cousins may not be the best choice. The idea of a real daycare flitted through his mind. There was a good one a block over from the clinic.

Maybe Dilly would enjoy being with other children her age in a busy environment. Daycare would be good for her. It was past time to ease off his dependence on Hope.

His mother-in-law would scream blue murder at first, but once Mercy was in Hollywood Hope would be back and forth a lot, seeing to Mercy's career. She'd lived that way before Janna's death. It seemed reasonable she'd want to do it again.

Everything had changed since Mercy had come home. And now, it looked as if it would all go sideways again.

Elle would be here with her brood. He'd be a face-to-face uncle rather than some guy who called at the holidays. Dilly would have cousins and another aunt.

With all that going on, he'd have no time to miss Mercy. No time at all.

But he already did.

Chapter Seventeen

MERCY ARRIVED AT THE office after hours to meet with Logan to fill him in on her news. When she stepped inside, he was on the phone. His voice rose. "Damn it, Jamie, can't you keep it together long enough to get there without me?" He dropped his head into his hand. "Fine, I'll take you." He tossed the phone down.

He looked up and his handsome face went blotchy with embarrassment. "Sorry you had to see my temper."

"It's okay. That was your brother?"

He shook his head in sad acceptance. "I want to tell you what's going on with me—us—my family." He sighed long and deep as he gathered his composure. "Jamie's finally going to rehab and he wants me to take him. Mom's a wreck and Dad's washed his hands of the whole mess."

This was what Karen had hinted at. How she gleaned all the gossip without sitting in a coffee shop all day was beyond her. "I had no idea you were dealing with this. I don't remember hearing about Jamie being troubled back in school."

Logan leaned back in his chair and squared his shoulders. "It started with football injuries in college. The coach wanted him playing, Dad couldn't afford to send him without a full ride, and the doctor gave him some heavy pain meds to get him over the hump."

"I see." She knew plenty of decent people who'd gone down the same road. "Prescription drugs can be hard to kick."

"Especially when the user likes them. Jamie got through college, but he never got clean."

"Is that why you came back from Tacoma?"

He nodded. "I'd like to say Jamie tried, but once he got a job he had more money. By then he'd developed a talent for lying. He could get prescriptions anywhere. He's a charmer, my brother." He snorted. "Anyway, I have to hand-deliver him or else he won't show up and that would kill my mom."

"How can I help?" She refused to burden Logan with her impending departure.

"Just be here. I have some appointments you can handle. Anything I need to sign can wait." He gave her a ghost of his usual grin. "I'm grateful."

"How long will you be gone?"

"A couple of nights tops. We'll fly because I don't want him to spend any more time worrying about this than necessary. The longer we delay, the greater the chance he'll change his mind and run again."

"Again?"

"He's taken to disappearing and I'm sick of tracking him down and dragging his ass back home. Dad's written him off, but my mom's hanging on."

She nodded, overcome by his pain and disillusionment. "I understand."

His gaze sharpened. "That's right. You've kind of been where I am." The vague reference to Janna's rebellion was a kindness. They both knew what he was saying.

She offered him a wan smile. "Let's hope Jamie has a happy ending. I'm overdue for seeing one."

He rose from his chair and enveloped her in a grateful hug. "You're the best, Mercy."

"You're the only person who believes that," she quipped.

He pulled back to consider her. His eyes crinkled at the corners in humor. "I'm not alone in thinking you're special. Clay's halfway in love with you."

She shook her head. "That's where you're wrong." She stepped out of his arms. "Now go, before Jamie changes his mind."

"I'll see you in two days," he said and grabbed his cell phone. "Call me with questions. I'll be available." He left with a grim but determined glint in his eye.

The thing about being halfway in love was that Clay was also halfway out of it.

It wouldn't be right to leave Logan hanging. She was grateful to him and she owed him a lot. He didn't deserve to fall behind in this fledgling business just because of her.

She'd happily give him his two days. More like three or four if she wanted to give him any kind of notice. She called Karen to tell her she'd be busier than usual at the office and it was unlikely she'd be at the kennels for the next couple of days. She didn't mention why. Let Karen get her gossip elsewhere.

What Logan had said about Clay being in love with her set her back to where she'd been the night before: pining and feeling broken. If she went to him, he'd only repeat the nonsense he'd said before. How ending things now was better than waiting. How Dilly wouldn't be affected by their split. He'd said Mercy belonged in Hollywood.

She didn't.

She belonged here, with him and Dilly.

It rankled that Clay had said he and Dilly wouldn't be enough for her. He assumed she'd regret choosing them over her career.

He couldn't be more wrong.

But how could she get through to him that what they shared didn't have to end? They'd both been wrong to make that assumption. Just because his marriage to Janna had gone sour and Mercy hadn't had a relationship last a full year didn't mean anything now.

Now was what they had.

Now was what they wanted. And any missteps in their pasts were just that . . . steps that had been mistakes.

Being with Clay was meant to be. But she was beyond figuring out how to get through to the stubborn man. Everything was a jumble with one clear shiny bit of joy: Dilly. No matter what happened, she'd have Dilly in her life.

"CLAY, ARE YOU INSIDE?" Nate's voice pulled Clay from his memories of living in the old mobile.

"In here," he called out the open door. "I've been looking through boxes I stored during construction of our new place."

Nate poked his head in and smiled. "I'm delivering a bundle of sweetness."

"Thanks, Nate. Dilly, come on up." The stairs to the door were old but sturdy. Nate held her hand as they climbed.

"What have you got there?" Nate asked as Dilly clung to Clay's knees and demanded kisses. Clay bent to her and smooched her into giggles.

When Dilly had had enough, she ran off to look around.

"I found a box full of my old gear from when I was a kid." He slipped his hand into his old ball glove. "I'll pass this along to my nephews if they have any interest." Dilly ran through all the rooms checking behind doors and closets, leaving the men to talk. "Mercy left yet?"

"Nope. She's still feeling her way through. I'd say she's overwhelmed. All kinds of calls from agents and business people who didn't know her name last week. We keep handing out her agency's phone number. But the press is calling, too. It's crazy."

Clay's belly rolled. This was all Mercy had wanted. Attention, adulation, her name on everyone's lips. He'd set that knowledge aside as she'd worked her way into his heart. The heart he massaged as he stood there. "An overnight sensation, as they say."

Nate snorted. "I'm not sure this sudden popularity is making her happy, though. In fact, she's damned uncomfortable. Unhappy, even. She's walking around stone-faced. If I didn't know better, I'd say she was hurting."

He narrowed his gaze. Nate seemed offhand, but with the Talbots, you never could tell. "What does her agent say about all this attention?" He already knew she was hurting. So was he. But better a clean break than a long, drawn-out process. He'd been through that kind of ending before. He didn't have the strength for another.

"They want her to come stay with them at their house, like a hideout. They're fielding calls from all kinds of people. Some big-name stars want to cast her as their leading lady. It's big time, all right. Big time. But mum's the word around town. We're not to talk to anyone about this."

Dilly came out from the back rooms, and Nate took her by the hand. "All I know is Hope's aflutter about all of it and Mercy's keeping to herself. I've given up trying to figure her out." He cocked his eyebrow at Clay. "You have any idea why she's hesitating?"

"Me? No. No idea." He gritted his teeth.

"Maybe she's grown attached to someone?"

Clay shook his head. "I wouldn't know."

"Maybe Logan Hughes. He's a good man. Steady as a rock." Nate turned to leave. "If you're done out here, I'll walk you back to the house." He didn't wait to see if Clay agreed or not, just moved off with Dilly.

"Come on, Daddy," she said, calling back to Clay while tugging on her grandfather's hand. "I wanna call Auntie Mercy to see if she'll put me to bed tonight."

Nate laughed. "She's been doing that a lot lately, eh, Dilly?"

"Yes, and she reads me stories and kisses me night-night."

Nate threw him a glance over his shoulder. "She does? Tell me all about it." He halted and waited for Clay to catch up with them. "Maybe you could talk some sense into Mercy about making a decision. Next time she's here helping put Dilly to bed, I mean."

"There won't be a next time," Clay said and moved on past them. Bitterness welled. What the hell was it with these Talbots? They were nothing but trouble, always had been, and always would be.

But there was one he didn't want to live without. He'd thrown Mercy out of his life and denied that what she felt for him was real enough, strong enough to withstand the career pressure she was under.

Maybe Janna was right all along. He was a cold bastard who didn't deserve happiness.

Hell, even his old man was right.

AFTER DINNER, HE SNAPPED at Dilly when she persisted in asking for Mercy, "Don't ask me again," he said. "She's not coming. Not tonight."

"How come?" Dilly whined in a way that grated on his last nerve.

He clamped his mouth shut, took her by the hand and led her upstairs. "It's bedtime. I'll read you your favorite story."

"No, I want Auntie Mercy." She dragged her feet until he picked her up.

"You can't have her." And neither could he. He'd made damn sure of that. In the end, Dilly cried until she fell asleep. Clay slid down the wall outside her room and sat on the floor staring at the ceiling with all the negative voices in his head battling for top spot.

AFTER DINNER, MERCY took a call from Esme again. After she hung up, Hope's eyes were gleaming with ambition. "Well, what did she say?" Hope asked. "She must have been furious that you're not going right away."

"You heard me explain about Logan."

"I heard hogwash and vague nonsense. Refusing to be specific about why you can't leave him right now just makes you look obstinate."

"What I said was sufficient. No one needs to know the details."

Her mother pursed her lips. "By no one you mean me."

"Yes. You." Mercy shouldered past her mother and headed toward the door to the garage. She needed out of this house, away from her parents' worry and their leading questions.

She needed time to mull her conversation with Esme. There'd been two more scripts delivered. Esme was emailing them now. She'd print them in the morning and take them to the office to read between appointments. She'd already informed the various people that she, and not Logan, would be seeing them. It was odd how comfortable she'd become dealing with the intricacies of selling houses.

She opened the door, but her mother's voice stopped her. "Mercy, come quick."

She headed toward the kitchen, where she found Hope staring out the window overlooking the street. "Clay's just pulled up. And he's coming in with flowers and a box in his hand."

"Roses and chocolates," she said on a soft breath that hid her thudding heart and ratcheting nerves.

Her dad came to join them at the window. He nodded. "Better get on out there and see what's what."

"What's what?" Hope said. "I'll tell you what's what. Mercy's going back to Hollywood no matter what Clay says. I don't know why he'd come around here and—"

"Hope," Nate said, "shut it. This is between them and it's time we let it be."

Mercy looked from one to the other of them. Her mother's face went red and Mercy figured her tongue must be swollen from biting it, and her dad looked calm, collected and carefully observant.

She smoothed her jeans down her thighs. She shook her head in doubt, unsure of what was happening. Clay was at the front door. The doorbell rang. Her belly rolled. "I thought he'd said everything he needed to say."

"I've got a feeling he's come up with a couple more things," Nate said. "Some men are slow at finding words."

Hope looked at him and the oddest light came into her eyes. "Oh, Nate, do you think?"

Mercy felt his hand on her shoulder. "Go on out now, Mercy. And listen to what he says and what he doesn't say."

She nodded and felt the icy grip of dread in her chest. What new hell did Clay have in mind for her? Was he angry that Dilly had asked for her? Nate had told her about his conversation with Clay when he dropped off Dilly this afternoon. She'd wanted to call and talk with her niece, but hadn't found the courage.

Now, she had no choice but to face Clay.

CLAY WAITED AFTER RINGING the doorbell, aware of Nate and Hope watching from the kitchen window. The irony was that he'd waited many times for their other daughter to join him in his car and they never saw a thing. He could hardly blame them for their curiosity now. His throat dried to a husk as he stood there aware of each breath ticking off the time.

Finally, Mercy opened the door, her eyes wide with an unreadable mix of emotions. One emotion rose above the others as she took in the sight of the long-stemmed roses and the box of chocolates in his hands.

"You look confused," he blurted.

She nodded. "I deserve to be." She looked toward the car. "Where's Dilly?"

Of course, she'd want to know if Dilly was safe and happy. One more thing to love about Mercy. "She's with Karen and Beau."

Mercy nodded but still looked skittish.

He and the Talbots had traveled a strange path these past few years, connected and disconnected through grief, love, and hate.

And Dilly.

"Why are you here?" Mercy whispered.

"For a date. Sorry for the short notice, but I wanted to make sure of a few things before you leave for L.A."

She tilted her head. "A date?"

"These are for you." He handed her the box of chocolates and the bouquet.

"Thank you. They're lovely." She took a sniff of the flowers but her eyes looked watery and she fought to hold in a smile as she drank in the rose scent. She set his gifts on the hall table and stepped outside, holding the door closed at her back. "Why did you bring me roses and why are you in a suit?"

"I've spent a lot of time waiting outside this house for a girl. But I've never rung that doorbell and arrived to take one out on a date. I'm tired of being a coward about wanting you in my life. There are a lot of things I regret about my comings and goings from this house, but all that is behind me. From here on in, we move forward together."

He offered his arm. Mercy took it.

When they reached his SUV he opened her door for her. "Climb in, I won't bite," he said and handed her in like the precious gift she was. He started the engine while he still could. His fingers trembled. She laid her hand on his and stopped him from putting it into reverse.

"What we need to say can be said here."

"Right," he said and hesitated. He clasped the steering wheel to steady his hands. No words came although he opened his mouth. His throat tightened. "I don't deserve another chance with you, but God, have mercy . . ." He needed to be put out of his misery, but he couldn't pull up the words he needed to do it. He shook his head. "I love you. I want you. Dilly loves you." His eyes stung as floodgates opened in his heart.

She placed her long delicate fingers on his cheek. "Clay, look at me."

He did and the love he saw in her gaze would have dropped him if he weren't already sitting.

"I love you, too," she said clearly. "I want you, too. Dilly's my child as much as she was my sister's," she said fiercely.

"More," he said and knew it was true. Mercy loved Dilly as much as any mother could.

He shook his head. "God help me, I want you here, and I want you there where your career is. I just want you happy. How do we make this work?"

Her voice went breathy. "Lots of people live away from Hollywood but still work in movies. We can do that. I don't want to get caught up in the machine. I want to be happy and me happy is having you and Dilly. The rest is nothing, means nothing without you."

He dragged her into his arms and pulled her as close as he could. "I hate bucket seats," he said. She laughed amid a wash of tears. "Don't cry. God, don't cry." He'd made too many Talbot females cry today.

Then she kissed him. Took him to her lips and kissed him deep and long. "I love you, Mercy. I love you." All the voices from his past drifted to silence as she kissed him. "I don't deserve you, but I'll try my damnedest to try every day for the rest of my life."

"Take me home, Clay. I want to be there when Dilly wakes up."

"You will be."

"Tomorrow and always."

Epilogue

Mercy, Clay, and Dilly walked the gauntlet of reporters and television news crews. Dilly blew kisses to all of them. She'd already stolen some hearts the previous week when she'd done the same thing at a movie premiere.

Clay leaned close to Mercy's ear. "Our sweet girl loves the limelight. Wonder where that came from?"

Mercy chuckled. "Funny how that is." Once inside the huge theater, they took their seats and waited with all the other hopeful nominees and supporters for the awards ceremony to begin.

Amid the chatter, Mercy pointed out different people who had befriended her. She'd come to admire many of them in the last months: directors, publicists, producers and more. A great many of her favorites lived the way she did: in a home far from the craziness of the business where they could pursue their normal lives with a normal family.

If the Talbots could ever be called normal.

Hope had taken to the stage with aplomb and brought the house down with her portrayal of Big Mama. Next, she said, was a musical. The family had yet to explain her singing voice wasn't all she believed it was. No one wanted to poke the bear.

Nate had taken up woodworking and put his workspace in the garage to good use. He'd taught Clay a lot, which was great because Clay and Mercy would soon need a cradle.

She slid her hand across her still-flat stomach and crossed her fingers for a boy who looked like his daddy. They'd chosen not to know the baby's gender until the birth. Nate had suggested that the anticipation would make for a lot of fun in the months ahead.

Clay leaned into her ear. "What did Esme say about the baby?"

"She told the director on the way here. We'll talk tomorrow." She hoped that they could film around her body's changes, but if it turned out they couldn't, she'd happily walk away from the role. Her priorities had shifted and her heart had never been more full of love and hope.

After she and Clay had promised their lives to each other, Mercy had gone underground; completely unavailable to anyone from the movie business. Those three days of silence and lack of response had helped her cause. When she appeared unattainable the frenzy had whipped higher and the Chastain Agency had dictated terms that made her head spin. She got everything she wanted in her contracts and more.

But best of all, she had her sister's child as her own, a solid husband to love and cherish and life roles she was excited to play: wife, mother, friend, and dog rescue fundraiser. Her poop scooping days were over.

"Elle called," Clay said in her ear, "and she's settled whatever it was she needed to take care of and will move in next week."

"We can tell Dilly she'll have cousins living in the house out back?"

Clay nodded in between craning his neck to ogle the rich and famous people sitting around them. He leaned in. "God help the men of Welcome because Elle Foster is back to stay," he whispered.

"Why would you say that?"

Clay chuckled softly as the lights in the auditorium dimmed. He whispered in her ear, sending thrills to parts south. "You'll find out."

The End

If you enjoyed *Finding Mercy* and have ever found a wonderful romance by reading reviews, please pay that joy forward by sharing a few words about how *Finding Mercy* made you feel when you closed it. A review doesn't have to be long, or a retelling of the plot, just a few words on how you felt when you finished. Did you sigh at the end? Feel happy?

Good news! There are more *Return to Welcome* romances. The next one is *Loving Logan*, the story of Logan Hughes and Elle Foster.

If you want to hear about exciting new releases and deals you can subscribe to Bonnie's Newsy Bits on my website. Readers can download a free e-book when they subscribe.

Over 40 romance titles are listed on my website at https://www.bonnieedwards.com/.

Don't miss out!

Visit the website below and you can sign up to receive emails whenever Bonnie Edwards publishes a new book. There's no charge and no obligation.

https://books2read.com/r/B-A-JXD-GKHQ

BOOKS 2 READ

Connecting independent readers to independent writers.

Did you love *Finding Mercy*? Then you should read *Loving Logan* by Bonnie Edwards!

She lives by three rules: Don't date. Don't sleep with the boss. Don't believe in happily-ever-after.

Elle Foster left Welcome broke, pregnant, and with a bad-girl rep.

Now, she's returned to Welcome still broke, with four children, but has vowed to never get pregnant again.

Logan Hughes is younger and establishing a new business. Adopted, he wants nothing more than to have a family of his own.

He needs an assistant and Elle needs the work...

A pirate raider lurks inside Logan and when he lets him loose, even a determined woman can fall under his spell. And that sexy pirate may make Elle Foster break all her rules.

Can Logan give up fatherhood for the one woman he wants more than life itself?

About the Author

Bonnie Edwards has been published by Kensington Books, Harlequin Books, Carina Press, and more.

With over 40 titles to her credit, her romances have been translated into several languages. Her books are sold worldwide.

Learn about more exciting releases and get a **free** romance by subscribing to her newsletter, **Bonnie's Newsy Bits** through her website.

https://www.bonnieedwards.com/

Cheers and happy reading!

Bonnie Edwards

www.ingramcontent.com/pod-product-compliance
Lightning Source LLC
Chambersburg PA
CBHW020235260626
47156CB00002B/682